Also by Diane Chambers Dierks:

Fiction
Already There

Non-Fiction
The Co-Parent Tool Box
Solo Parenting: Raising Strong & Happy Families

back to life

DIANE DIERKS

Aha! Publishing

This book is a work of fiction. Names, characters, places and incidents are products of the author's imagination or are used fictitiously. Any resemblance to actual events, locales or persons, living or dead, is entirely coincidental.

First printing 2020. Printed in the U.S.A.

10 9 8 7 6 5 4 3 2 1

Cover photograph by Billy Dugger.

Brian Andreas quote used with permission.

For Laura

In my dream,
the angel shrugged & said,
if we fail this time, it will be
a failure of imagination.

& then she placed
the world gently
in the palm of my hand.

-Brian Andreas

prologue

2013

THE RE WILL ALWAYS BE SOMETHING EERIE about a cold and misty September morning for me, especially since one ended in my death. Friday the 13th began less than ominously, but since I'm accident-prone on a good day, the mishap wasn't necessarily surprising except for the finality of it. Even though I heard the diesel engine roar to a crescendo, I thought the Port Authority bus was traveling away from me, which in retrospect makes no logical sense from a physics point of view. But logic is secondary to survival when a bus is coming at you full speed. In my defense, I had forgotten the city recently made 21st a one-way avenue. Since they say habit takes about 90 days to take root, and I was only on day 80-something, I feel marginally justified in the mistake. Besides, why do those buses look the same in front as they do in the back? Nevertheless, preoccupied with getting to a meeting on time, I scurried across the street like a dazed squirrel, and I lost the gamble.

Since that September day, I have wracked my brain over and over to remember what led me to that particular moment, but I only have a few distinct recollections of the morning right before the accident. I can't remember what I had for breakfast, whether or not I had made my lunch, or if I had slept well the night before. Honestly, I can't remember much about that entire week, but I do recall random details just minutes before the accident, like speeding toward the city, approaching the Fort Pitt Tunnel, and running behind as usual. An inconsistent rain slowed traffic to a crawl through the underpass. The city skyline was wrapped in a dark haze as I made my way out of the black toward the bustling downtown. The so-called light at the end of the tunnel was not present that morning, which I typically look forward to as I head toward the job that makes me a little crazy. I hadn't thought much of my tardiness up to that point, until I remembered the meeting Cam Fletcher reminded me of when I was leaving the office at 6:30 the night before. "Eight o'clock sharp," he had announced casually with his usual doubting arrogance. It was 7:58 when I glanced at the clock to calculate how many minutes it would take to drive down Holland, park in my usual spot, and run into the building as if I had my coffee and thoughts prepared. About five.

Fletcher's gonna kill me, I thought as I sped toward 24 Park Tower, the posh Pittsburgh high rise that housed our ad agency, and I rounded the corner of Holland and 21st. It would have been the second time in a row that I'd shown up late for a meeting with Tamborlin, our biggest client. Not because of an accident in the tunnel or a flat tire, or any other respectable excuse. I was just late. I'm always late.

I haphazardly pulled into the parking spot in the garage across the street from our building, gathered my purse and briefcase, locked my car (I think, but am not sure), and quickened my pace as I walked out of the garage to cross

21st Avenue. I stepped off the curb with my eyes fixed on the twenty-four building, while trying to avoid getting soaked by the sudden downpour. And then as they say, everything went into slow motion.

Halfway across the street, running off-balanced and knocked-kneed in my pencil skirt and five-inch pumps, I belatedly realized my dilemma. I glanced at the bus driver, a blurry figure behind the giant sloshing wipers, and knew I was on the wrong end of the bus. He was checking his side view mirror as he pulled away from the curb and didn't look ahead to see that I had occupied the space he was about to dominate. I tried to hurry my step, but because the bus was traveling toward the middle of the street as I was, its flat front met my sprinting body head on. Upon impact, my limp frame flipped over and landed on the damp pavement ahead of the bus, just about the time the driver became aware of my decision to hesitate. His brakes squealed, but not in time to avoid the 50-year-old, 130-pound lump of flesh that now lay behind his massive vehicle's tire, which had rolled over me like a speed bump. *Fletcher's gonna kill me.*

"Oh my God, oh my God!" I heard first in the distance but then much closer. Tandem screams were followed by a freakish silence, as a crowd gathered and quietly murmured, and the whaling bus driver shouted in a Spanish accent, "I didn't see her! I swear I didn't see her!" I wanted to answer, "It's not your fault! I am a stupid woman who forgot what I was doing." But nothing came out. My head and chest pounded in pain. Then numbness set in, as I felt the warmth of blood seeping beneath me, carrying my feeling away with it.

A cacophony of muffled voices on cell phones sent out pleas for help. The dazed bus commuters, with mouths gaping, must have been shocked into disbelief at my mangled body.

back to life

They're all going to be late for work because of me. Like me. Everything. Late. *I'm cold.*

Two men kneeled helplessly at my side telling me to hang in there. One covered me with his suitcoat. "Everything will be okay," he assured. The other asked if I was breathing. He must have lowered his cheek to check for breath because I remember the scent of Aqua Velva aftershave just before he snapped back in a panic saying he didn't know. Soon the faint sounds of approaching sirens turned to blaring horns and confused chatter. No one said so, but I was fairly sure I was not going to make it. How do you survive getting run over by a bus? Had I been able, I would have laughed out loud with my usual twisted humor, as they placed the oxygen mask over my face. I could imagine the conversation around the water cooler the next morning. *Say, what happened to Kate yesterday? Oh, I heard she got run over by a bus.* Then their nervous laughter would turn to horror, as they realized it was true. There was just something funny, or deserving, about that.

In and out of consciousness, I felt my partially numb body bouncing as they loaded me into an ambulance, a needle being poked in my arm, and a dog barking in the background. *Max.* My chow, Max. If he were here, he would lick my face to snap me out of this nightmare. *Oh, Max.* Someone needed to call my neighbor to look after my sweet 10-year-old boy. He would be so worried. Or mostly hungry. But who would think of that? Maybe Deirdre. *Oh, no, Deirdre.*

The paramedics lifted me out of the ambulance and rushed through the entrance of the emergency doors of a hospital, I presumed U of P Mercy since it was nearby. There was a lot of commotion and orders being barked, but my eyes were now plastered shut, despite my willing them to open. I thought again about Deirdre. The wedding. *Oh God, the wedding*

4

is less than a month away. How beautiful she had looked in that mermaid gown at Laramer's. *I've ruined everything.*

I couldn't keep track of time. It felt fast, then slow. Something was helping me breathe, but then it seemed to come to an uneventful halt. The pain subsided significantly. *Ahhh.* Morphine maybe.

"Mom?" I was startled by Deirdre's frantic voice. She pressed a warm cheek to mine. I wanted to jump up and tell her I was all right, as I always did when I really wasn't. But my brain was no longer in control. *What's happening?*

"What is it?" I heard her brother Sean answer, in a strange little boy voice. *Am I dreaming? How did they find out about the accident? How did they get here so quickly?* Hours may have passed. I couldn't be sure.

"I don't know…Mom…Mom...please open your eyes," Deirdre pleaded with a quivering voice I'd never heard before.

Then everything went eerily quiet. Not even the usual ringing in my ears could be heard. Silence.

Regret is a terrible emotion. It can be so debilitating that the fear of reexperiencing it can drive us to even more regrettable decisions. Yet it always feels so important, so right somehow, to attempt to fix what we regret wasn't right the first time. How does one go back and wait patiently at the curb? Had I known then what I know now, I could have saved myself a lifetime of pain. Literally.

My name is Kate Mulligan (don't laugh) and I got a second chance at life.

one

JUST LIKE WHAT I HAD HEARD ABOUT NEAR-death experiences, I levitated, gazing at a body lying still on the hospital bed below, everything shrouded in white. At first, I couldn't make out who it was, but when I saw Deirdre and Sean crying over it, there was no mistake it was me. Time tumbled backwards. There's the bus, and people yelling around the broken body. It *was* me. The cross and Claddagh necklace was mine. The diamonds in it were sparkling among the wreckage. I marveled at how little I cared. *Wow. This is crazy.* An unfamiliar peace came over me. In true cliché fashion, I looked skyward and saw a bright white light that I suspected was a sign of what I was supposed to do next. I had no fear – only immense curiosity and awe. *So, maybe this is it.* I almost laughed at my giddiness but felt certain that the next thing I would see would be the stereotypical pearly gates attended by Saint Peter.

Everything went dark again for a few seconds, followed by something that resembled a giant screen reflecting familiar images. *Oh, yeah, this is the part where my life flashes before me.* Next came a stinging twinge of sadness and grief. *This is what I'm leaving behind. Wait...wait....not so fast.* Kate, this is your life. *Wait! I said...wait.* There was my father, staring down at me on the day I was born in 1963. He was smiling and cooing. My

6

mother, in her 1950s smock dress with the patent leather belt, waved from behind the wheel of her new Chevy Bel Air. My nine-year-old brother Daniel….he was gasping for air before he drowned in the pond at the edge of the corn field. *I should have saved him. But I didn't know.* The funeral. *Awful.* My first sexual experience in the back seat of Charles Davenport's '69 Corvaire. *Also awful.* The senior prom with Blake Tanner. *Dreamy.* My first date with Sam. *Nice.* The wedding and my mother crying. *Why?* Giving birth to little Deirdre. *Incredible.* Getting a job at the ad agency. *Nervous.* Look at her smile with no front teeth! *Sweet.* Going to the hospital again to have Sean. *Painful, then perfect.* Sam in bed with that woman. *Unforgettable.* Difficult divorce. Juggling work and daycare. *Exhausting.* First date with John. Marriage too-quickly to John. Annulment. *Depression.* Deirdre graduating from high school. *Proud.* Breast cancer. *Shock.* Sean graduating from high school. *Relief.* Remission. *More relief.* Sean is going to college. Look at him with his mortar board. *Proud.* Blake Tanner calls and says he's now divorced. *Dreamy.* First date with Blake. He's more annoying than I remember from high school. *Disappointing.* Deirdre announces her engagement. *Bittersweet.* Working overtime to pay for the wedding. *Exhausted.* Forgetting that 21st is a one-way street. *Over.*

I slumped forward with shame. *That's it? Then this? I don't get it.* Confusion, then anger, permeated my now transparent form. I wished for something different. I wished my "film" would have had me feeding starving children in Kenya or climbing Mount Everest or smiling a lot more. Every image seemed somber and serious. *Didn't I laugh more than that?* Overwhelmed, I waited for the next terrible thing to happen. *Maybe this isn't heaven after all.* What felt like a heart in my chest raced with fear. The light came on again, too bright for me to see anything. Instead, I heard a voice coming through a white cloud. An image appeared from nowhere.

"Good morning, Katherine," a bald man with a round face greeted me. I hadn't been called that in a very long time.

"Good morning." I was dumbfounded. "Am I dead?"

He smiled with adoration, as if he knew me.

"Not exactly."

I hesitated, and then felt alive. "Oh, I get it. I'm dreaming." I tried to relax, preparing to see what might come next before I woke up. *I think they call this a drug-induced coma.*

"I'm afraid you are not dreaming. Let's just say you are at a crossroads." His voice was calm and assuring.

"Crossroads?" I asked with skepticism, then fear. "Like purgatory?"

"This is your time, Katherine, to decide" said the man before me. I could feel his softness, even though I couldn't touch him.

I put the back of my hand to my cheek to test for skin. It was clammy and cold. "Are you sure I'm not dead?" I begged. He remained silent for what seemed like eternity.

The man with the soft round face came closer and knelt beside me, where I sat on something warm. "Some people," he explained, "have a tougher time in life than others. They leave before they have a chance to realize their full potential."

"You mean like Martin Luther King or Janis Joplin?" I inquired, feeling stupid.

He chuckled with kind, reassuring eyes. "Well, I suppose. But ordinary people, as well. Like you."

"Me?" I pulled back anxiously. "I'm not really sure where I am or who you are, but..." He came closer and took my hand in his. It felt strong and soft. Then he stood up and pulled me up with him.

"C'mon….let me show you something." The man with the soft round face, still holding my hand, led me through a mist of clouds and into a landscape that was breathtaking. We were on a precipice, surrounded by blue sky, mountainous peaks, and foliage painted in colors I had never seen before. A large lake below glistened with the reflection of what looked like a giant Crayola box. Every sense was stimulated. I could hear a brook rushing in a hurry toward the river, and a cool breeze that seemed to make the leaves dance on the trees. The fragrance of honeysuckle led my eyes toward a spray of yellow flowers at my feet. I reached down and plucked a bud from the vine and sucked the nectar from it like we used to do when we were kids. The bittersweet taste reminded me of my youth and I closed my eyes to take it in.

"Where are we?" I asked in wonder.

"This is Quietude," he whispered in reverence.

I wanted to laugh. *Quietude?* That sounded like something out of a bad romance novel.

"You don't believe me?" He looked concerned.

"No, it's just that…well…I don't know. This is beautiful and all, but what does it mean? Why am I here? What are the crossroads you mentioned? Where are we going? I mean, what…?" I felt frustrated and scared at once.

"Katherine, I don't think you are ready for this yet. Quietude. It requires your soul to be more at rest."

I was now more confused than ever. I felt a chill and folded my arms. Isn't heaven supposed to be where we achieve rest? That's when I noticed the blood was still wet on my sleeve. I gasped.

"It's okay. Don't be afraid," the man with the soft round face said as he put his arm around me and pulled me into himself. I burst into tears.

I cried for a long time with my face buried in his chest. I shook like a leaf, feeling foggy, needing to be held so my body would not fall into pieces again. I wasn't sure why I was in this place and who this strange, but soft man was, and what I was supposed to be doing or deciding. For a moment, it just felt safe to be able to let it out. *I must be dead, but isn't it supposed to feel good?* I wondered if I was entering a more dreadful place that I had not planned to go when I died. Guilt washed over me.

After what seemed like hours, the man with the soft round face put his hands on my shoulders and squared me up in front of him. He looked directly into my eyes. His were clear blue. I saw my reflection in them as he gazed into my soul and brought me back to the moment.

"I am going to give you a second chance," he said in a low, but reassuring voice.

His hands gripped my shoulders and I began to tremble again. "What?" I was still trying to grasp his words.

"A second chance at life. Katherine, I know all about you. I know how hard you tried to make everything right. I know you have so many regrets that we don't even have time to name them. You wish you would have made better choices, chosen different friends and partners. I know you wanted to see yourself differently. I know every pain you've ever felt, every tear you've shed, every curse word you've uttered. I know your heart, Katherine, like no one else could ever know."

Then he was silent, still looking intently into me. I felt naked and undone. And strangely relieved. My mind raced with wonder, then fear and confusion.

"Who the hell are you?" I finally asked with a surprising crossness. "What is this? Am I dead? Are you Jesus, or something?"

10

The man with the soft round face smiled. "I've been known by many names…but that's not important." His face was angelic. And for a moment, I wanted to touch it and see if he was real, but I was afraid to find that it wasn't.

"There's a lot in you that is unresolved. You are not yet ready to be done with life, so I want to give you a chance to discover love in yourself, for yourself, with my help."

"Okay…tell me…what does that mean exactly?" I was exhausted with fear and doubt.

"Not many people get this chance because they are not capable of learning the deeper lessons," he explained, "but there are a few, like you, who I sense have the ability to make amazing self discoveries." Then he said something that made my legs go numb.

"I love you, Kate." I was struck by his sudden informal mention of my name. "I have always loved you. From the day you were conceived until today when you misjudged the bus. I love you now as you stand here in anger toward me because you don't understand. That's one of the things I love about you. You long to understand and be understood. If I told you that I understand you completely, would you trust me for the rest?"

I was dumbfounded. I had longed all of my life to be told by a man that I was completely understood. Now, here he was. With a soft round face, liquid blue eyes, and a voice that melted my heart. He was right here in front of me, but I couldn't determine how or what or why. Finally, I agreed because I wanted it so badly.

"Yes, I will trust you." I drew in a long breath and tears stung my face as I exhaled.

The man with the soft round face stepped away from me and waved his hand in a circular motion, revealing a brass chalice. He placed it on a bright white platform and turned back toward me.

"I trust you," he said, then paused, "to trust *me*."

I searched my heart for the meaning of his words. *He trusts me to trust him?*

He went on. "And I trust that no matter who you encounter, you will be a positive influence and teach without even knowing you are teaching. That's your gift."

His words warmed me, but I remained puzzled by this whole experience. Still, I wanted to hear more. I was not used to anyone knowing me in this way. *How could he know me like this? He must be God. I must be dead.*

"You are not quite expired," he declared, as if he knew my thoughts.

"Now isn't that funny?" I guffawed. "That's sort of like being slightly pregnant, or not quite human, isn't it?" I lost control and burst into laughter. The man with the soft round face smiled back at me, apparently delighted in my attempt at humor. If he *was* God, then he was used to this kind of conversation with me. He was used to the comedy of errors I called my life.

"Let me explain further," he said gently. "I'm going to make you an offer, but there are some very important components to it that you need to consider before accepting."

Suddenly, I felt like Peter Graves...*here is your mission if you choose to accept it.* I began to laugh again in disbelief.

"I'm sorry," I exclaimed, "It's just that this is all so surreal."

"I know. You have always found humor in the grimmest of circumstances. Remember that time you were sitting by yourself in the hospital, hooked up to the chemo line? You wanted to cry because your daughter had to leave you there while she went to work, and it felt so lonely and hopeless. I'll never forget how you joked with the nurses about their orthopedic shoes. Remember that?"

Yes. I did remember that. In amazement, I stared at his clear azure eyes again. "How...? I mean, yes... I couldn't understand in this day and age why they couldn't make nurse's shoes more attractive than those whitewashed duplicates of what my 80-year-old grandmother wore!"

"That's how you got through the day, Katherine. But I saw your tears that night when you slept on the bathroom floor by yourself. I soothed your stomach. Do you remember the moment it felt warm again? Do you remember?"

Chills ran over me. Yes. I remembered distinctly. All of a sudden, the nausea had left. I had been praying to just die right there on the floor. Then a warmness came over me and the nausea left for the night. I remembered.

"That was you?...that was *you*?" Another chill went up my back and I felt a cool breeze. "Well, if that's true, why did you let me get there to begin with? Why?" I searched his gaze for answers. He was silent, which angered me more. I pulled up my fists and buried my face in them. The tears were flowing easily now.

"It wasn't my doing or my choice." He fell silent again.

"If you had the power to stop my nausea, why couldn't you stop me from getting cancer to begin with? I don't get it," I said, barely able to complete the sentence between sobs. "What was cancer supposed to teach me? What was any of it for?"

"All I can say is that I went through it with you."

I still didn't understand.

"Kate, look at me," he said informally again as he took into his hands my damp face, now dripping with a mix of

13

mucus and salty tears. His eyes were as kind as ever. "Yes, I have power, but you live in a flawed world. It is imperfect and stained and toxic. But love always triumphs. Even in sickness."

"Okay, if that's true," my voice quivered and gasped to catch a breath, "then why didn't you create perfect beings to live in a perfect world? Why not that...God...or whoever you are? Was it some sort of sick joke of yours to create us and then put us in a world that cannot possibly bring us any comfort or happiness?"

"There will be plenty of time to answer these questions when your soul is at rest. Until then, you have more to do and you must trust me to try again, or I will send you back to your children. Either way, I'll be with you."

"Send me back? What in the world does that mean?" I was exhausted.

"Like I said, I have an offer for you."

Oh, yeah. That Mission Impossible thing, I snickered to myself.

"I will allow you to go back to a place in time of your choosing...to recreate your life in any way you want," he explained patiently.

"Go back? You mean like being reborn?"

"Well, not exactly. More to a time and place where you feel you could make a fresh start without guilt or regret, whatever age that was. You could start there."

Thoughts of Daniel raced through my mind. I should have saved him. I was only thirteen. But if I could just go back and save him from the pond. That alone would be worth starting over.

"Okay, I'm listening. So, I go back to age thirteen and save my brother. Then what? Then I can reach Quietude?" Just saying that word felt ridiculous. There was an anxious knot in my stomach.

14

"Well, it's not quite that simple," said the man with the soft round face.

"Kind of like not quite dead," I mused, wiping my face with the back of my hand.

"If you decide to do this, you must live your life from that point until your death…whenever that happens." He fell eerily silent and for a moment, he became a blur.

"Oh." It was a lot to take in. "So, I'm confused. Who will I be? Will I still be me?"

"Of course. I wouldn't want you to be anyone else," he said adamantly. "But you will know what you know now. None of your memories will be gone. You will be fifty years old in your mind and heart, but with a thirteen-year-old's body."

"Now, *that's* funny!" I twirled around in child-like amazement. "I've always wondered why we couldn't start with aged wisdom and just get dumber as we grew older and weaker, ya know? I mean if we were smart and had a hot body to boot, can you imagine what we could accomplish early on? Instead, the smarter we get, the more decrepit we look. That's grossly unfair! If we could just have all that wisdom as a young person, we wouldn't make all the stupid mistakes that end up…"

"Killing you?" The man with the soft round face interrupted.

"Yeah. Something like that. So, what if I say yes? Then what?"

"I send you back to age thirteen and you start all over. That's all. Then you get to live your life with what you know now."

I was skeptical. "Wait a minute…there's gotta be a catch. There are no second chances, no free lunch, no do-overs."

He shrugged his shoulders as if to remind me of the faith he talked about earlier.

"Will I be able to talk to you?" I continued as I began to seriously consider the offer.

"Like you always have."

"Oh." That's not what I wanted to hear.

"What about Sean and Deirdre?"

His silence and sober face answered me.

"Oh. I guess I would have to live the same exact life to have them."

"Yes," he said gently.

"But I could save my brother and my mother would be so happy and not depressed, which would save her, too, wouldn't it?"

"Those things will depend on her."

I thought on that for awhile, still convinced this was some sort of trickery. I needed to weigh all the options.

"So, what if I choose not to take your offer?"

"I will send you back to where you were after the bus hit you. I will give you another chance to live out the life you had made for yourself."

I felt sick. This was not a choice I wanted to make.

"Will I be okay or will I be..? That bus ran right over the middle of me. Will I walk again?"

"That is yet to be seen." He looked genuinely sad for me. "Faith is more important than answers."

"Can't I just go to this Quietude place and be done with all of it?"

"I'm afraid that's not an option. Like I said, you are not yet ready. I must either send you back to your original life or let you start over."

"If I start over, what will happen to my children? Will they come here? I'm so confused." I fought the urge to burst into tears again. I couldn't imagine a world without them, and I didn't understand these parallel lives.

"To the life you just left, you will be gone, but I will comfort Deirdre and Sean. I will watch over them while you are...busy...with your other life." He spoke as if he knew them intimately. "I will be in Quietude with them when they arrive and when you arrive here again – for good – eventually they will be with you and you with them. Either way, they will be safe and cared for."

I had trouble wrapping my head around this idea. I felt comforted by him yet torn. This felt more like Let's Make a Deal now than Mission Impossible. *Door number one or two?*

He had apparently read my mind. "There is no right way to do this. I will love you no matter what you choose. I will be here for you either way. Only you can decide which life you desire to live. I will support you."

Flashes of Daniel and my mother returned. *I could save them. Finally, I could really save them. Deirdre and Sean would be okay. He promised. This is my chance to make everything right.* Like jumping off a cliff, I made up my mind to avoid the agony of choosing.

"Okay...okay...I'm ready. If I have to choose, and you tell me that my children will be okay, then I am willing to try."

"Kate." He hesitated. "This is final. There is no trying. If you start over, you cannot return to your old life. Is that clear?"

"But you'll be with me, right?" I pleaded.

"Like I always have."

I wanted to know my relationship with him would be different, special somehow. That it would be better, closer, more real. But it was clear he was not going to give me those assurances.

"You will know of me differently now," he went on. "You will know what to expect when life comes to an end. That is more than what others know. That has to be enough."

"That faith thing, huh?"

"Yeah. That faith thing. It's enough, Kate. It's all I need from you."

"Okay, let's do it." I felt exhilarated. "One more thing…will it be 1976 when I return? That will be weird."

"Yes. That will be a challenge with what you know. You may be tempted to warn others about what may happen, but understand that since you are starting over now, life events may not happen as you once knew them. You will not be able to predict life based on having lived it before. Do you understand?"

"Not really. It's all very confusing." My head began to pound. I massaged my temples and drew in a deep breath. "But I want to try. I do." *Who is this guy?* This was not how I pictured God. This guy looked more like Uncle Fester from the Addams Family. I was reeling with both excitement and dread.

He turned toward the white platform and lifted the chalice. It had a purplish liquid in it that looked like wine. "Drink from this cup. All of your past mistakes will be no more. A new life begins now and there is no limit to what you can do. I will be with you always, Katherine, until the end of the age."

He put the cup to my lips and I drank. A cleansing warmth rushed through my body, much like that time on the bathroom floor. I can't describe the peace. I was overcome. Then asleep.

two

1976

THE FIELDS WERE AS GREEN AS I HAD remembered. I was flying on my purple Schwinn with chrome fenders and white-walled tires down the country road toward my family's home. The smell of pink lilacs in bloom that lined the Ferguson's white picket fence was enough to bring tears. *I'm back. I'm really back.* But my thoughts turned quickly to not being late. *I'm always late. What time is it?* I looked up to see the sun high in the sky. *About noon.* The warm summer air blew on my face with a reminder of how refreshing it was to take a dip in the pond. *It was lunchtime when I left him. Lunchtime. About noon or sometime shortly after.* I had to get focused. *Faster, faster. Don't be late.* I heard the crackle of freshly tarred gravel bounce between the bicycle spokes as I pedaled fiercely into the driveway. I hopped off the bike with surprisingly youthful ease, and then took pleasure in noticing my soiled white Keds as I clicked down the kickstand to park the bike for later. I was in awe and a little light-headed at what had just transpired. I could hardly contain my excitement, feeling a flutter in my chest as I approached the front door. This was the serenity of the Mulligan homestead in Clearfield, Ohio.

Surprisingly, for a fleeting moment, I thought about Cam Fletcher and what had happened at that meeting with Tamborlin. Were they attending my funeral or feeling pity at my bedside when told I would never walk again? I shook my head to jiggle those thoughts out of my mind. I don't have to worry about any of that anymore. That's all over. But Deidre. Sean. *They will be okay.* He said they would be okay. *Focus, Kate, focus.*

I started opening the screened door slowly, not sure what I would feel or think when I entered. Just then, I heard the faint, but happy screams of children in the pond a hundred yards from the house. "Daniel," I whispered to myself. I wasn't sure exactly what day it was and how soon I needed to find him. I darted back toward the driveway and ran across the road and into the field, through the tall alfalfa that eventually would feed the cattle for the winter. The pond where I had spent hours with my brother in our young childhood, fishing, swimming and sunning, was at the bottom of the hilly field.

"I'm coming," I whispered. "I'm coming, Daniel." When I saw him, I stopped dead in my tracks. He was exactly as I'd remembered. Skinny, wiry and full of energy. I plopped down in the thick, tall grass just to watch him. I picked up a blade of it to see if I could still make it whistle between my thumbs. Dad had given him his summer crew cut as usual and his neck was the color of radishes. A childlike joy took over. *Waaaaaaah!* I was thrilled at the sound, which resembled the loud slow cackling of a sick duck. I whistled with the grass between my thumbs, which startled Daniel, who had been playing water tag with our cousin, Cherry. I had forgotten how tiny she was then.

"Katie! Come in with us. The water's warm...honest, it is!" His smile was wide and innocent. His voice small and boyish, so clear and playful.

I sat dumbfounded, taking in the familiar sights and sounds, yet not sure what to do next. I had been plunked down in the middle of this small farm that I called home as a child, but it was oddly surreal – a dream that was not really a dream. The pond was glassy and gray as I had remembered, except for the ripples Daniel was making as he bobbed up and down. My grandfather took pride in stocking it with bass and bluegill for his fishing pleasure, and my grandmother had nurtured the ducks that waddled there daily to bathe and frolic with their ducklings. A lump grew in my throat as I realized that I would see them again. Grammy and Gramps, as I had known them. I had a sudden urge to run up the hill to the farmhouse where they lived. To put my arms around her and tell her how much I missed her. She was probably making bread. Her gnarled hands, stricken with arthritis, would be kneading the dough into submission while she told the same stories we had heard all of our lives about the life she had as a girl. One came to mind that she liked repeating about how it was nothing to chop off the head of a chicken for dinner, only to see its body run around without its head. That always made us grimace and laugh, which I loved. I snapped out of my thoughts, knowing there would be time for Grammy. Right now, I had to worry about Daniel or this whole thing would be for nothing.

I noticed how yellow the ducklings were against the blue-gray water, dutifully following their mother, and I saw Daniel and Cherry bobbing up and down, which made me smile. Daniel. I couldn't get over how much I had forgotten about him. And how vibrant everything around me looked. Had I noticed this as a child, or had I simply taken it for granted because I had known little else? This was the kind of place I had dreamed about retiring to someday in my first life. *Interesting.* I didn't realize I had already had it.

Daniel looked up and saw me sitting alone in the grass and called out to me a second time. I had no memory of this particular moment, which made me slightly nervous. But the man with the soft, round face did say that things would not be exactly as I remembered simply because I would change the course of events by returning. I wondered if this was the day Daniel had drowned or if it was another day. For a second, I panicked and wondered how quickly I needed to be ready to jump in. My mind was racing, trying to remember the events of that day and whether or not they included Cherry.

"Hey, Daniel," I yelled back. "What is the date today?" I noticed how high-pitched my voice sounded.

"What?" he responded with annoyance. "Are ya comin' in or what?"

"First tell me what today's date is!" I yelled while cupping my hands around my mouth so he would be sure to hear me from a distance.

"What do ya need to know *that* for? We're on summer vacation!"

"Just tell me you jerk!" I was surprised at how easily I was able to lapse into my childish banter with him.

"It's the eighteenth or nineteenth or somethin' like that," he said.

"Okay. I'm comin' in a minute," I responded, my heart pounding. Daniel died on the nineteenth. Today might be the day. It probably is the day, since I had asked to be returned at this precise time. I was afraid to leave Daniel to go into the house to find out for sure. I decided to stay right there just in case. *Was it possible to make the same mistake twice? Of course. I had a*

22

long history of that. I simply couldn't blow it this time. There was too much at stake. For a split second, I remembered Deirdre and what she was like at age thirteen. Would I have expected her to know what to do at this age? I marveled at the fact that I had never thought about that before.

I rose from sitting in the field and was surprised at the lightness of my gangly frame. I looked down at my chest and burst into laughter. So, this is how it felt to be minus my breasts *before* cancer! I was wearing a multi-colored, flowery bathing suit with a ruffle around the waist that made me feel like one of the ducks flapping around in the water. I walked slowly toward the pond and as Daniel's face came into clearer view, I had to hold back the tears. *God, it really is him.* It had been so long, and I had blocked out his memory for so many years on purpose so I could forget the guilt. Now, here he was in plain view. I stood at the pond's edge and stared at him while he and Cherry giggled at playing water tag.

"What's wrong with you Katie?" Daniel noticed my staring.

"Uh, nothin'. I was trying to play the role of a thirteen-year-old but found it incredibly uncomfortable.

"Well, c'mon. We need another player. Cherry can't swim worth a lick."

"Shut up, Daniel, or I'll tell Katie your secret!"

"What secret?"

"Nothin'. Cherry's bein' stupid."

Cherry climbed out of the pond, using the rope ladder that Gramps had attached to the small wooden dock he had made. Dripping wet with teeth chattering, she declared, "I've gotta go. It's lunchtime and I told mama I'd be home by noon."

"When do you have to be back up for lunch, Danny?" I inquired.

"Ya mean when do *we* have to be home?" replied Daniel. "Mommy said we could stay here all day if we wanted."

"No, she didn't," I corrected. "We probably should head up to the house, too. I'm kind of hungry, aren't you?"

"No! I wanna stay here. You go on, I'll catch up to ya in a few minutes."

That was it. I remembered. This was déjà vu in its truest sense. *No! I wanna stay here. You go on, I'll catch up to ya in a few minutes* rang over and over in my head for years after that. Those were Daniel's last words to me. I recalled being frustrated with Daniel because I was hungry, and he was being stubborn. So, I left him there, which I was never supposed to do. Swimming alone in the pond was breaking Gramp's rules.

I always resented that my mother put me in charge of keeping an eye on Daniel from the time he was a toddler. There was only four years difference between us, but because I was a girl and the older sibling, mother expected me to take on a responsible role with my brother. On June nineteenth, 1976, I decided I was tired of being my brother's keeper, so I walked away and left him there to die – at least that's how it felt. The guilt came rushing back in full force.

"Daniel, I am so sorry!" I cried out spontaneously.

"Huh?" Daniel scrunched his face in confusion, while at the same time shading his eyes from the sun.

"I'm sorry," I said in a quiet voice. "I'm...just...sorry."

"Ya got that right, fraidy Katie!"

I smiled through the tears at the nostalgia of hearing him call me that. He was always the first one to take a risk, while I would warn of the dangers.

C'mon Katie, let's climb up that tree!

No, Daniel, it doesn't look safe. Remember, Gramps told us to stay off of it because it's dying, and the limbs are probably rotten from the sun?

What's the matter fraidy Katie? You're such a sissy!

And he would climb the tree anyway. On June nineteenth, 1976, I decided I was tired of reminding Daniel to abide by the rules, and there were grave consequences because of it.

"You're actin' awful strange," Daniel said before he plunged back under the water to retrieve his goggles. When I saw him disappear, I panicked and jumped in after him. The water was starkly cold against my lean milky white skin and for a moment, I lost my bearings. When I popped up next to Daniel, he was cheering because I had decided to join him after all.

"Yeeeeeeeee! Wanna play Marco Polo?" Daniel screamed in delight.

I grabbed him and held on as tight as I could. "Danny! Please let's go to the house. Please!"

"Hey, hey! Get your grubs off me! I thought we were gonna play some more!"

"No, let's just get out and go eat lunch, okay?" I pleaded in fear.

Daniel gave an angry look and then started swimming toward the dock.

"Okay then. I'll go, but not 'cause *you* want me too!"

"Okay, Danny." I was breathing hard from the excitement, but relieved that my little brother – my precious little brother – had agreed to live, letting me off the hook for a lifetime of guilt I could finally avoid. "Thank you," I whispered under my breath, as I watched Daniel's skinny body climb up the rope ladder and run through the field toward my parents' house. I swam to the pier and thought I could die right then and there and be happy that I chose this new path. I thought of the man with the soft round face and wondered if he was watching from afar.

Worn out from saving lives – mine and my brother's – I stepped through the door of my childhood home. The smell was exactly as I had remembered it. Murphy's Oil Soap combined with the aroma of simmering vegetable soup on the stove. My mother, Sarah Mulligan, had two occupations – housekeeper and cook – and she was always doing one or the other, or both at the same time. The worn yellow linoleum below my feet felt hard and dimpled.

My heart thumped with anticipation. How would I react to seeing a younger version of my mother?

"Katie Ann?" she yelled around the corner before seeing me at the door.

"Oh, there you are. Didn't I ask you to have your brother home by noon? It's 12:15 and I've got errands to run after lunch."

I stood surprised. Seeing my mother was like looking in the mirror. *Wow. I had no idea I looked so much like her.* I did the math and figured she was about forty-one or forty-two now – younger than me. *Amazing.*

"Hey, cat got your tongue? I'm talking to you, young lady." She stared with a familiar sternness. I don't know why I had expected my mother to scoop me up in her arms and cry with joy that I had saved my brother. But it made sense that she could not be happy about something she didn't know would have happened if not for me. There was something unnerving about the idea that I was the only one who knew I had just spared the entire family, and their small community for that matter, an enormous amount of pain and sadness. Memories came flooding back from that terrible day, sending a cold chill up my spine.

Katie, where's your brother?

He's still at the pond. I tried to get him to come, but he wouldn't come. I'm hungry.

You know you are not allowed to leave him there alone!

She had stormed out of the house, angry with me, and came back ten minutes later, screaming and yelling to call someone, anyone.

Run up and get your grandfather. I need to call your dad!

What's wrong?

She wouldn't answer.

Where's Danny?

She was on the phone with my father. Then I heard her scream...He's gone! He's nowhere to be found, but his towel is still on the dock...

Within twenty minutes my father and grandfather were searching in and around the pond. I watched the two strongest men I ever knew bob up and down, catching breaths intermittently, until Gramps took one last dive and came up with an expression of terror I never wanted to recall again. "I found him!" And then the two strong men brought up Danny's limp, waterlogged body that had gotten tangled in some brush at the bottom of the pond. They tried to revive him, but it was too late. I'll never forget how my father collapsed on top of my brother, sobbing and screaming for him to not be gone, and then my mother knelt down and began to hit my father on the back, yelling, "Don't let him go, damn it, don't let him go!" But he was gone. In those days, an ambulance was not something that could be summoned by 911 in five minutes. A few volunteers from the local fire department that Grammy had called showed up first and then an ambulance arrived a little while later, and that's when my brother was put on a stretcher and carried up the hill with a sheet covering his face.

My mother didn't talk to me for a week after that. And then when she began to speak again, it was as if she was one of those people from *The Invasion of the Body Snatchers*. It seemed she had been replaced by someone in a pod who looked exactly like her but had no soul.

"Katie," my mother interrupted my thoughts to bring me back to the present. "I will not tolerate this kind of disrespect, you hear me?"

"Yeah...but Daniel kept fighting with me," I defended softly, while looking around, still fascinated with my surroundings.

"Well, every time I think I can count on you, Katie, you seem to disappoint me. Now get your wet suit off and get dressed for lunch. I don't have all day."

That stung me in a familiar, but forgotten, way. It reminded me of what my ex-husband had done to me so often and in this context, I realized how similar he and my mother actually were. *Classic.* I wanted desperately to ask her important questions, like, "Are you really happy in this life?" or "Doesn't perimenopause suck?" But I had no credibility. Questions like that would go unanswered and probably land me in some sort of doctor's office, so I kept quiet, which was my first encounter with the reality of my choice to come back. *I can't really be who I am in this world. At least not for awhile.* The thought of having to endure days and weeks of being a child again caused slight panic. *I don't know if I can do it.* But I knew I had no choice in the matter now. I tried to keep reminding myself that I did it for Daniel, and for my parents. I had to push through the panic and revel in the prospect of possibly experiencing a mother who wouldn't be depressed and a father who wouldn't drink so much to numb the pain. I wanted to think I had prevented the catastrophe called my childhood.

28

Lunch was heavenly. Homemade bread and vegetable soup made with the harvest from our family's garden was my mother's signature lunch. As a child, I had despised the garden that she used as punishment when Daniel and I argued. "Obviously, you two are bored, so get out there and weed the garden," she would yell. It was the reason I had decided not to put in a garden when my children were at home. That supposed place of new growth and hope symbolized failure for me. Failure to live up to my mother's strict standards. Now that I'd had children of my own, I felt sorry for the younger version of myself. *It wasn't me. It was her.* My mother placed a bowl of soup and bread in front of us, and I realized how much I had taken the simple things for granted and remembered craving those exact foods when I would feel unusual hunger pangs during my cancer days. Comfort food was my mom's specialty, even if she lacked the ability to show it physically to either of her children.

Sarah Stone Mulligan was raised in a large family that included eight children, four girls and four boys. I remember her telling stories about how her older brother dropped out of school to work odd jobs because their alcoholic father couldn't stay sober long enough to hold down meaningful employment. Of course, I didn't hear these stories until I was a teenager, and only then it was because my mother was touting the hard work ethic held by her brothers and wondered why I was being so lazy in not completing the simple chores she had assigned to me. Although I now understood how she felt, I wish I could tell her that my laziness was a simple childish attempt to say something in protest that I didn't know I needed to say out loud to her. That something was *I need you, Mom. I need you to stop working and cleaning and making lunch and just love me. I don't want to end up like you!*

I spent the afternoon riding my bike around the old familiar country roads and visiting with Grammy and Gramps. They were precious. I had forgotten how quiet Gramps was and how animated my grandmother could be. I was amused by the way she waved her hands when she talked. She was in her early sixties and had deep wrinkles in her forehead that made me want to tell her that Botox was an amazing remedy. Yet she wouldn't be Grammy without them. She was weathered from working out in the hot sun and had little wispy gray pin curls that framed her aged face. Gramps tried to ask a question and she totally ignored him. He shook his head and walked away, giving me a wink as if to say, "she'll pay attention to me when her little muse is gone."

Soon it was bedtime and I found my old pink satin nightgown balled up in my dresser drawer. There was a rose appliqué just below the satin bow on the front of the gown and the hem was ruffled so that when I twirled around, it poofed out like a ballerina's costume. Seeing it crumpled up like that felt oddly sad to me. I thought if I'd had kept that gown in my first life, I would have washed and dried it gently, ironed out all of the wrinkles, and hung it on a padded satin hanger just to look at it so I could savor that Christmas morning when my father first gave it to me.

I love it, daddy! It's beautiful, I exclaimed at age nine.

You're welcome princess. I know how much you love pink… and soft things.

I made a mental note to save it for my adult life this time around. The gown was originally full length to my ankles, but I wore it for years after that. As I got taller, I didn't get much wider, so by age thirteen, the gown still fit my small frame, but had shortened to just below my knees. I took the gown out of the dresser drawer and laid it out on the bed, slowly smoothing

30

it with my hands. Just then, my mother appeared in the doorway.

"It's almost nine, Katie, stop dawdling and get your PJs on," my mother screeched with an unnecessary tone. *Seriously?* I didn't remember her being quite this harsh, an attitude apparently reserved for those she supposedly loved. She had a beauty that was innocent yet striking. My friends used to say she looked like Doris Day. They never saw the side of her, though, that could bring Joan Crawford to mind. There had to be some sort of underlying pain that drove her to work so hard at being inaccessible.

"We need to give that thing away," she said as she snatched the gown from the bed. "It's way too short for you now."

"No." I felt tears coming as she looked at me sternly. Just then, my father came into the room. He had returned from work late. Daddy was a lumber salesman and he traveled occasionally to other states, but mostly he worked steady hours. Sometimes he had late dinners with local builders.

"What's going on here?" He smiled at me and my heart melted. I had forgotten how handsome he was as a middle-aged man. My mother glared at him, which stung me. I knew that look. It was the one I used to give Sam sometimes when he returned home late, looking a little too satisfied. I shook off the thought. *Not Daddy.*

"I was just telling Katie that this gown is way too small for her now." My mother pretended to be tidying my room.

"I'd like to keep it anyway, Mom. It's my favorite gown, even if it doesn't really fit anymore." My father smiled, with his hands tucked halfway in his front jeans' pockets. I wanted to snap a photograph of him with that look. I don't remember him admiring me, but it almost felt as if he was. I got a lump in my throat and looked away, so he wouldn't notice my lip quivering.

"C'mon Sarah. What's the harm in lettin' her keep it?" He sounded annoyed with her.

My mother threw the gown back onto my bed and abruptly walked out. My father walked toward me, bent over and gave me a hug. His whiskers rubbed against my youthful skin and I smelled a scant scent of whiskey on his breath. *No big deal*, I thought. Builders liked wining and dining with lumber salesmen.

"You better get to bed like your mother said," he admonished.

"Okay, Daddy."

He walked out, shutting the door behind him. I sat on the edge of my bed and stared into space. It was all too much to process. My father's late arrival. The looks they exchanged that I hadn't noticed before but felt so familiar to me now. I couldn't quite grasp what it all meant, but I resolved to keep a closer watch. *What other disasters did I need to help this family avoid?*

I invited Daniel to sleep in my room, in a sleeping bag next to my bed, which he loved to do. As much as he acted like he hated me, he was nine and didn't like sleeping alone. I lay there, with the moonlight softly shining through the window screen, staring at Daniel while he slept. I was inexorably vigilant, not able to take my eyes from him until well after midnight -- until the threat of death on June nineteenth was behind me. When midnight came, I wiped the joyful tears I had shed in silence from my cheeks and said a prayer of thanks for the courage and wisdom to right the first mistake in my life.

࿒

Feeling rested, I was up the next morning, ready for whatever was ahead. I had forgotten how soothing the sound of crickets outside my open window could lull me into a deep sleep. The constant hum of the box fan sitting on my desk chair also gave me a sense of constancy and comfort. Cool Ohio summer nights allowed us to tolerate the humidity of the day without air conditioning.

At the breakfast table, Daniel came running with more energy than I ever remembered, but then again, this was the first day of the rest of a life with Daniel for which I would have no frame of reference. By this time in my first life, Daniel was gone, and my parents had turned to ice. Today would have been the funeral planning and tomorrow the wake. I felt a sense of joy and relief at knowing I had saved my entire family from the extreme pain of losing a child. I was now confident I would not have to watch my mother sink into deep depression and my father turn to alcohol to self-medicate. I felt alive with the possibilities of experiencing my parents in a brand new way. *Maybe, just maybe,* I thought, *I can finally learn to love them.* I caught myself smiling into my bowl of Raisin Bran. Yet, there remained a slight uneasiness in me from the events of the night before. I quickly pushed it out of my mind and savored the moment.

Daniel plunked down his G.I. Joe in the middle of the breakfast table just in time to have our mother shout, "No toys on the table, Dan! If I've told you that once, I've told you a thousand times. Now, what are you gonna eat this morning?"

I wanted to tell my mom to calm down. *He's only nine.*

"I want Cream of Wheat! With lots of sugar on top!" he said energetically.

"That will take too long. How about cinnamon toast or corn puffs? Or you can have some Raisin Bran like your sister."

"Ooh yuk…that stuff makes you poop! Ya hear that? It will make you *poop*, Katie," Daniel teased as he got within inches of my face.

I didn't feel the slightest annoyance. I enjoyed the fact that my brother was able to ignore our mother's foul mood.

"I love you, Daniel," I said drawn out and jokingly, which I remembered always made him retreat.

"Gross," he said as he sat back down to play with his G.I. Joe.

Not surprisingly, Daniel got his Cream of Wheat. The squeaky wheel gets the grease, and it was so true in this family. I never squeaked so I never got what I wanted. I simply accepted my mother's abrasions, while Daniel charged right through them. A memory surfaced of a therapy session I once had after my divorce and I shuddered. *How can I say what I want without sounding like my mother?*

three

1978

IT NEVER OCCURRED TO ME WHEN I MADE the deal to come back that having a fifty-two-year-old brain in a now fifteen-year-old body would be extremely lonely and difficult, and sometimes hilarious. But then again, many things never occurred to me when I made this decision to attempt a perfect life. In the past two years, since I returned to my childhood, I learned things that I missed the first time around – or maybe I wasn't supposed to know because of the grace of God. I was now a teenager who actually *did* know everything, which is knowledge I have to use sparingly and with sensitivity. Deirdre was like that. Her brother, not so much. I had more arguments with that girl about her clothing and what she did with her time. I desperately did not want her to turn out like me. All that lecturing and fighting got me nowhere then, but she turned out better than me anyway. I missed her terribly.

"Katie," my friend Lisa Keebler interrupted my thoughts.

"Yeah," I answered, still staring into space.

"Should I wear the bell-bottoms or the skirt?"

The only people I knew as a child who had whole-house or even window air conditioning were Lisa's family, which is why we spent a lot of time in the summer at her house. Lisa's dad, Chuck Keebler, was a lawyer who my dad called a "sleezy ambulance chaser," which I didn't understand until much later in my first life when I had my first car accident. I was 27 and had been vehemently pursued by a tall, greasy-haired guy who promised to get me a million-dollar settlement if I would only claim whiplash. I ignored his phone calls, but years later wished I would have at least heard what he had to say. A million dollars could have changed my life.

Lisa eventually ended up being a salesclerk at the local discount department store, I'm sure to the disappointment of her highly educated family. She had the opportunity to do it and I didn't. Or at least I thought I didn't. I always thought if I had been Lisa, I would have gone to Harvard and made something of myself. But I wasn't Lisa, and no one told me I could be something if I wanted to.

"Kate, what's wrong?" Lisa asked convincingly, eager to hear the answer.

"Nothin'."

"I can see it in your eyes, Katy-did. Are things still bad at home?"

"Kind of. Mom's still checked out."

"Do you think she and your dad are gonna separate?" asked Lisa with a sordid anticipation.

"I hope not," I said. "I don't think my mom could handle my dad leaving her." Underneath, I was angry at my father ever since I discovered his "secret" a year ago. All those late nights with customers turned out to be something else entirely. I was amazed at how such a detail could have slipped by me in my first life, but I chalked it up to having lived fifty years before I turned fourteen. It was about a year ago. I had been sorting laundry in my parents' bedroom, since my mother frequently left me to manage the regular daily chores. I had opened my dad's sock drawer to place the clean ones there and an envelope fell out that appeared to have gotten stuck behind the drawer above. I reached in and took it out, noticing it smelled of sweet perfume. It was a little mangled from having been stuck behind the drawer, so I thought I should straighten it out a bit and put it back where I found it. The sweet aroma intrigued me and I wondered if it might be a love letter from my mom – and I craved to hear a positive voice from the woman who was now in a medication-induced sleep on the couch most of the time.

Before finding the letter, I was at a loss as to why my mother had gotten so depressed. I had saved Daniel from drowning, and in essence, saved my family from the worst grief and pain anyone could ever endure. So, why couldn't my mother pull herself up and live her life? I also felt a pang of trepidation, as I had recently noticed things about my father that were never apparent before. Since my first husband had cheated on me, I told myself that I was simply paranoid and generally distrustful of men, which would explain my recent suspicions about my father. I didn't want to believe my dad could possibly betray my mother like Sam had done to me. But it was difficult to ignore the late-night meetings at the office, the whispered phone calls after my mother had gone to bed, and the faint smell of this same perfume on his collar before I placed his shirt in the washing machine. I gently removed the paper inside the envelope and began to read.

April 9, 1972

My dearest Patrick,

No words can describe how I feel for you in this moment. Our weekend together last month has left me missing you more now than ever. Please tell me that we can be together someday. I know that you have a wife and two children, but I also know how terribly miserable you are being married to Sarah. I would never deny you the love you deserve, my Darling. I have never denied that and I never will.......

I continued to read but failed to comprehend any further. *The love you deserve...our weekend together...my darling...* It was signed, "Yours forever and always, Marla." I plopped backward onto the bed, tipping over the laundry basket, and let the letter drop to the floor. It was true. My suspicions were confirmed. At fourteen, I had no business knowing this. But I knew I was not truly fourteen. For a minute, I felt glad I had not discovered this letter in my first childhood. Or was there even a letter then? I felt protective of her – the younger Kate. But at the same time, it would have relieved me from my guilt. All along I thought my mother was depressed because I failed to save Daniel. Now, it was apparent there may have been more to the story – or not. Maybe my father had not had an affair the first time around. If he did, I would have been oblivious to it. Regardless, I had lived an entire life of burden. Had I learned this as a fourteen-year-old, would it have resolved my guilt or would I have grown up to hate my father? Which is worse? I spent the rest of that day sitting at the pond by myself, trying to decide if I had made the biggest mistake of either of my lives by coming back.

I never mentioned the letter to anyone, especially not to Lisa, who tended to be a gossip regardless of where the information originated.

"Katy-did! Are you listening to me?" Lisa shook my arm.

"Uh…yeah…" I was jolted out of my angry thoughts.

"What is it?" she cajoled.

"Nothing, Lis. Nothing." I knew better than to give any more details, ever since Lisa had spilled the beans about me making out with Charlie Davenport in the back seat of his car.

That was one experience I actually wanted to repeat this time around because I had always felt fondly toward Charlie and thought he was an amazing lover, probably because he was my first. I thought it would be fun to see if I still felt that way about him. Instead, it was horrible. He had fumbled around trying to unbutton my blouse and managed to slobber on my face while trying to deliver a passionate kiss. I suddenly remembered in the heat of the moment that in my first life, he had finished in record time, letting out an embarrassing noise to indicate he was in a foreign land. I wondered if that's why I originally thought he was so amazing – the fact that he had seemed to get so much pleasure from simply being with me for only a few minutes.

"Please take me home," I had said after he slobbered on me. I couldn't stand the sight of his boyishness. I felt like a pervert.

"Uh, okay," he said, smoothing his cowlick nervously while trying to find his keys. Charlie started the car, took me home, and I never went out with him again. And he never asked.

I knew I was too young to have sex, but it had been a long time, so I thought it wouldn't hurt to explore. I was wrong. It felt eerily dirty to even think about it with boys my age.

Apparently, though, Charlie had reported to the rumor mill that we had sex even though I had stopped him at first base. Lisa was all too happy to *pretend* it wasn't true, thinking she was protecting me. I was mortified because I *knew* it wasn't true – this time.

The next thing I knew, every guy at school was looking at me differently, which I had always thought meant they were finally noticing my breasts! Now, I was well aware what those hungry looks were all about, so I went straight to the source – Charlie. He denied telling anyone, although he said he "may" have mentioned it to his friend Ricky, who would not have told anyone. According to Lisa, our friend Betsy told her she had slept with Ricky because he pressured her. "Katie and Charlie did it, so what's the big deal?" he had convincingly said to Betsy.

"Now Betsy's mad because you are denying it!" Lisa had pleaded with me. "Betsy was so angry, and you know how I don't like people to be upset."

"I'm denying it because it didn't happen." I emphasized.

"Okay, whatever. Skirt or bell bottoms, Kate? You haven't answered me!"

"The bell bottoms. Wear the bell bottoms. The skirt looks too...too slutty."

"Thanks a lot, Katie. Now you think I'm a slut?"

"No, it's just that...I don't know. We're going to the library, not a concert. Boys get the wrong idea, ya know?"

Lisa looked at me as if I had two heads.

"You mean like *Charlie*?" she teased.

"No, like all of them!"

"Shut up. I think Tom Clayton is really cute, don't you? He's not like that."

"Okay, Lisa. You're right. I'm sure Tom Clayton has nothing but good intentions where you are concerned," I replied in a mock British accent.

Lisa picked up a pillow from the bed and threw it at me. I laughed and threw it back at her as we giggled. Old women still like a good pillow fight.

༚

It was a Saturday in the summer of 1978, and the public library was in downtown Clearfield, which was nothing more than a few streets with mostly mom and pop shops and the occasional empty storefront that had gone out of business with the latest coal mine layoffs. Lisa had her skirt and boots on, and I was in my bell bottoms, with ball fringe on the hem that I had attached so they would look unique (and because I had grown an inch over the summer). We had the crazy idea that we might find some boys there who would think we were smart.

"Shhhh" Lisa put her finger to her lips as we walked through the door. She was mocking the librarian, Mrs. Walker, who glared at us over her horn-rimmed glasses as we entered. I felt a little guilty because I knew she would be annoyed with us for a couple of hours, but I didn't have a choice.

The smell of leather-bound books on the shelves at the Clearfield Library was intoxicating. It always brought back fond memories of the first time I stepped into the bookmobile at school in the third grade. I was fascinated that I could get books for free that would open up the whole world to me.

"Look, there's David Parmeter," Lisa whispered. "He always looks at those *National Geographic* magazines at that table by himself. You know he's just lookin' at the pictures of those native women with naked breasts." Lisa snickered and I tried to pretend I was amused. I followed Lisa as she intentionally walked toward Tom Clayton's table, looking around as if she were focused on something else.

"Hey, Lis," said Tom Clayton, as he looked up briefly from the *Car & Driver* magazine.

"Oh, hi Tom," Lisa answered in a surprised tone.

I don't think he saw me standing behind her, so I kept quiet, not really interested in talking to Tom Clayton, who was the captain and quarterback of the Bannon County High School football team. He was a nice enough kid, but I think he got hit in the head too many times when he was younger, so even though he was a senior this year, he was twenty years old because he had been held back twice before. He could throw a killer Hail Mary pass, though, that won us the regional championship last year. That was one of my first pleasant surprises in this life. In my first life, we hadn't done that, so it made me wonder what had changed in the course of this life that would have allowed us to manage the victory.

Tom was sitting next to Dirk Matthews, a heavy-set fullback, also a senior on the team, who had zero personality.

"What are you guys readin'?" Lisa asked with her I'm-too-dumb-to-see-what-you-are-reading voice.

I took a seat across from Dirk, while Lisa sat in front of Tom. Dirk was flipping through a *Sports Illustrated*. He looked up at me and gave me a half-smile, as his leg jumped up and down under the table. He tapped his fingers on the magazine, obviously uncomfortable.

42

Lisa was whispering something to Tom, who was half paying attention, looking up from his magazine occasionally to appear interested. She was obviously flirting, and he knew it, but Tom was the kind of guy who could get any girl he wanted, and Lisa was just one of many admirers. I wanted to tell her that she was beautiful, and smart, and kind, and that she deserved a life and an education and a guy who would adore and respect her. Not this dimwitted jock who was five years older than her and who had no intention of loving her. But I knew better than to think a teenager would listen to sage wisdom. It hurt my heart to witness her lowering herself to his level.

I watched Mrs. Walker behind the librarian's desk. She occasionally looked over at our table, waiting for an outburst she could scold. Dying with boredom, I got up from the table and walked over to the desk.

"How can I find information about applying to Harvard Medical School?" I asked seriously.

I noticed Mrs. Walker holding back a grin, pursing her lips as usual.

"My, my, young lady, that would be an ambitious endeavor for you," Mrs. Walker spoke in a low tone. "Or are you inquiring for your brother?"

I was annoyed at the reference. In larger towns, I'm sure it wouldn't have been a strange question to ask, but in our little blue collar environment, where most everyone was a coal miner or steel worker, a girl going to college was simply unnecessary when men could bring in fifty dollars a day or more. The women were just expected to have part-time jobs and be full-time mothers.

"No, I'm inquiring for myself," I answered to the discerning Mrs. Walker, who walked out from behind the desk and led me to the card file – organized with the Dewey Decimal System. I marveled at the work of the past. Now with the internet at our fingertips, the rows of wooden cabinets with tiny little drawers have been replaced by a simple computer screen and keyboard. When I first arrived here, I'd had to watch my impulse to simply say, "I'll just Google it" when I needed information. That usually brought strange stares. I think most people who knew me in this life accepted me as being a little odd, so I allowed myself that perception to make up for the occasional mistaken references to the future.

She was giving instruction while looking up the information, but I was not listening because I was too distracted by her orthopedic shoes that had a stream of toilet paper trailing behind the left one. I wanted to burst out laughing, and probably would have if Lisa had been standing there, but a fifty-two-year-old teen knew better, so I graciously walked behind Mrs. Walker toward the bookshelves, trying to step on the trail of paper to break the connection. I noticed a group of middle-schoolers laughing uproariously at the table next to the card file. Mrs. Walker paused to shush them and went on her merry way. I felt a bit of affection for her, knowing that Mrs. Walker would die within a few years of a stroke, but not before she suffered for several months in a nursing home. But I remembered what the man with the soft round face had said about not being able to predict the future this time. I secretly hoped this woman's fate would be different – at least less painful and sad.

"Thank you," I said to Mrs. Walker as she handed me a slip of paper with several reference numbers on it. She then walked off with only a few inches of paper still attached to her shoe. I smiled and eagerly went about looking up the information to get into Harvard Medical School. It was both frightening and exciting. I had always wished I could have pursued a medical career, but by the time I knew that's what I would have loved, my children were small, and I was divorced and there was no possible way to do that without killing myself. *This time around I'm going to do it right. I'm going to do it my way.* Thoughts of my dad suggesting I become a secretary made me more determined. I wanted to show Patrick Mulligan that I would, under no circumstances, be anyone's Girl Friday.

I poured over the booklets and pamphlets about Harvard University, wondering if I had the courage to do such a thing. My parents would be less than enthused about it. Me in a big city, going to school all by myself without knowing a soul? My father was recently enamored with the fact that I had received the fastest typing award in my class. The IBM Selectric was the newest technology out there for typing a term paper and I was pleasantly amused at its simplicity. I was a star typist and Daddy encouraged me to take office practice classes instead of things like chemistry or biology because I would obviously "make some boss a good secretary one day." I paused at the advice, wondering if Marla had been his secretary. A wave of nausea came over me at the thought. He was disappointed when I told him I had changed my mind and was going to pursue the college preparation track at school.

"Aw, Katie, whatdaya need all that for?" He had said one night at the dinner table. "You're pretty and talented in so many other ways. There's a nice fella out there whose gonna wanna marry you and give you the life. A nice doctor or lawyer or something'."

I could see the hurt in his face as I thought, *or a lumber salesman?* I didn't really understand why he was so opposed to me going to college, other than that he was more afraid I would end up an "old maid" as they called unmarried, presumably lonely, women in those days. He had no idea how much I had enjoyed being a single woman after my divorce from Sam. I loved my father despite his chauvinism. I knew he was just ignorant to what was to come in this crazy world. Just like I had taught Deirdre, a woman needs to be able to take care of herself. If a man comes along to help, great. But you can't count on that.

"What if that guy never comes along, Daddy? I need to make sure I can take care of myself, don't I?" I had said while passing the peas across the dinner table.

"Well, look at your mother here. She loves being home with you kids and she does a great job. There's no need for two people in the same family to be out working. That's what's wrong with kids these days. They have no supervision. No supervision I tell you."

I had been observing my mother during this conversation. I could tell in her eyes that she would not defy my dad's advice verbally, but she looked at me as if to say, "Go, Katie, go! Don't do what I did." For the first time in my new life, I thought that maybe she did love me. Maybe she always loved me, but I just never knew. Kind of like the night in my bedroom when my dad was defending my desire to keep the nightgown Mom wanted to give away. Maybe they both loved me in their own way but had no way of expressing it to me in the way I needed. Maybe I remembered it all wrong. If that were true, it's possible I made a lifetime of mistakes based on false assumptions about them and me.

"You ready to go, Lisa?" I said, holding three catalogs that I had checked out to peruse at home.

"Already?" she said, annoyed.

"I asked my mom to pick us up here at 2:00. She'll be here any minute, so we should go wait outside. You know how she gets upset if she has to come in looking for us."

"Okay," Lisa responded reluctantly. "Bye boys." She made it a point to tug at her skirt as she got up and I saw Tom Clayton get a little red in the face as he stared at her bare legs protruding from the skirt. I was sure my mother would make a comment about Lisa's attire after she dropped her off at home. I was not allowed to own a miniskirt, nor did we have the money for clothing that could not be worn to school. On one hand, I felt sorry for Lisa because she was missing out on the best part of herself, but on the other hand, her courage was admirable. I needed to find a way to combine my wisdom with that kind of courage.

On the way home, I stared out of the car window. It was a rainy August afternoon, which made it a little stuffy in our un-air-conditioned vehicle. My mother's silence didn't help. My thoughts drifted to Deirdre and Sean. I thought about them daily and missed them desperately, but also knew that if I was living this life as promised, the man with the soft round face had also kept his promise to be there for my kids. I still did not understand where they were. Did I die and was I already there with them in heaven or was he taking care of them in their grief in a world that didn't include me? I hoped the former was true because the thought of them grieving one minute for me broke my heart. They were too young to be grieving. Deirdre was about to be married – for that I hoped they were continuing to live because I thought Deirdre had much better instincts about relationships and men than I did. I thought my daughter would be happy with Jake, the son-in-law I had looked forward to having.

I had moments of wanting to pick up the phone to call Deirdre to apologize for being so mean to her when she was sixteen, or to call Sean and tell him I understood why he needed his privacy. I thought that every mother should have to relive her teen years before raising her own because there was so much to learn from them. I felt guilty, knowing I had made my kids' lives more difficult than necessary. It was all much clearer now. *God be with you, Deirdre and Sean.*

four

1980

"DANIEL'S DONE WHAT?" I HAD TO ASK MY mother again because I thought she had just said he was in juvie for vandalizing the junior high school building.

"He got in trouble," she said with a blank look that I knew too well. She was zoned out on Valium again.

"How? With whom?"

"He and that so-called friend of his, Andy Larson, climbed over the fence and on to the school property tonight and broke a few classroom windows."

"Why?" I was a little dazed at the news. I knew my brother was a little hyperactive and unruly at home, but this was beyond my comprehension.

"Beats me. Your father is beside himself. He's down there now, figuring what to do to get him out. I'm sure we'll have to pay for it and it's not like we have extra money lying around."

In the last couple of years, things had gone very badly in the housing industry. Mortgage rates had gone up into the double-digits, which caused my father's lumber sales to plummet. Jimmy Carter wasn't doing any better this time than he did in my first life. But the promise of Ronald Reagan was just around the corner. Now, at seventeen, I was allowed to start acting like I knew a little about politics, so I was enjoying the rhetoric with my teachers and other adults. My parents, though, were suffering the fallout of a bad economy and now a wayward son, which broke my heart.

"Is there anything I can do?"

"Yeah, can you talk some sense into him?" She looked worn out. She was wearing a housecoat that she probably had worn all day. *Just a little lipstick, mom, would do wonders.* She was pale and sad looking.

"I'll try. When do you think Daddy will be back?"

"Who knows? It's late, I'm going to bed." She started to walk away.

"Mom?"

She turned around at the interruption and took a deep breath.

I said, "I love you."

She nodded and hesitated. I waited. I could even see it in her eyes. She couldn't do it. She couldn't say it back. She never could. She turned back around, and I went after her.

"Why? Why can't you say it?" I insisted. She turned around.

"Say what, Katie?"

"I love you. Why is that so hard in this house? Do you know how important that is? I love you, Mom. Now you are supposed to say, I love you, too, Katie. And then we hug. And then we are free."

"Oh, stop being so melodramatic. You watch too much television." Her tone belied the glisten in her eyes.

We both stood silent for a few seconds, paralyzed.

"There's leftover spaghetti in the fridge," she finally said to break the silence. "Like I said, I'm going to bed." With that, she turned and walked down the hall into her bedroom. My heart dropped when the door clicked shut. *Melodramatic. I hate that word.*

I sat alone and ate the almost-burnt spaghetti that I had warmed up in the sauce pot without enough liquid. Living without a microwave oven was more difficult than I remembered. My father and Danny came home while I was eating. Daniel had a scowl on his face and made a beeline down the hall to his room and slammed the door. *Two down, who's next?*

"Katie, I don't know what's got into him. Why is he so angry? I work to take care of you guys and do everything I can in this God-damned world to keep a roof over our heads and this is what I get?"

I sat silent. I knew he wasn't talking to me. I was getting straight-As and working toward valedictorian in a year. He went on for a few minutes and then burned out.

"Where's your mother?"

"In bed."

"Figures." He finished a glass of milk and started to walk away.

"Hey, Daddy."

"Yeah?" He looked back.

"I love you." I figured I might as well give it another whirl.

He softened and sighed heavily. "I know you do. I wish things weren't so crazy. We'll talk later, okay? I'm just mad right now." He shook his head and walked back out the front door. I knew he was going to the Route 26 Bar to drown his worries.

As far as I knew, Marla was no longer in the picture, but if she was, she hadn't gotten her wish to be with my dad. Even though he had strayed, I respected him for staying with my mother. In those days, what else was he going to do? She had no way of making it on her own. He was stuck and I could see it. I understood the pain. I felt sorry that he didn't have a good option, but selfishly thankful at the same time. If he would have left, Mom and Danny would have counted on me to be the stability. I wanted to believe my dad was sparing me that duty, but I couldn't know for sure.

I could hear rain coming down on the metal awning over the front porch. *Yeah, we'll talk later.* I realized in that moment that there was no difference in how I felt as a teen and how I felt now as an adult in a teen's world. Only now, I was saying what I didn't have the courage to say as a child. But it made no real difference in those I loved. I could love them better, but it didn't make them love *me* any better. I heard my father's old Ford truck speed out of the gravel drive, and I prayed he would come home in one piece. I simply couldn't live with myself if he died because I had let my brother live.

Days turned into weeks and weeks into months as I tried to ignore my family's drama and work toward my own goals. It was December, 1980. Reagan had won the bid for President and my father seemed a little more hopeful, although his drinking persisted. My mother became increasingly difficult to live with as she stopped doing anything productive in the house, so I had become the mother of my out of control brother and a surrogate wife to my father, just like I had the first time around. This time, though, I was much more outspoken with Daddy, but I had never experienced Daniel this way, and I found myself coddling him, protecting him. I needed him to be okay. He *had* to be okay. It seemed, though, that the harder I tried, the more rebellious he became. On the last day of school before the Christmas break, he came home with alcohol on his breath, and I nearly killed him.

"Is that whiskey I smell?"

"Naaa, you're crazy, Kate," he said with a slur.

I grabbed his arm as he walked by and he pulled away, looking at me with glassy red eyes. There was fire in them, full of anger, but he couldn't control his speech.

"What the hell, Danny? Are you trying to self-destruct? 'Cause if you are, you're doing a damn good job of it."

"Who asked ya? You're not my mother." He walked away with a crooked gait.

"You're only thirteen-years-old, for God's sake." I yelled after him, and then slammed the dish rag onto the kitchen counter.

That day I made an excuse for him, like I often did for my father, to keep the peace. That day I also went out and found a bottle of wine for myself. Even though I was aware that I wasn't old enough to drink, I knew what I could do to take the edge off, and I found an older boy who was willing to buy it for me. Boone's Farm. Apple wine. It was the worst I had ever tasted, but it served its purpose. I sneaked around the corner of the little market, with my brown bag in hand, and sat on the railroad tracks situated on the hill directly behind the little market near our high school. I took big gulps of the elixir so I wouldn't have to taste the bittersweet on my tongue. I sat there, the sun going down behind the line of trees in front of me and thought about the bus accident. How quickly I had made a decision that would change the course of my life, or death, forever. As I sat at the tracks, I secretly hoped the train would come quickly and finish the job I had started. Not once in my first life had I wanted to end it all, but this time around, I was more impatient with how things were going. I had saved

Daniel, so what else was needed? Did I really need to live life better to prove something to myself? Or to someone else? More and more, I was learning that I had way less control than I ever realized about the events that were happening around me. The best I could do was make good decisions on my own and hope that things would turn out better.

I finished half the bottle and was feeling a sufficient buzz. I slowly poured out the rest between the railroad ties where I sat. After emptying the bottle, I threw it into the trees and heard it smash into pieces. I got up and stumbled a little since it had been years since my body had experienced alcohol. I began to cry, and then sob. I hated my life. As much as I hated to admit it, I hated my life. When I was a child the first time, I had way more optimism. Of course, that made sense. I didn't have an inkling about the trials of the coming adult life. I was ignorantly blissful. Now, as a grown woman, pretending to be a child, I am more pessimistic than ever. My brother was heading toward disaster and I had no control of it. My parents were miserable but staying together anyway – something that was a foreign concept to me. My father was not the man I thought he was, and my mother was to blame for some of that. I had been losing weight recently and had difficulty sleeping. I knew what this was, but there wasn't much available besides Valium to help. I had tried to take one of my mother's pills a few days before and all it did was make me sleepy. I felt alone and defeated.

"Where are you?" I cried with my face toward the dark summer sky, standing with my arms raised as if I deserved a miracle. "You said I wasn't finished yet, but I don't know what I am supposed to be finishing!" Tears were stinging my cheeks as I walked unsteadily along the tracks toward my car that was parked across the street from the market. I knew I wasn't in any shape to drive. Just then, a shadow appeared in front of me. My heart began to race as I recognized it to be a male figure in shorts and a t-shirt.

"Who's there?" I said softly. It was just light enough to make out his shape.

"Gabe. Who are *you*?" the moonlit silhouette answered.

"Gabe who?" I said, feeling silly. "Who *are* you?"

He then came into view. A boy younger than me, with curly hair and a sweet face.

"Kate," I responded. "Sorry. You scared me."

"Didn't mean to. Kind of dangerous out here in the dark, don't you think?"

"I dunno. Are you dangerous?"

He smiled and I felt relaxed. For some reason, I knew I could trust him.

"Nah. I just like to do this when I'm trying to clear my head," he said while rubbing his shoe on a railroad tie. "You know. Walk the tracks."

"Me, too. I've had a little too much to drink, though. I was headed to my car, but I don't think I can drive yet." I felt a silly smile emerge that I knew was a telltale sign of my inebriation.

"Drink? Really? Where'd ya get it?"

"Friend. I think he thinks I'm gonna pay him back. Not gonna happen."

He smiled. "Yeah well...do you have any left?"

"Sorry. I just emptied the bottle and threw it across the tracks."

"What a waste."

"Yeah. I only wanted a buzz, not a hangover."

"Wanna walk with me? I know we're going in different directions, but..."

"Sure. It's not a problem."

"I'm headed to my car over there." I pointed to the parking lot across from the market.

"I just live over the hill on Michigan Street. Want me to walk you to your car?"

"Okay, thanks." We walked about a quarter mile. I couldn't believe I had gotten that far from my vehicle. Gabe and I talked about school. He was only fifteen but seemed much wiser than his years. He was having trouble at home, too. His dad had died, and his mother was not dealing with it very well. He had gotten a job at a local gas station to help her out, but that caused him to fall behind on his schoolwork. He wanted to be an engineer and was worried he wouldn't get into a good school if he started his high school career with mediocre grades. I assured him that he could work hard and make it up, but then I remembered that there were not so many options for disadvantaged kids to get a proper post-high school education in these times.

We got to my car and continued to talk. I liked Gabe. Gabe Michaelson, I eventually learned, although he seemed hesitant to reveal his actual identity. I wondered if he made it up. Even so, he seemed caring and real. He seemed troubled like me, but it was comforting. When I was feeling sober, I bid him goodbye. He said a simple, "Take care now."

I asked, "See you again sometime?"

He just said, "Probably," and gave me the same smile he did when I first saw his face. I got into my car and drove off, watching him in my rearview mirror as his gangly frame shuffled down the street in his shorts and oversized t-shirt. We hadn't exchanged phone numbers or any contact information, so I chalked up our meeting to a much-needed chance encounter.

After a few weeks, I tried to find him again. He was the first person I had encountered in this life who seemed to understand me, and I felt myself craving his companionship. I made numerous phone calls and looked in all of the local high school yearbooks that I found in the library. I checked out all the houses on Michigan Street and every gas station in Clearfield. Nothing. Then it dawned on me one day. Gabe Michaelson? *Really?* I laughed at myself and the obvious sense of humor the man with the soft round face possessed. Not surprisingly, Gabe Michaelson did not exist in this world. But despite my lack of faith, the cries from the railroad tracks had not gone unnoticed.

five

Spring, 1981

"KATIE!" LISA YELLED ACROSS THE DAIRY Queen. "How'd you know I was here?"

She was sitting there with Betsy, who wasn't all that glad to see me since she apparently couldn't get over the Charlie Davenport debacle.

I ignored her question and posed my own.

"Guess what?" I said while pulling the letter from my macramé purse. Cher's *Dark Lady* was playing on the radio behind the counter a little too loudly.

"Here," Lisa said eagerly, while pushing her cherry Mister Misty across the table for me to take a drink. "I can't drink the rest of this. It's giving me a serious headache."

"Guess what?" I repeated, annoyed, realizing she hadn't heard me the first time.

"I don't know. What?" She said hurriedly, without much interest.

"I got in!" I unfolded the letter and ran my hand over it like a television model selling the latest gadget.

"Whaaaat?" She looked confused, slowly guessing the meaning. "Are you serious?" She snatched the crisp letter from my hand.

"Harvard. Yes indeed." I put my hands in my shorts pockets and rocked back and forth on my toes.

"Oh my God, Katie!" I saw tears in her eyes, which made me realize why we were still friends. As ditsy as she was sometimes and often selfish, she really did love me.

Betsy tried to act like she was busy stirring her chocolate malt. "Congratulations," Betsy finally said, dispassionately.

"Thanks," I replied with a respectful smile.

"So, when do you go? Oh, Katie. I'm gonna miss you so much." Lisa got up and threw her arms around me. We hugged for a few seconds. "Sit down. I wanna hear all about it."

We spent the next half hour talking about the plan. It was the spring of 1981. Graduation was just around the corner. I had indeed qualified for valedictorian and the school of my dreams had said "Yes" to my impressive application and well-written, mature-beyond-my-years essay about the future of cancer research and my hope for a cure. I felt a little scandalous about some of it, since I had inside information that could eventually change the world of cancer treatment, but unfortunately had not studied it much in my first life. I just knew enough from my bout with breast cancer to talk with marginal intelligence about it. In a few short months, I would be leaving the Mulligan farm behind and going to Cambridge. I was ecstatic, but terrified. I had never approached something so daunting before, and I knew I would have to work my way through. Even though they were giving me a scholarship, it was not going to take care of everything there.

Earlier in the day, I had gone to the mailbox with tempered nervousness. I waited until I got into the house before scanning the pile of mail. When I saw the correspondence, nestled between the electric bill and a K-Mart ad, my heart skipped a beat or possibly two, which took my breath away. I carefully ran a letter opener through the delicate parchment-colored envelope with the crimson *veritas* logo. Opening it slowly, I told myself to not get my hopes up. *You can always transfer to Harvard from Ohio State later if you have to.* When I read the words, "It is our pleasure to inform you..." I couldn't read anything else. I just kept reading, "It is our pleasure to inform you, it is our pleasure to inform you, it is our pleasure to inform you." I sat down at the kitchen table and tried to slow my breathing. *Yes!*

"Mom?" I ran toward the back of the house and knocked on her bedroom door. "Mom? Are you awake?"

I heard a faint noise, as if she was mumbling something. The door opened and a disheveled woman I had come to accept as my mother stood there with darkened, deep-set eyes. For the first time, I noticed defined wrinkles on her forehead as she frowned.

"I got in," I said excitedly. "To Harvard. They said yes."

"That's nice sweetheart. Give me a minute and I'll be out shortly." She closed the door to the dark room.

My heart sunk. I knew she would be out when the drugs wore off. I wished so badly that I could call my dad. There was no telling when he would be home from work, and he wasn't accessible in the field. This was one of the few times I missed having cell phones.

I was pretty sure he had broken off the affair with Marla since the telltale signs had gone away a year or so ago, but that didn't mean he wouldn't find someone else to give him what my mother couldn't give any of us. I hoped he was working today and not doing something that would cause a big to-do between he and my mom and ruin my day in the spotlight.

That's when I put my schoolbooks in my room, grabbed the keys to the Catalina, and left to see if I could find Lisa at home or at the Dairy Queen. When I got to the house at 452 Ivy Lane, my first thought was, *someday I'm gonna have a house like this. That's what happens when you go to Harvard, right?* Lisa's mom answered within seconds of my pressing the doorbell.

"You look awfully chipper, Katie," said Mrs. Keebler, with her newly coifed hair in a Princess Diana feathered look. She had always kept up with the latest styles, which put years between her and my mother, who was about the same age.

"That's because I just got into Harvard!" I squeezed my hands in front of my face, which I'm sure looked as if I was about to explode in excitement. I couldn't help myself. I wanted to tell the whole world.

"Aw, Katie. That's wonderful. I'm so proud of you." She hugged me like a mother should.

"Thank you, Mrs. Keebler. Is Lisa here?"

"No, she and Betsy are at the Dairy Queen. You need to go right now and tell her. Oh, I'm so happy for you." She had her hands clasped together with an ear-to-ear smile that I wanted to photograph in the worst way. *That's exactly the reaction I'm looking for.*

I sped off to the Dairy Queen downtown, which was only about three miles from Lisa's place. I wondered if my mother cared that I took her car without asking, but then again, she was in no shape to drive, so I justified it by thinking that having the car was keeping her from doing something stupid. Another co-dependent move, but at least this time around I knew I was doing it.

Lisa and I stayed at the Dairy Queen for about an hour until it was time to go home and scrounge up some dinner. When I pulled into the driveway, I was surprised to see my dad's truck already there in the garage. It was only a few minutes after five and he normally didn't get home until six or later. I walked in and my mother immediately began scolding me for taking the car without asking.

"Katie, you know I don't mind if you drive my car, but you need to tell me. What if I had plans to do something?"

Yeah, right. Plans.

"Sorry, where's Daddy?"

"He's out in the garage," she said while stirring something in a stock pot that smelled like chili. I was pretty sure she hadn't remembered the news I told her earlier. At least I preferred to think she hadn't remembered.

I found my father in the detached garage behind our house. He was under the truck looking at something.

"Daddy? You under there?"

"Yeah, Kate. Tryin' to figure out what's wrong with this thing."

"Can you come out? I've got something important to tell you."

"Just a minute." He fumbled around for a few more seconds and then slid out from under the truck on a crawler board. I noticed he was graying at the temples, but even with sweat on his brow and greasy hands, he was the most handsome man I knew.

"What is it?" He was frowning a little, but I knew he would be happy for me.

"I got in," I said softly. "I got into Harvard."

"What?" He rose and grabbed a towel to wipe his hands. "Harvard? Wow." He smiled through the worry.

I put out my arms to accept a hug and he reciprocated. I could feel the warm dampness of his sweat through the cotton shirt. Even so, I wished I could stay in his arms forever.

"So, what does this mean? Are they gonna pay for everything?"

I knew money would be his first concern.

"Well, not all of it, but I promise, Daddy, I will get a job and pay for anything that isn't covered. I really want to do this."

He stood there staring at me as if he didn't want to disappoint me with what he was about to say. Unlike my mother, at least he was aware of what he was about to say and do.

"I just worry about you being in a strange town like that with no friends or family. All by yourself? So far away?"

I guess I expected him to react that way, but I had hoped he would be slightly more bright-eyed about the whole thing. I knew he was just being a dad and the excitement would register after he had his questions answered.

"I know, Daddy. I'm a little scared, too, but I have to do this. I just have to do this for myself."

"What about Ohio State? It's not so far away and your cousin Larry is going there. He could watch over you."

I hated Larry. He was a self-centered jerk.

"I know," I said while lowering my head, feeling somewhat dejected. He was right. I knew not a soul in Cambridge and it was a lot to take in for a small-town country girl.

He detected my disappointment and put his arm around me, leading me back to the house.

"We'll talk more about it with your mother later. For now, I'm really proud of you, Katie. Harvard, huh? Wow. That's really somethin'. My little girl wants to be a...doctor, is it?"

"Yep. Dr. Mulligan. Has a nice ring to it, don't ya think?"

"I don't know. I still think you'd make a good secretary or office manager or somethin' like that. Right here in Clearfield. Everyone already loves you, so there'd be a bidding war to hire you." He laughed with that familiar guttural sound that made it uniquely my father's.

"Yeah, right. Not everyone thinks of me like you do. But I've worked really hard for this. The classes and the term papers and all the homework. I'm the valedictorian. I want that to mean something for later on."

"I know," he said while opening the door to the kitchen. "but that also means you will be moving to a big town somewhere to do what you want to do. I doubt you'll wanna replace old Doc Pope in town. Or would you?" He looked halfway serious.

"Ya never know. I could end up being the town's family doctor down on Main Street." I knew I was saying that only to appease my father.

"Did you hear the news?" My father was speaking to my mother, still standing at the stove.

"News?" She turned toward him with a genuinely puzzled look. I breathed a sigh of relief. She really hadn't remembered.

"Katie got a letter from Harvard and they've accepted her."

She dropped the spoon in the pot and rushed toward me. She was wearing an old pair of jeans and a sweatshirt that looked like she had picked it up off of the floor.

"I can't believe it. Harvard said yes?" She pulled back from the embrace and stared into my eyes. "You did it! All that you've worked for. You did it!"

My father quickly countered. "Well, I told her we need to talk about this. You know. Her bein' in such a big place with no kin or anything."

My mother waved him off and pulled me to the chairs at the table. I loved her when she was coherent.

(Wait a minute. I stopped myself to observe what was going on. This is where the videographer pauses to interview the characters on *The Office* or *Modern Family*, before getting back to the comedic action. In my fake documentary, I would say, "In my first life, I have no memory of my mother ever caring about who I was or who I would be in the future. Hmmm…I'm not sure if I remembered it wrong or maybe it was my fault for not trying harder." Then there would be an awkward stare into the camera, as I actually thought about believing the words I had just said.)

"So, what's the next step?" my mother continued, with excitement. "Do we visit the campus?"

"That's a long drive, over there to Massachusetts, ya know." My father was drinking a large glass of milk, leaning against the counter.

"Drive? We'll fly," she said. "I'm ready to go right now."

We talked excitedly for a long while, my father interjecting his cautions, while my mother acted like a crazed schoolgirl. I could tell they were both nervous and proud – my mother living her dreams through me, my father not sure he wanted his daughter to be so high-brow. He prided himself in coming from humble means and living simply. He was wise to be worried about what education and money might do to me and I appreciated his guarded support. I knew he was probably wondering how he was going to tell his friends and co-workers in a way that would not have them thinking he was a bragging man. *Brag about me, please, Daddy. For once, brag about me.*

Danny emerged when my mother called him to dinner. She quickly told him the news, to which he muttered a squeaky "Great." His voice was changing, and it was comical how when he was tired, it pitched high then low. "Now maybe I can have the bigger bedroom, huh?"

I pushed his head as he sat staring into his bowl of chili. He smiled and murmured, "Cut it out, Kate."

I worried what would happen to Danny without me around. I hadn't planned on having to choose between keeping my brother alive and fulfilling my dreams. I hoped there was room for both.

I graduated from Bannon County High School in May of 1981 and began my journey toward Harvard by slowly pulling away from my family. I was saddened, almost grieving, that I had spent only five short years in my return to childhood and wasn't sure it had been good for my family. Or, as it turned out, my friends.

It was June nineteenth. The same day my brother had died in my first life and was saved in my second. This time, something else died in me. I had gone to Lisa's house to pick her up for a girl's night out. It was a clear, summer Friday night. The moon was full and imposing. This time when I rang the doorbell, I was met with a somber-looking Mrs. Keebler.

"Hi Katie. Lisa's in her room." She walked away without another word.

I walked down the hallway, painted in a bright yellow, and she was spread out on her stomach on the bed, in her sweatpants and Bannon High Tigers sweatshirt. About a dozen used tissues were crumpled up alongside her.

"What's the matter, sweetie?" I said, while I sat down and rubbed her back. I heard her sniffling from the tears.

She turned her head to look at me and I knew it wasn't good. I sat there quietly for a moment and then she spoke.

"Oh, Katie. I'm pregnant."

I was speechless. Pregnant? What? Who? My mind was racing.

"I'm sorry." I didn't know what else to say. Then I had to ask the obvious question. "Who? Whose baby is it?"

"Tom's." She whispered.

"Tom...Clayton?"

"Yes, Tom Clayton."

I stood up and began to pace. This was not how things were supposed to be. She never got pregnant in my first life. She was supposed to go to cosmetology school and marry that guy she met who bagged groceries at Kroger. They would have three boys and she would actually be happy. I remember talking to Lisa as an adult, after we both had children. She complained about Robert, but I think she really loved him. But Tom Clayton? He was cute, but he was a loser. A real loser.

"Katie, what are you doing?" She had sat up and was gathering the snotty tissues on the bed. While watching me pace. Her face was red and swollen.

"I don't know. I guess I'm in shock."

"You're in shock? How do you think I feel?" She blew her nose forcefully.

"I'm sorry, Lisa." I couldn't help but think that it was my fault. I had warned her about Tom Clayton. She was flirting with him way too much and I didn't trust him. Maybe I had protested too much, which caused her to see it as a challenge. Maybe she was trying to prove something to me by conquering Tom, despite my warnings, and now she is facing this. *Oh, God, what have I done?*

"This is all my fault," I said anxiously, and felt the tears sting my eyes.

"What?" Lisa stopped crying and frowned at me.

"I don't know. I can't expect you to understand. But I shouldn't have scolded you about him. I shouldn't have said you were too good for him. Do you remember that? I should have left you alone. And now, you are pregnant with his child? I am so sorry, Lisa. I'm so sorry." I was in a full-blown sob now. Lisa stood up and began to console me.

"You're talking crazy, Katie. You didn't do anything. I'm the one who is to blame. I should have known better. I'm just a weak person. A very weak person."

"No!" I grabbed her by the shoulders and stared into her eyes. "You are not weak. You will have this baby and be a wonderful mom. I know it. You are human, Lisa. Just human."

I never told Lisa that I'd had an abortion when I was only nineteen in my first life. I had hooked up with a guy I met at a disco bar, we had a one-night stand, and low and behold, I turned up pregnant. Not even knowing who he was and how to make it right, I borrowed three hundred dollars from my cousin Cherry, the only one who ever knew about it, and got rid of it when I was five weeks pregnant. I knew right away that I was pregnant because my periods were never late, and I started feeling nauseated in the mornings on my way to work. I went to see a doctor at three weeks, and he told me it was too risky to do it so early. He said I should come back in two weeks when there was more inside me to abort. Those were the longest two weeks of my life. I never forgave myself for that little "mistake" and it occurred to me as I was standing next to Lisa that my abortion had not been part of the movie clip of my life that I saw before I met the man with the soft round face. I felt a momentary and strange sense of gratitude toward him.

"Katie? Are you okay?" Lisa was staring at me with a confused gaze.

"Yeah, sure. I'm sorry." I grabbed her hands and pulled her back down to the bed. "What are you going to do?"

"I don't know. My dad wants me to get rid of it and my mom is very angry about that. I know she's disappointed, but she doesn't believe in...you know." She put her head down and I knew exactly what she was feeling. Shame.

"You're eighteen, Lisa. You do what you want to do. This isn't anyone's decision but yours."

"But what do I do, Katie? What am I going to do?" She began to cry again.

We sat there on her bed for a long time without saying anything. I just held on to her while she cried. Finally, her mother knocked on the door and came in.

"Lisa, you need to eat something. Dinner is on the table. Please come and eat."

Lisa didn't reply. I looked at Mrs. Keebler and shook my head, as if to say, "I'll make sure she eats." She shut the door quietly.

"Lisa, I need to tell you something." I knew I was taking a risk, but I just couldn't bear her pain any longer. "I was pregnant once and I had an abortion."

She turned her head toward me abruptly.

"When? Why didn't I know about this?" She seemed hurt by the news.

I struggled with how to tell the story. I certainly couldn't tell her it happened in my first life. That would sound crazy. But I wasn't yet the age I was when it actually happened. So, I quickly came up with a story.

"Last year. A guy from Turner High. You didn't know him."

Lisa's mouth was agape, obviously stunned.

"Why didn't you tell me, Katie?" She stood up. You went through something like that and I didn't know about it?"

"Please don't be upset. I was just so embarrassed. My parents never knew. The guy gave me the money and I had it done out of state. He took me to Indiana. It was awful. The whole thing was awful." Lisa was listening intently. "But I can tell you this. I will grieve the rest of my life that I made that decision so quickly and didn't even consider the possibility of having the child. I was too scared and too cowardly."

There was a pause while Lisa was thinking about what I just said. She finally responded, "I don't know what to do."

"Have you talked to Tom about it?"

"Not yet. My mom says I need to very soon. My dad thinks I should just get the abortion and not say a word."

"Well, your parents love you and want to do what's best for you, but I think it would be unfair to not let Tom be part of the decision, don't you?" I couldn't believe I was saying that, given my feelings about Tom, but I was now speaking as a fifty-something mother, not as a friend.

"That's what I think, but I don't know how. It's all so unbelievable, ya know?"

"I know, sweetie, I know."

"Obviously, I won't be going out tonight. I'm a wreck."

"Me, either. I'd rather stay here with you, if that's okay. We can watch a movie or something. Something funny. What do ya say?"

"You're sweet, Katie. I think I just want to hang out in my room. I have a lot to think about. You go ahead and go with Sheila and Betsy. But please don't say anything to them, okay?"

"Of course not. This is your news to tell whoever you want to tell. But I do think Tom should be the next to know. Who knows? Maybe he'll step up and be responsible."

Lisa rolled her eyes to let me know she knew better.

"I doubt it," she said with a slight smile. "You're the best, you know that?" She put her arms around me again and I realized in that moment how much she and I were like sisters, not just friends. There was nothing I wouldn't do for Lisa Keebler and I knew the same was true for her. I got up to leave.

"Katie?"

"Yeah?"

"Thanks for telling me. You know. About your experience. But I'm still mad that I never knew."

"I know. I'm sorry. I should have told you."

"Yes, you should have. But it makes me feel better. That perfect Katie wasn't so perfect after all." She smiled for the first time since I had arrived.

Perfect Katie. I was stunned.

I left with a heavy heart and wondered about the child I had lost. Would I see him or her when I finally made it to Quietude? There were so many questions and no way to get the answers. For the second time in this new life, I wanted to be taken from it in the worst way. His words echoed in my soul.

"This is final. There is no trying. If you start over, you cannot return to your old life. Is that clear?"

"But you'll be with me, right?"

"Like I always have."

Where are you? Where the hell are you?

six

Fall, 1981

WHEN MY MOTHER DIED IN MY FIRST LIFE, I remember how the memory of her began to slowly fade after a time. So, I would study a photo of her to refresh the memory of her almond-shaped eyes and the vibrant smile she flashed when she wasn't depressed. I was so afraid to lose the ability to conjure up an image of her in my mind that at times, I would close my eyes and replay a memory of a conversation with her just to assure myself that she really had existed. My mother had been gone, but I could always bring her back with photos and memories when I felt the need to be near her again. I never imagined when I made the decision to return to my childhood that remembering my own children's faces would be so difficult and so very painful. This time, I had no photos to take me there. I had only my memories, which after eight years had faded and transformed into something I feared was not real. I was so thankful when I would have a dream of Deirdre or Sean, when I could see their faces or hear their voices. That would sustain me for weeks. The only thought that made the other times bearable was knowing that I would see them again when this life was over. I had been assured they would be safe and content. That didn't replace the ache in my heart. It just gave me hope to keep going for another day.

Hope. That thing with wings that Emily Dickinson talked about. It perches in our heart and keeps it fluttering and alive. Without hope, life would be a prison, which was how I felt on the lonely and rainy drive toward Cambridge in August, 1981.

As the windshield wipers clunked back and forth, my father sat quietly, listening to his favorite Kenny Rogers cassette. I wondered what he was thinking. Did he hope I would succeed, or did he secretly wish me to fail so he wouldn't have to worry about me? I was caught between two worlds. One held my haphazard memories of regretful mistakes, personal foibles and wonderful joys. The other held more regretful mistakes, personal foibles and wonderful joys. The two were not the same worlds. Only I was the same. Coming to terms with the fact that I was not making much of a difference in either one was a difficult concept to process. The only hope I had besides knowing I would be reunited with my children someday was that I could make a difference in this new life and maybe not live to regret it all.

"You hungry?" My father interrupted the rhythm of the windshield wipers – and my secret thoughts.

"I guess so."

"I need to stop and fill up soon, so we'll grab a bite then, alright?"

"Sure." I was still lost in thought.

"You okay?" He reached over and turned down the volume on the stereo.

"Yeah, just a little nervous, that's all."

"Nervous? You're gonna be the envy of every girl on campus, Kate."

That made me smile. My father had no idea how much I didn't care about being envied by other girls. Little did he know, I just wanted to be accepted by the men. I wanted to know I could compete with them – the students and the teachers. I wanted validation as a woman. I wanted to know that I mattered in the world as much as they did. Yes, I wanted to be understood and valued and respected by women, too, but to get it from the men would make this crazy, whirlwind second life of mine worthwhile. I wanted to matter this time because I had something to contribute, not because I was pretty or could cook or knew what I was doing in the bedroom. I just wanted to matter.

Daddy and I arrived on the campus of Harvard University at 2:00 pm on a Sunday. I could tell he was a fish out of water. He had not gone to college and if he had, it wouldn't have been anything close to this caliber. I sensed his discomfort around people he assumed were intellectual types who didn't have any horse-sense, as he would call it. But I was so proud of him for being there with me. My mother had planned to come but, as I should have expected, she was not feeling well the morning of our departure and gave me a perfunctory hug and wished me well as she made her way back to her den of despair. I was only half disappointed since I knew not having her on the trip would relieve both me and my father from having to manage her moods.

It pained me to realize that I could have done this very same thing the first time around and my father would have supported me, but I didn't know that then. I hadn't known enough to try. I hadn't given him a proper chance to show me he would have stepped out of his comfort zone to support me if I would have simply believed he would. I felt courageous and proud of myself and of my father. Maybe this time, I understood him a little better. Maybe this time, I understood him as a parent.

"This sure is a big place," he said as we walked toward the admissions office where I was to pick up my new student packet of instructions. "Won't you feel kind of lost?"

"I'm sure at first it will be hard, but I'll get used to it."

"What if you don't like your roommate? I mean that could be awful if you have to live with someone you don't care for, ya know?"

"I know, Daddy. You're worried about everything right now, but once I get settled, I think you'll see that I will be safe and happy here. I promise."

A man approached who looked like the quintessential bearded Harvard professor, with jeans and a patched corduroy jacket. My father stared at him as he walked by.

"Really, Katie? Do you really think this will make you happy? All these strangers in a town you don't know?"

I stopped on the sidewalk under a huge old oak tree and he continued ahead of me until he realized I was no longer by his side. He turned to see where I had gone.

"What's the matter?" He turned and walked back toward me. He was dressed in his favorite polyester golf shirt and jeans, an outfit I'm sure he felt was fitting of a special occasion like this one. I wondered in that moment how my mother could be so cold to him. I also knew that he couldn't possibly know that I had spent years as a single woman by myself, sometimes in strange places without knowing a soul. He didn't know that I knew how to stay safe and watch my back and fend off inappropriate men. He didn't know and it struck me how much I needed him to care.

"I love you, Daddy. I love you for caring." I reached out and gave him a hug. He felt stiff in my arms. He was not very comfortable with public displays of affection. He patted me on the back and then pulled away, putting his hands in his jeans pockets as he often did when he felt vulnerable. He looked away for a moment, then gave me a closed-lip smile while letting out a sigh.

"Of course, I care. And I worry. It's my job." He hesitated. "I'm sorry your mother isn't here. You know…" he trailed off, looking past my shoulder as if he was staring at her in the distance.

I did know. As much as I believed my mother was truly proud of me, she couldn't seem to slay the demons within her when it counted the most. Surprisingly, I didn't feel anger toward her in that moment. Just pity.

I linked my arm in my dad's and started walking toward the building with him again. "Okay then," I said. "You do your worrying since that's what you will do no matter what I say, and I'll just pretend you're okay with me hanging out with all of these book nerds."

He laughed heartily and all seemed right with my world for a change. But it was only a matter of weeks before I got reports from home that things were going haywire. In fact, things were worse than ever before.

꙳

My mother called me the weekend before Thanksgiving to tell me that Daniel was in trouble again. This time, he had been caught selling marijuana on the street corner near the high school. She said my dad was beside himself with anger.

"He's…well…you know, taking to the bottle again. We miss you, Kate. When will you be home?"

Taking to the bottle again. As if that excused her somehow.

My heart sank thinking about what was happening to my family the minute I went off to forge my own life. I wanted to say to her, *Suck it up Mom. He drinks because you close yourself up in that dark room and Danny just does whatever the hell he wants.* I knew it was futile.

"I've got a paper due on Monday. As soon as I turn that in, I will be on the bus home." Just the thought made my stomach turn.

"Dad says to leave in the morning, not at night. He doesn't want you hanging around the Greyhound station after dark, okay?"

"Okay, Mom. I'll get a ticket tomorrow. I'll try to leave before noon. I might not get into town until close to midnight, though. Will you be able to pick me up or do I need to call Lisa?"

"The way your dad is feeling today, he'd probably drive to Cambridge to retrieve you. But, no, I will pick you up."

"You promise?"

"Katie! Of course, I promise. What kind of mother do you think I am?"

You don't want to know the answer to that.

The drive back to Clearfield on the bus was long and uncomfortable. I had too much time to think about what I would do when I got in the middle of my parents and my brother. My mind drifted to memories about what I was doing at age 18 the first time around. I think I was settling in at my new job at Tamborlin, the firm that ended up being our biggest customer at the ad agency. That's how I landed the job at Schuster and Bates. After about five years of working for

Tamborlin, in their satellite office in a town near Clearfield, I was sent to an all-day advertising meeting at the S&B corporate offices in Pittsburgh. John Schuster liked my looks, I think. It certainly wasn't my brains because I hardly spoke at the meeting. However, during the break I must have impressed one of the ad managers and the next thing I knew, I was a young woman in her twenties working admin for the largest advertising agency in Pittsburgh. Without a college degree, I started as a secretary to an ad manager and worked my way up to assistant manager of the manufacturing group after about twenty years. I marveled at the thought of having moved to the big city when I was only 23 years old. Especially with no idea about how to live alone and pay my own bills. I had lived with my parents right after high school until Lisa and I moved into together when we were 19, renting a small apartment on Buckeye Avenue near the railroad tracks, until she met Robert and left me without a roommate. Luckily, that's when I was offered the promotion and off to Pittsburgh I went.

Along the way, there were lots of political maneuvers that worked against me and promotions that passed me by. But there is something to be said for staying power and after a while, I think John Schuster began to trust me simply because I was loyal. I knew I would never rise to a full-fledged manager because I was a woman without an education, never mind that I had educated myself over a 25-year span to know exactly how to look, speak and connive in the world of ad sales. Even my female co-workers and superiors treated me as if I was merely Schuster's sympathy hire instead of someone who had common sense to know how to relate to people. Eventually, I ended up working for that idiot, Fletcher, when it should have been me who got his position. He was an outside hire who was the son of a cousin of a brother of someone in Schuster's family, or something like that. So, the sales department was as far as I got, but I was determined to be good at it even if it wasn't my life's passion. It wasn't until my second life that I came to understand that my success in my first life was largely attributable to my father's sales abilities and incredible work ethic. "Do it well, whatever your lot in life," he would often say when my brother or I would complain about a chore or school project. I was always told I looked like my mom, so I think I felt I had to be like her. But dad and I were more alike than I ever gave us credit for, and it took me a lifetime to appreciate that, which bolstered me this time around.

Now I wanted to go back to my old life and tell John Schuster and Cam Fletcher to go to hell. I dreamt of the possibilities as I stared from the bus window out onto the dark, dashed pavement going by, line after line. I fantasized about finding those guys and giving them a piece of my mind, but unfortunately, they wouldn't have any idea who I was or what I was talking about. I was finding fantasies like that fell flat and were a complete waste of my emotion. *Stay in the present* was my constant reminding mantra.

My mother was waiting at the bus station, surprisingly, and we had a quiet drive home. She asked the expected questions about how I was feeling, how the bus ride was, and if I was happy to be home for the holidays. But I was not in the mood for small talk.

"Was dad still awake when you left?"

She seemed hurt that I shifted the conversation to him.

"I don't know." There was silence for the final ten minutes until we pulled into the driveway and parked in the garage.

"You know, Katie," she started while gathering her purse and sweater from the back seat, "I'm not your enemy."

I stopped and thought about what I should say. When nothing came, I opened the car door and got out. I made my way into the house and found my dad sitting in the dark in his recliner, with a glass of Scotch and water – his classic drink of choice. I went over and turned on the lamp beside his chair. His face was worn and tired. His eyes glassy. He was wearing the fleece robe I had bought him three years ago for Christmas.

"Hi there," I said, as I plopped down my suitcase.

"Hey," he blurted out, clearly startled from his stupor, and stood too fast, steadying himself against the side table. When he gained balance, he reached out and hugged me tight as I heard my mother's bedroom door slam shut. I could smell the liquor on his breath, as he pulled back from me and stared into my eyes.

"Let me take a look at my girl."

"So how are you, Daddy?" I smiled, shoving the worry about him and the tension with my mom down to a familiar depth.

"Oh, you know. Life's got its challenges. But things are better now that you're home." He returned my smile in an attempt to appease me.

"Your job okay?"

"Yeah, sure...same old same old. How're the studies coming?"

"Same old same old." I didn't really want to talk about me. "Actually, it's pretty exciting," I corrected.

"That's great, Katie. Really great." I couldn't tell if he was incredibly sad or just alcohol worn.

The elephant was getting restless, so I gave in.

"Mom told me that Danny's been acting out again."

81

He became silent and sat back down in the chair. He motioned for me to sit across from him on the couch.

"What's going on with him? I don't understand. And you. Look at you." I shook my head and turned away. It was difficult to see him like this, even though I had seen it a hundred times before. This time, though, I felt indignant. I was doing my level best to make him proud and this is what I got.

"It probably isn't the time, Katie." He got up from the chair, trying to escape my inquiries.

"Sit down!" I was surprised at the force of my voice.

He complied, reluctantly.

"I leave for a few months and suddenly everything is falling apart. Danny's out of control, Mom's back in the darkness and you...." I still had trouble naming it.

"Yeah, what about me? Now you sound like your mother." He knew how to disarm me. There was nothing worse than being compared to her.

It was my turn to leave, sure that this late-night conversation was misguided and headed nowhere.

"No stay," he pleaded. I saw tears in his eyes that were more than the glossiness of his inebriated state. "I'm sorry. That was unfair."

"Very." I sat bent over, staring at my Reebok tennis shoes. It was time for a new pair.

Silence passed between us for thirty seconds. Finally, he broke in with, "I don't know." Then more silence. "Well, we probably can't solve anything at this late hour."

"No probably not, but tomorrow it will be more of the same and nothing will get resolved then either." I felt a lump in my throat growing. The thought of having already lived beyond the age my father was now coupled with wanting so desperately to fix him. It was overwhelming. I got up and knelt next to him as he took another sip from the highball. "Can't you see that this whole family needs help?" My voice shook with both anger and sadness.

"Not you. You seem to be the only one who has any sense. But your brother? Your mother? I have failed them, Katie. I've failed."

"How? How have you failed? Mom is like a zombie most of the time and Danny, well, I don't know why he is the way he is. But you have done everything to take care of us. Everything you knew to do."

I did know that Danny was the way he was, in part, because of his biology. He got the gene from both sides of the family. But that wasn't my dad's fault. If anything, the fault he had was in sending the message to his children that life is best dealt with through the lens of the bottle. I rejected the message, but Danny embraced it wholeheartedly and with more intense means. My father looked at me with both admiration and confusion.

"Well you're the only one who appreciates me around here," he slurred. "The other two? They just suck the energy out of me. Suck it completely out."

His sadness quickly turned to anger, as it often did when he wasn't in his rational mind. He got up and took a second again to get his balance. "You all want me to stop drinking? Okay, I will if the rest of you will just cut me a break." He raised his hand and threw his drink across the room. It smashed against a silk flower arrangement on the hearth of the fireplace. I startled at the sound of glass smashing against brick. "There," he said with a smile. "I'll start right now."

"Dad! Don't do this!" I immediately got up to clean the mess. Luckily the thick glass broke in mostly large pieces. The smell of whiskey made my stomach turn.

"Do what?" He was red-faced. "Sit here and try to pretend? Ask your mother what I've done that makes her the way she is. She'll tell you all about it and she'll never let me forget it either."

"I know. I already know." I laid the pieces of glass on the hearth and turned back toward him. "And trust me, that's not what makes her this way. You could be a saint and she would be the same."

He took in what I had said and rubbed his face with his hands in frustration. I saw his anger surface again.

"I knew it. I knew she would tell you. She was always trying to pit you and your brother against me."

"That's not how I know. I don't need to tell you how I know, but it doesn't matter now. It's over, isn't it? The affair. It's over?"

He sat back down, hunching over to rest his forearms on his lap. His work-worn hands were trembling, and he clasped them between his legs. A minute later, he was sighing heavily and apologizing. "Of course, it's over. It's been over for years."

We sat silent for what seemed like hours. I sat on the floor, hugging my knees and at a loss about where this was going. Eventually, I broke in with my own tears.

"Daddy, I can't expect you to understand what I am about to say, but twenty years from now, you will be proud of me. You will be proud. But it's going to take some time and I need the time to focus, not worry about all of you. Please don't make me regret all of this later. Please."

He looked up quizzically. "You're not making any sense. I'm already proud of you." He sighed heavily again. "Maybe you're right. It's too late to do this."

"I know you can't understand. But for once in my life, I want to know that in the moment, I am doing the right things, making the right decisions, saying what I should say to make it all better — so I don't live to regret this very moment." By this time, I was rocking back and forth, engulfed in my own personal turmoil that had nothing to do with the present.

He knelt down beside me and covered me with his arms. I sensed he was more sober than he had been when I first entered the room.

"I don't know what's going on Katie, but it's going to be okay. You can't fix this. You can't regret it when it's not yours to fix. This isn't your fault. This isn't your fault." He was rocking with me. He placed his tear-drenched cheek on my shoulder, and I was undone with grief. "I swear this isn't your fault."

I could have died a second death right then.

seven

1982

THERE HE WAS, JUST LIKE I HAD REMEMBERED only I was less intrigued by his charm than I had been in my first life. Sam. The one who had given me two beautiful children, but who had also turned my life upside down with his selfishness. My heart began to pound the minute I saw him. I had thought that at some point we would run into each other, but because we didn't travel in the same circles and he didn't grow up in my hometown, I hoped I could avoid him this time.

I was doing the historical math in my head. We had met at a party around this same time. Christmas, 1982, over winter break. Possibly on this very same weekend and maybe even a Friday night like tonight. He had come home from college and I had been hanging out with Lisa, who wanted to go to a party a girlfriend invited her to, where she thought her next beau might be found. Now, here we were again in this new life, on quite possibly the very same weekend. Sam and I at the same bar. We couldn't have planned it better if we tried, which felt eerily like something divine was at play. Only this time, I was dragged to a bar by my cousin Cherry, which was not much different than Lisa insisting I accompany her to a party for

86

similar reasons. Sam appeared to be with some old friends, flirting with a group of girls at a nearby table. I scoffed to myself at his perfectly pressed khakis and Izod sport shirt. Bright coral, no less. What once impressed me was now a deterrent. The guys I actually liked at Harvard were the ones who were not so pretentious. I thought that alone was a great improvement over my first stab at life. I sipped my rum and Coke, with a certain air of superiority, while listening to Cherry drone on to some random girl she knew from high school, who had made herself at home at our table. Cherry was recounting an argument she had with her boyfriend the night before. The girl pretended to listen as she scanned the crowd for prospects. I tried to show some interest but couldn't keep my eyes from Sam and the way he was working the room. At one point, he looked at me, but I quickly looked away, not wanting to make eye contact. But curiosity got the best of me and eventually Sam locked eyes with mine, which brought him to our table.

"Sam McConnell," he said suavely, extending his hand toward me. I returned the gesture and he pulled out a chair to sit. I searched my brain for the memory of how he had introduced himself before, but I drew a blank.

"Kate Mulligan," I said without thinking. I wanted the discomfort to be less obvious, but given my secret history with him, I was verbally paralyzed.

"Are you from around here?" He continued, rather loudly since the DJ was back from his break and spinning Loverboy's *Working for the Weekend*. A bunch of girls had jumped up and were dancing with drinks in hand. Sam sat down, uninvited, next to Cherry's friend and gazed at the dancing girls. Cherry stopped talking for a second to look him over, but then resumed her story without missing a beat.

"Yeah...grew up in Chandlerville and graduated from St. Olafson High School," he said proudly. "You?"

I was slightly amused because I happened to know that he had only ended up at St. Olafson because he got kicked out of public school for being a bully. This was going to be a somewhat enjoyable test to see if he could tell the truth or not.

"Clearfield. I'm a student at Harvard now. Second year." I was probably too anxious to impress, but this was Sam after all. Getting the one up was way overdue. He seemed annoyed by the loud music as he strained to hear my answer.

"Did you say Harvard?" I had forgotten how piercing his eyes could be and how perfect his skin and hair were when he was a young man.

"Yes," I affirmed with a little more humility in my voice.

"Wow, that's a bit out of my league," he said jokingly. "I'm third year at Kent State," he said almost apologetically, as he summoned a waitress by holding up his empty glass toward her.

"That's a good school." I said tritely and was embarrassed that I couldn't think of anything more intelligent to say. All of the sarcasm that I had practiced after our divorce, in case I ever had the chance to confront him, was no longer accessible. This was not the Sam who had hurt me. This was a younger, more innocent version of him, who became something else later. Maybe it was because of the bad chemistry between us, or just because people change when they are challenged. In reality, he should have ended up with one of those dancing girls he was admiring. It occurred to me as he fidgeted with his empty glass that maybe Sam wasn't comfortable in the presence of girls who didn't swoon over him at first glance. Information I wish I had known before.

"So, Harvard, eh? What field?"

"Pre-Med."

"Nice. You must be a smart one. Not many girls have that kind of ambition."

"What about you?"

"Marketing. I've always been told I could sell ice to the Eskimos, so it just made sense to do what came natural, ya know?"

I never noticed until now that his two front teeth were not perfectly aligned. Sam had always been difficult to engage in conversation. Most of the time during our marriage, we talked without even looking at one another. I wasn't sure if it was bravery on my part or that I had just learned to be more direct in conversation, but I was noticing many things about Sam McConnell's face and mannerisms that seemed new and different.

"Uh huh. That makes sense." My heart was no longer beating out of my chest, but I felt strangely unmoored.

"Why medicine? You have doctors in your family?"

This one I could answer.

"Oh no. My dad is a salesman like you and honestly, I will be the first one in my family to even get a college degree."

"What? That's great. Congratulations."

"Well, I haven't done it yet, but so far, so good."

"I'm sure you will be great. Dr....what was your last name again?"

"Mulligan."

"Yes, Dr. Mulligan will see you now." He said with feigned reverence.

I laughed in appreciation of his attempt to relax me. He had sensed my discomfort and like a true salesman, put me at ease with a little humor. He smiled back at me, knowing he had succeeded.

I can't lie. For a moment, or even a few moments, I felt a surge of maternal longing. What if? What if I gave into this feeling? What if I pursued something with Sam again? I wondered if I could make the timing work. If he and I could reproduce Deirdre and Sean. I ached for them and this would be one way to bring them back into my life. My mind raced with the possibilities and what would have to be done to make it happen. Yes, I would have to delay my education. The first time we met, I wasn't in college. I was working for a local PR firm and Sam was finishing his bachelor's degree in marketing. All he cared about was finding a woman who would put him on a pedestal, which I didn't do very well, but I could try again. My father hadn't been too keen on Sam, but that's because he saw us fight so much before we ever said, "I do." I could control that, couldn't I? A wave of nausea came over me and I excused myself from the table. Sam looked confused, but I had to get to a bathroom.

Sweat poured over me as I leaned against the bathroom wall, not sure if I was going to vomit or just needed a splash of water on my face. I looked into the mirror and saw that my mascara was running down my cheek. A girl about my age walked in, looked at me, and laughed as she went into one of the stalls. "Yeah, been there before. They make the drinks a little stronger here than in most places. You'll puke it up, but then it will pass."

I remained silent. *Oh, honey, if you only knew.*

I composed myself and walked back out into the bar, determined to be civil to Sam, but not give into anything that would change my previously charted course. The irrational thought that I could somehow reproduce the same children was delusional and I knew it.

After pulling myself together, I sat back down at the table where Sam sat alone. Cherry and her friend had joined the dancing girls, as a disco ball turned to the beat of a Pointer Sisters' tune.

"You okay?" Sam said with more concern than I had ever witnessed in our entire marriage. He reached out and touched my arm, which sent an electric pulse through me.

"Yeah...I think whatever they put in this drink is getting the best of me." I pulled my arm away and he picked up a napkin and fiddled with it.

"I know what ya mean." He chuckled while rolling up the napkin like a joint. I watched with interest until he looked up to meet my gaze. "Hey, I'm only here for another week or so, then I have to go back to school...and I guess you do, too." Those familiar dark brown eyes were flanked with the longest lashes I'd ever seen. "I was thinking maybe we could go out? You know, get to know each other better?"

There it was. That irresistible smile. It was a sweet invitation, but underneath was the old innocence that drew me in but felt disingenuous at the same time.

"Oh, I don't know." I hesitated, trying to think of a way to nicely decline his invitation. *Wow. It's Sam and I'm having trouble rejecting him.* I marveled for a moment at how memories are always more intense than real life is in the moment.

"What about now? We could get a bite to eat and then drive out to those nice homes on Prospect Lake to look at the holiday lights."

He seemed more desperate than I remembered. It crossed my mind that if I had played a little cat and mouse with him the first time around, maybe he would have respected me more in the long run.

"That's very sweet of you," I finally answered. "But I'm here with my friends as our last girls' night out before I go back to school. I'm headed back earlier than most because I'm working on a big project. You know...it wouldn't be fair to skip out on them." I tried to sound convincing, but most of it was a lie. I could feel the color rising in my face. I didn't have the heart to tell him that we had already been married before and it didn't turn out so well.

"Oh, okay. I see." He shifted around in his chair and then pretended to see someone he knew across the room. "It was nice meeting you. Maybe we'll see each other around some other time."

"Sure," I said with a more genuine smile. He got up and walked toward the dance floor. The rest of the evening I was distracted by his presence, wondering if I would ever see him again. Cherry eventually noticed.

"Hey, that's some hunk you were talking to, Katie."

"Yeah, he's cute, isn't he?"

"You can't seem to take your eyes off of him. Did he ask you out?"

"Yes, but I don't have time for that. Guys complicate things."

Cherry looked at me as if I had three heads.

"I'll never get you," she said as we walked out of the bar to her car.

"Hey, you okay to drive?" She looked a little wobbly.

"Probably not. What about you?"

"I'm good. I barely had one drink."

"Cool." She threw me the keys and we climbed into her silver Chevette. I was distracted by the thought of how odd it was that Sam would never meet the children we had created in another life. He wouldn't grieve them and somehow that seemed grossly unfair.

The drive to Cherry's apartment was quiet. We made arrangements to get her car back to her in the morning and I watched her fumble with her keys before finding the right one to let herself in. I wondered how this Cherry was different from the one who had left my brother in the pond before he had drowned. Would her life turn out better with less guilt or would it simply go the same way? Once alone in the car, I moved in and out of quiet sobs on the drive home, wishing the radio had not been playing the song that had played many years ago on this same weekend when Sam and I had our first date. *Hard to Say I'm Sorry,* indeed. I guess some things are burned into memory for no apparent reason.

Saturday was quiet and uneventful. Lisa and I went shopping for Christmas presents. Danny slept most of the day and mom and dad were at least being civil to one another, for my sake, I think.

According to Danny, they had been fighting about everything but the weather lately, and they were not in particular agreement about that. He was a source of much of their arguments as he was flunking most of his classes and managing to dodge the cops as he regularly violated his probationary terms. Sometimes I looked at Danny and wondered what he was getting out of destroying his life. Destroying everyone's life. I was thankful to have college as a respite, but every time I left to go home, I felt as if I was abandoning my child. My baby. The very thing I came back for but had no power to fix. The child was screaming for its life and I wanted nothing to do with it. Nothing to do with the dysfunction, the illness, the brokenness that defined my roots and who I had become in my first life. I wanted to abandon it to become something else, but there it always was when I returned. As broken, and sick, and weak as I had left it. It both saddened and angered me.

On Sunday morning, I drug myself out of bed around ten o'clock, Surprisingly, my mother was up and making breakfast. I smelled the coffee brewing and heard the bacon sizzling in the kitchen where my mother stood dutifully.

"You're up bright and early this morning," I said to her. I had forgotten how ugly her pink flowered housecoat was. I'm pretty sure my dad hated it, which I assumed was the reason she wore it.

"Early? Katie, it's after ten in the morning. I've been up since seven." Her brightness told me this was one of her good days. When she wasn't doing so well, darkness circled her expressionless eyes.

"Okay. Where's dad?"

"He just went out to get the paper."

I saw my father walking through the front door, with paper in hand and holding on to a white coffee cup with *Best Dad* scrawled across it in letters painted by my four-year-old hand.

"Morning, Katie. Want some coffee?" he said energetically and put the paper down on the table in front of me. He started talking about a big weather storm coming in that night, but his voice became muffled as I stared at the front- page story of the *Clearfield Dispatch*. The headline said, LOCAL MAN KILLED IN DEADLY CAR CRASH. Somehow the name McConnell jumped off the page at me. *Twenty-year-old Sam McConnell was killed instantly after striking a utility pole on Clarendon Street early Saturday morning around 3:00 am. Autopsy results are pending, but alcohol is believed to be involved.* The photo of a mangled truck sickened me.

I fell into a seat at the table, while the distant sounds of my father's voice trailed off. My throat fell into my chest and then everything went blank. The next thing I heard was my mother's voice as I lay on the kitchen floor, passed out from the shock.

"Oh, dear." She grabbed my shoulders. "Katie, are you okay? Are you okay?" Her hands shook with frantic force. I opened my eyes but couldn't focus.

Sam is dead.

My first thought was strangely that Sean and Deidre would be angry with me for killing their father. *I should have stayed with him.* It didn't make sense. Was I waking up from a nightmare? My head was pounding.

"Thank God! Are you okay?" I was surprised at my mother's genuine upset.

"Yeah," I managed to whisper.

She helped me to a chair at the dinette set, where I saw the headline again. It was true.

"I need to go lie down." I got up and my dad grabbed my elbow to help me down the hall. He looked back to make sure my mother had stayed in the kitchen before he spoke.

"What's going on?"

"What do you mean?" I asked, confused.

"Is this a hangover or something?"

"No, not at all." I searched my groggy mind for an excuse. "It's that time of the month. That's all."

He nodded in agreement.

I slept most of the day, sipping water now and then, but had no appetite or motivation to face the world.

Sam is dead.

eight

1983

I FINISHED MY SECOND YEAR AT HARVARD with relative ease. Organic chemistry was a bear, but I was intensely motivated. Sometimes I felt a little guilty because I had experience under my belt that made me unfairly competitive. Even though I appeared to be a peer to my classmates, there was something in how they responded to my old soul that made me wonder if they knew more about me than I thought.

I had a lackluster relationship with my first- and second-year roommate, who didn't believe in wearing deodorant. I was not upset when the second year came to an end and I could put that awkwardness behind me. She was nice enough but avoiding her proved to be more labor intensive than it was worth. Against my usual needing to please everyone, including a smelly roommate, I finally gathered the courage to tell her I had found another roommate for year three even though I hadn't. Her response was "Good. Your tidiness was a bit much for me anyway." The nerve! It was one in a long list of lessons this old soul would learn about assuming I could make do in a relationship if I just overlooked the obvious.

As the school year came to a close and summer was near, I was sad to leave the one friend I had made who would be the greatest memory of my second year. Angela. Yes, it's corny when considering the root of her name, but she became an angel to me in the usual way angels tended to present themselves to me in this life – with subtlety and awe.

The first time I saw her was in the campus community room, near the cafeteria. She was sitting cross-legged on a couch, totally engrossed in a literature textbook. I glanced over at her and immediately did a double-take because she was a mirror-image of Deirdre. At first, I thought I was hallucinating. I had just returned from the winter break and was deeply depressed about Sam's death. I had tried to talk to someone about him, but no one had any sympathy for me. As far as they were concerned, I had only met him at a bar so there was no need for dramatics. I had talked to my father about my guilt – that if I had said yes to his offer for a date on that Saturday night, he might not have died, but my dad was more glad that I wasn't with Sam or I would have been dead, too. There was no one to talk to about what I was feeling. On top of that, I had accidentally mentioned Deirdre to my mom in a moment of weakness, saying something like, "Yeah, Deirdre always liked that, too."

"Who?" she asked, confused.

"Oh, just someone at school," I answered, with a lump in my throat. I only *wished* I could see her at school. Then, *voila.* There she was and I rubbed my eyes to refocus. The same auburn curls, pulled up on top of her head. The high cheekbones, with a natural blush. The same slope to the nose and perfectly shaped lips. She even wore a cross around her neck, just like Deirdre often did. I walked closer to her, thinking it was a phantom I created to cope with the trauma of recent days and distant times. She looked up.

"Hi," she said, a little startled, since I was clearly walking toward her with purpose.

I noticed the closer I got, the more she took on her own distinct identity, which was a weird relief. But still, the resemblance was uncanny.

"Hi. Do you mind if I sit here?" She had been taking up the entire couch with her tall, lanky body and bookbag.

"Oh, of course." She quickly moved to the end of the couch and gathered her things closer to her. Even her voice sounded similar to Deidre's.

"Which prof do you have for Lit this semester?" I asked, trying to sound my age.

"Foster. He's pretty good."

"Oh, yeah. I had him, too. Last semester."

She put her book down to be polite. I felt intrusive, but too intrigued to care.

"I'm Angela," she smiled and extended a hand.

"Kate," I answered. Her hand was small and warm. I wanted to hold on to it in the worst way. Looking more closely at her face, I noticed that she resembled Deirdre more from her profile than straight on. Her face was longer and her mouth smaller. I wanted to just sit and stare at her while she read, but I figured that probably would be creepy.

"So, where's your home?" Angela continued. She shifted from her cross-legged position and turned both knees toward me, which I took as an invitation to have a conversation.

"Ohio, and you?"

"South Dakota," she replied, almost embarrassed.

"Hmmm...I've never been."

"No kidding. Who would purposely travel to South Dakota?"

"Oh, I don't know. I've always thought seeing Mt. Rushmore would be cool, but never had the chance."

"Do you know that's what *everyone* says?" She laughed out loud.

"I guess they do," I said sheepishly. "I had a friend who lived in Las Vegas for awhile and no one ever believed that she was telling the truth. She would get so annoyed when others would say, 'You mean people actually live there?' 'No, it's populated by aliens.' She would answer." We both laughed at that and became fast friends.

Every day for about two weeks, we found the same table at dinner or the same couch after meals to meet and talk. The more I got to know her, the less she reminded me of Deirdre in appearance, but it was exactly the kind of relationship that Deirdre and I had enjoyed when she became an adult. Conversation was always easy and supportive and full of love and care. Angela was intelligent and witty, like Deirdre, and seemed to fall into my life at a time when I had lost all hope that I would ever see my children again.

I'll never forget that snowy evening in January, after I first met Angela, when I looked out of my dorm room window and spoke out loud to the man with the soft round face. The snow was falling gently against the sill. I lifted the sash to let some of it fall on my hand. It was cold and real and miraculous. All I could muster was a simple "thank you" as I stared up into the dark, cloud-insulated sky. *Thank you...for being there.*

At the end of the semester, Angela and I had agreed on rooming together for our third year, but until then, we were saying goodbye for the summer. We vowed to write to one another during the break, but neither of us did. There were plenty of moments when I longed for Angela's friendship, but other things got in the way – like the distraction and humiliation of my little secret family world.

༄

The summer was full of activity and the usual family drama. I tried to stay out of the house by spending time with Lisa or Cherry. Lisa had a one-year-old little boy – Tyler. When I came home during the last break and found out she had decided to keep the baby, I was elated. She and Tom had moved into a little apartment. Mrs. Keebler watched the baby while Lisa went to cosmetology school and Tom got a job in a local factory, making athletic shoes. I wasn't sure they would survive as a married couple, and Lisa probably would regret having a baby with Tom at some point, but I knew she would never regret allowing Tyler to come into her world. It was one of the few things about life I knew for sure.

There were lots of discussions that summer about what to do with Danny, who had overdosed the day after I returned from school. More than once, half-empty glasses of my father's bourbon went flying as my mother predictably slammed the bedroom door. One day on the way to Sharonville to see Danny, I had a flashback of my mother trying to shew us out of the house because Danny and I were fighting too much. "You kids are gonna drive me to Sharonville if you don't stop!" I never really knew what that meant until I got older and learned that it was the infamous home of the state mental hospital. I had never been there, and quite frankly, never thought I would need to go to Sharonville, but there I was, walking down the cold dark hallway toward the visiting room, with spotted green industrial tiles on the floor and the smell of old wood and disinfectant in the air.

At first glance, I didn't recognize his face. It was sunken and pale.

"You gotta get me outta here, Katie."

"You're here for a reason," I said, while staring at his bony fingers that were nervously tapping the cafeteria-style table. His nails were bitten far below the fingertips, which were red and swollen. He looked much older than his fifteen years.

"But I'm not crazy," he said in a near whisper. "You don't understand. These people are not like me. They have real problems."

"And what do you think you have?"

"I know I messed up, but I can stop. I know I can. I don't need to be in here." He looked older but acted more like a nine-year-old than a teenager. Hyper, distracted, paranoid, but with a touch of innocence that was almost believable. He really thought he was convincing me of the lie he was telling. I thought about the day at the pond and wondered if he had matured at all or if I had simply saved an eternal child.

Danny began to get agitated and I moved around the table to his side. I put my arm around him. He stiffened and pulled away. Nearly six-foot-tall, he sat like a frail stack of bones.

"Are you eating anything in here?"

He brushed the back of his hand against his cheek to clear what looked like a tear and wiped it on the leg of the blue scrub-like uniform issued to him by the hospital. "Not really. Most of the time, I can't tell what it is they're feeding me. It all tastes the same."

"I'm worried about you, and I don't understand..."

"Stop," he interrupted. "I don't need you to understand. That's all I get from mom and dad. *I don't understand why you do this*," he mocked their words, but I understood why they said it. I understood why any sane human being would say that about their self-destructing child.

The whole interaction with him was heart-breaking. I knew he needed something more like the Betty Ford Treatment Center that was recently in the news, but unfortunately, it would be years before centers like that would be commonplace and substitutes for the likes of Sharonville. For now, he had to endure his addiction as a stigmatized mental illness.

"Just hang in there, Dan." I whispered and put my hand on his forearm. "Mom and Dad will be up to see you next weekend and if you just do what they tell you here, maybe they'll let you go home soon." It was the most encouraging thing I could think to say. He shrugged and seemed annoyed by my attempt to wrap it up so I could go.

I walked away from my brother after a short interchange of perfunctory sentiments, and when I looked back, he was gone. That angered me. Maybe I wanted him to be like Sean was when I used to leave him at daycare. Nose pressed against the window, screaming for me to come back and not go to work. Pleading for me not to abandon him. But I went back at the end of the day and took Sean home, proving that he could handle time without me. I always came back and he learned not to cry. But Danny? He was his own worst enemy. He would abandon you before you ever had a chance to prove yourself. He knew exactly what to do to make sure no one could come back for him. It was a losing game, but one his fear and need for power would forever bait him to play.

On the way home, I cried tears tinged with guilt and frustration, as I thought of how I came back to absolve myself for abandoning him the first time. So, it was inconceivable that I would abandon him now, even if he was forcing me to. It was the beginning of a lifetime of strategizing about how to save Danny from himself.

nine

1984-1988

CANCER PRESENTED ITSELF IN THIS LIFE IN ways that were truly evil and unrelenting, as if it was laughing out loud at my foolishness. My cousin Cherry was its first victim. I had lost touch with her in my first life. But in this one, she and I remained closer – probably because Danny was around and they were buddies until high school, when he began to pull away from all of us. Cherry married a local business owner right out of high school and had a baby within a year. She then began to have seizures and horrendous headaches. Eventually, she was diagnosed with a brain tumor and barely lived to see her little boy's second birthday. Her husband, Craig, moved away to be with his family in Indiana, and it was as if Cherry never existed in our lives.

Then it seemed that everyone I knew had a connection with the "C" word. Lisa's mother died of breast cancer, which wasn't the case in my first life. Angela, my college roommate, had a brother die of leukemia and Sam's father lost his battle with lung cancer by the age of 60. He had smoked for 40 of those years, but until now, no one thought much about the connection between nicotine and death. I forgot that treatments were not as advanced as they would be in the future, so it was somewhat shocking that so many were dying around me. At the end of my first life, hearing the word cancer seemed less daunting than it had in the past, yet now I longed for a true 20-something attitude, when mortality was a thought you tucked away for a later day. It was all too real for me in this dual state of mind. And Cherry's end had flooded me with unbearable sorrow and guilt.

"Kate," Cherry said with labored breathing on the last day I saw her. The cancer had spread to an area of the brain that was beginning to affect her vital organs.

"Yes, sweetie, what is it?" I held her little one in my lap next to her bed, as he played with a Sesame Street toy.

"Do you think there's a life after this?" She stared at her son with sadness.

"I know there is." I said it with a quick confidence that surprised me.

"How? How do you know?"

"I wish I had an easy answer for that. I guess I can't imagine that this is all there is." I planted a kiss on top of her son's silky blonde head. "When I look at this little one, I want to believe there's a purpose for all of us here and afterward. When..." I stopped myself as I was about to recount a memory that was too long ago.

"When...?" she asked pleadingly.

"When I think of how wonderfully made this little one is, I have to believe there's a God who would give us more than what we can achieve here." I had recovered well. I stared at his soft little fingers as they gripped the Big Bird figure. I couldn't lead on that I was more confused than she was about such things.

"Yes, I hope so. I need to know I will see him…and you…and Craig. Everyone again someday."

"You will. I promise. And it will be a big party."

I thought of Danny's death in my first life and how many years I had wished that what I was saying right now would be true. I dreamed of entering heaven and seeing his dirty little face and scolding him for not listening to our mother. I dreamed of telling him I was sorry for abandoning him to die and that I had lived my life in guilt as a penance for my error in judgement. I wondered what all of it meant. What would I say to my little brother *now*? Would he even make it to…? A wave of noxious guilt flooded me.

"Can you put him next to me?" Cherry was holding out her taped and needle-stuck arms to embrace her son. I stood up with him and gently laid him down next to his mother. He was quiet and subdued as if he knew something more than we did, still fingering the play figure, seemingly deep in thought.

"Will Craig be back soon?" I asked, wanting to take it back as soon as I knew it sounded like I was in a hurry to go.

"Yes, he just went to get some coffee. You can go now, if you want. I'll be okay."

"No, I'll wait." I stared at my dying cousin embracing her toddler and wondered what in the world made sense about this picture. "This is a sight to behold." I smiled through the tears and Cherry attempted a smile through her agony.

I wished I had a smartphone to snap this moment, not to plaster on social media, but to remind me of what matters. To push me toward finding a cure for this dreaded, putrid disease. All I had was my eyes and my heart to take it in and haunt me.

I put my warm hand over the frail one that was folded around her child. Neither of us said a word while we listened to her little boy make unintelligible noises, presumably imitating Big Bird.

Craig, looking thin and disheveled, came back into the room and swallowed hard when he saw his wife and son in bed together – one with a lifetime of hope and the other with no hope of life. We locked eyes. I nodded and got up to leave.

"I'll stop by tomorrow afternoon, okay?" I was glad it was summer break and I had some time available to check in on her. At the same time, I couldn't stand to see her in this state. Everything in me was at war.

"Okay." She turned her hand that was under mine and squeezed it. "Love you."

"Love you, too, Sweetie." I rubbed her son's back. "Bye little guy. See you tomorrow." He looked up at me for a second, then quickly turned back to his toy. On the way out, I hugged Craig, whose face was a dam ready to break with a lifetime of tears.

That was the last time I saw Cherry alive. She died that evening, peacefully at home with her parents, husband and child by her side. I tried to call Danny, but he was nowhere to be found. He missed her funeral and I found myself as angry at God as I had ever been. What was I to learn from any of it?

That's when another angel appeared.

During my first year of medical school I felt antsy about my career. I wanted to specialize in oncology, but the current knowledge and treatments for most cancers were so much more antiquated than what the future would hold that I was sure it would frustrate me. I had done enough research in my first life about my own cancer that I at least had a good idea about where the research was headed. So, in a drunken moment, after a long day of grueling test-taking, I decided to use my brain and my supernatural experience to forge a career in groundbreaking cancer research. I say *drunken*, because it seemed the light bulb never truly went off until I had several shots of tequila in me. Devak Patel, one of my med school classmates and recent drinking partner, stood at the bar with me, while we lamented the day's exhaustion from Dr. Carr's microbiology class. Devak asked me if I had made a decision about my focus.

"Have you settled on a specialty yet?" He asked with a slight Hindi accent.

"I don't know. I think oncology. I have a heart for cancer patients."

Devak sighed in protest, while shaking his head. "I admire people who want to do that but talk about depressing."

"So, I suppose you are going to choose something that will always be uplifting?" I joked, while staring at the fourth or fifth shot I was about to ingest. I had lost count.

"I'm thinking thoracic surgery. Maybe transplants. Something that gives new life, ya know?"

"Wow, I'm impressed." I noticed my words were slurring quite a bit.

"Ya know, Kate. If you really want to make a difference in oncology, I think research is the way to go. I think we're on the brink of knowing so much more, don't you? There's so little to work with for those doctors now. Just think about what's happening with AIDS research and how cool it would be to be on the leading edge."

Even in my inebriated state, Devak was making a lot of sense. He drove me home to my apartment that night and I attempted to have sex for the first time in my second life.

Drunken sex, granted, but it had been so long, and I had waited because I never wanted to complicate my life with what had always tripped me up before – sexual attention from men. I was quite proud of myself to have avoided the trap all these years. At twenty-six, though, it just felt like it was time. Of course, Devak was totally unaware I was a second-life virgin, because in essence, I wasn't really. And he was too nice of a guy to take advantage of a clearly compromised soul. He politely rejected my advances, gently removed my heels and tucked me in bed.

I woke up with a bad headache and a new way of looking at my future. It appeared by the blanket and pillow placement that Devak spent the night on the couch and left before breakfast, but I was satisfied and certain we were still good friends. I was changed though. I knew what to do. *I'm going to find a cure for that devilish disease if it takes the rest of this life to do it.* I plodded toward the kitchen to get some water and saw a note on the breakfast bar, propped up by the bottle of wine we had emptied. *It's a faith thing*, it said. *Enjoy the ride. You'll be fine.* I laughed out loud. *It's a faith thing. Enjoy the ride.* My parting conversation with the man in Quietude, coupled with one of my favorite lines from James Taylor's *Secret of Life.* Devak knew nothing of my JT obsession and we had never talked about faith. I looked up and closed my eyes. *Thank you.*

∽

Med school graduation came quickly, almost too fast. I did an internship at Boston University School of Research, and I looked forward to a residency appointment. I hoped to get closer to home and was excited when I was accepted to the University of Pittsburgh Cancer Institute.

I sat for a minute on the stoop of the Bostonian rented row house I had been living in for the past year. It was spring of 1988 and the cool air chilled me as I wondered what the significance was of Pittsburgh. That's where the bus had hit me in front of the office building. That's where I raised my children and divorced my husband and fought the cancer demon. Why would I go back there? It was both scary and intriguing. I didn't want to go back, but found it drew me like a curious magnet. Life had been going somewhat as planned in the last eight years since I had embarked on the adult part of my second life, when I could block out my family problems and focus on recreating myself. But to be honest, truly honest, I had to admit that I was still me. And that made me a little scared and paranoid. Wherever you go, whatever you do, *you* are there. I think that was some lame wisdom from the *Brady Bunch* dad, but it was true, nevertheless.

Since my parents had not heard from Danny in three years, I began to let go of my fantastic dreams of being my family's hero. Occasionally, they would get word through the grapevine that he was living with friends, had odd jobs, or did another jail stint. Honestly, I think they were relieved to not have to deal with the drama of his life being out of control all of the time. A family can only take so much disequilibrium until it finally has to settle on something constant, even if dysfunctional, like the mobile over a baby's crib that goes around and round as long as each piece maintains its assigned place. I couldn't help but think that my return as a different version of me upset the mobile, and caused my parents to resent me, not think differently about themselves. Self-discovery with noble intentions, I learned, is a cruel and thankless endeavor.

I used to spend a lot of time regretting that I hadn't done something more useful with my life and thought if I had, I would be different. Changed. More proud. Better. In reality, in this new life, I was changed, but not fundamentally. I was still the gangly girl from Clearfield who had a screwed-up family and plenty of choices to regret. I was just a better version of myself. Me, but confident instead of anxious. Me, but humble instead of pitiful. Me, but undone, vulnerable, open and without walls. Me.

Pittsburgh was an opportunity to focus this life on a higher calling. Saving unknown strangers instead of saving my little pathetic corner. At least that's what I thought in 1989. The year I met Kentaro Ikeda.

ten

1989

IT WAS SEPTEMBER. THE INSTITUTE WAS ONE of many who were featured at a benefit being held to fund childhood cancer research. As a new recruit, I was expected to attend the benefit in my little black dress and talk to potential donors about the work we were doing and why funding from private corporations and individuals was so critical to the success of our many projects. At the time, I was on a team that was wrapping up a project about the differential metabolism of a certain chemical on human leukemic cells. The next big project would involve the antitumor effects of antibodies in mice and the evaluation of them in the toxicity of monkeys, as well as some other work involving genetic mutations. These projects would be geared specifically toward breast cancer, which was near and dear to my heart. I wished I had known more in my first life about the chemical nature of cancer and its path to destruction, but just knowing breakthroughs were on the horizon and I could add to them was exciting and the challenge intoxicating.

"I'd like you to meet Denise Robson. She's with the Susan G. Komen Foundation," said Carol Perry, one of my colleagues at the Institute. The Komen Foundation was fairly new, and I knew so much more about what they would do in the future. It was difficult to not burst out of my skin and tell her how great their work would actually be.

"What an honor," I said while reaching for Denise Robson's hand. She was a forty-something girlish looking woman, with permed blond hair and in a squared-shoulder business suit that stood out among the party dresses most other women were wearing. Her facial expression told me she didn't care about fitting in with the half-drunken party goers. She was here on business.

"No, the pleasure is all mine. I heard you and your team are going to be doing some ground-breaking genetic work that might be of great interest to us."

"We hope so." She was referring to what would later be a discovery of the gene mutation BRCA1 by one of their own grantees. I knew for a fact that the Institute was not originally the source of the discovery, and I wasn't exactly sure how I was going to lead the team toward it, but I felt a great responsibility to speed up the process without being the hero. The words of the man with the soft round face were ever-present in my mind and heart. This second chance was not about changing the course of history. This was about what I could learn about myself. I constantly had to keep that in perspective.

"What is going on with the Foundation these days?" I asked.

"So much. More than I can express in only a few minutes."

"Well, then have a seat." I motioned to the table where I was assigned for dinner.

"I'd love to," she said with a smile, and pulled out a chair at the table.

From where we sat, I had a vantage point toward the small orchestra that had been providing the background music for the cocktail hour. Denise Robson talked excitedly about chapter expansion outside of the Dallas area and the establishment of a toll-free helpline for women who had been touched by breast cancer. Her monotone voice could not overcome my sudden fascination with a certain cellist in the small ensemble across the ballroom.

"We're hoping to compile the stories of the women who use the helpline to inspire others going through similar circumstances," Denise's voice droned on.

He was an Asian man, maybe Japanese, but it was difficult to tell from that distance. The way he tilted his head and drew the bow across the strings was so sensual, I felt a strange sexual attraction to the movement. His eyes were closed and concentrating on something that sounded baroque, maybe Bach or Corelli. Regardless, it was mesmerizing and held my attention to the point that Denise had stopped talking when I failed to answer her last boring question.

"I'm so sorry," I said, knowing I probably needed to apologize for my lack of attention. "It was a late night last night and a long day today. Forgive me if I seem a little distracted. Now, tell me again about the toll-free number..."

Denise and I talked for about thirty minutes until the first dinner course arrived, and then we continued to make small talk during the main course and dessert. All the while, my eyes kept following the movements of the cellist, who eventually left his post as the keynote speaker took the podium. Something inside of me felt I needed to connect with him, but I had no idea how or why. By the end of the evening, I decided it was simply my hormones driving the desire and that the opportunity was gone and life would continue as usual.

After all the awards and table talk were over, my bladder was about to burst from the pre-dinner wine and post-dessert coffee. I decided to hit the restroom on my way out when I happened to pass by a small room where the musicians were packing up their instruments to leave. There he was. The cellist. I was gripped with a moment of now-or-never and in a split second, found myself saying, "Great job," as I poked my head into the small room.

"Thank you," the Japanese-looking man in a black tuxedo said with a voice as soft and clear as the bow was against his strings.

Surprisingly, I continued the conversation with a dumb question.

"Was that last piece Bach?" I wasn't really sure I even remembered the last piece, but I couldn't pull myself from the moment.

"No, Handel, actually. But I can see how you would think it was Bach." He seemed surprised at my interest.

"Oh. Of course. I'm not much of a classical whiz, but I do love to listen. It's very soothing." There was an awkward moment before I ended with, "Okay, then. Well...thanks again for the entertainment."

Thanks again for the entertainment? Good job, Kate.

I walked out of the room, feeling the beaded sweat of embarrassment on my forehead. Then I heard his voice again.

"Miss."

I turned to see him with my shawl in one hand and his cello case in the other.

"You dropped your wrap."

"Oh, thanks. I didn't realize..."

It was almost impossible to go forward without walking beside him through the exit door. I must have appeared totally humiliated because he resumed conversation with me that was clearly a rescue attempt.

"This was quite an event tonight," he said while we both walked and looked forward.

"Yes, I'm with the Cancer Institute and it's very exciting to see so much interest in funding the research we're doing."

"That's great. I admire those who are scientifically talented."

"Well, likewise. I admire those who have the kind of musical abilities that make you stop and stare. You know, I was totally mesmerized watching the ensemble tonight. It truly was beautiful."

"Thanks for the compliment, but I think we were supposed to go unnoticed, providing the background mood that would give those with deep pockets a nudge to go deeper."

"I think you did that very well, but for some of us, the music was very much appreciated for its artistry, not just its marketing value."

He smiled with lips closed, but I could tell he was enjoying the interchange by the way his eyes nearly closed with the expression.

He held the door open for me as we exited the building. Awkwardly, I slipped past him and attempted to make a goodbye gesture as I headed west on Centre Avenue. For some reason, I expected him to stay there, or turn in the opposite direction, or something to make it easy to part ways. Instead, he nodded at my gesture and continued to walk behind me. I began to walk more briskly, not really knowing why, but then I heard his voice call out in the brisk air.

"Miss…"

I stopped and turned to look at him. He held up a copy of the benefit program that I had apparently dropped while fumbling with my keys. *What a klutz I am! First the wrap and now this. He must really think I'm baiting him.*

"This yours?"

"Oh, oh, yes…thanks." I reached out to take it from him.

"It looked like you had written some notes on it…that might be important." He seemed nervously awkward, too, which was comforting. I noticed my handwriting as he handed the program to me. Denise Robson's name and phone number were scribbled across the top. I didn't really need it, but what could I say?

I reached to take it from his hand and clumsily dropped it again onto the rain-drenched sidewalk. We both scrambled to pick up the now soggy booklet that wasn't all that important, except it kept us connected for thirty more seconds.

"Hey," I said, totally surprising myself, as if it were someone else speaking. "Would you like to go grab a cup of coffee or something?" I froze as I watched an expression of regret (or maybe pity) cross his face. I would think at my (real) age, I would know how to do this better. But the first time, I married young, and then remarried on the rebound. I guess I didn't have much experience with this kind of thing.

"Thanks," he said apologetically. "But I have to get this thing back home…you know it's a pain to lug it around." He was referring to his cello, which I assumed he would put in a car nearby and drive off with it.

"I just live a few blocks away, so I'm walking tonight."

"Oh, of course, I just thought…" I just thought *idiot. I'm an idiot.*

117

"You are welcome to walk with me..." he gestured toward the direction of his apartment.

"Well, I'm just going to the parking garage." I pointed toward it, only a block away. All the gesturing and pointing made me nervous.

"Okay, then, I'll walk you to your car," he replied with a confidence that relieved me. "We've had our share of late-night muggings around here lately, so I'll be glad to escort you."

"Well, I'm on the fourth floor." I was trying to imagine him lugging that thing up the stairs or into an elevator to walk me to my car. I smiled at the ridiculousness of it.

He smiled back, this time with teeth showing. His prominent cheek bones and smooth skin were particularly attractive under the late evening streetlights. Everything seemed to glisten after the rain, including his face. He looked a tad exasperated and turned toward me with purpose.

"Let's do this right, starting with your name." Another open-hand gesture.

"Kate...Kate Mulligan." I smiled with embarrassed relief and extended my right hand to shake his. He clasped it gently. Not a handshake. It was more like he was grasping the bow, with all fingers curved. With a controlled gracefulness. I took in a deep breath. He replied.

"Ken...Ken Ikeda." This time he smiled with his eyes.

"Pleased to meet you, Ken." Playfully, I added, "Would you like to walk me to the entrance of the parking garage?" I joked.

"No, I would like you to walk me to my apartment. Then I'll unload this thing and we'll go get a cup of coffee. There's a little café near me that even serves wine, if you're up for it." I loved a man with a plan.

We proceeded to walk west on Centre Street, exchanging information. *Where do you live? Near the university on Baum Boulevard. Oh, I'm down here on Penn Avenue, above a violin shop. Oh, that sounds very romantic. Not really.* And so it went until we reached the entrance to his apartment building, a rustic wooden door with the numbers "733" across the middle, next to Josef Crane Violins. I wasn't sure if he wanted me to enter, so I offered to wait for him on the sidewalk.

"It's your choice, but I'd prefer you come inside and at least wait at the bottom of the stairs. You know…the recent late-night muggings."

"Oh, right." I felt silly again.

"I'm okay with you coming upstairs, though, if you want. I'll only be a second."

I had just met this man and I couldn't believe I was considering walking into his apartment. I would have scolded Deirdre for even thinking of such a thing at this age, which made me wonder how old Ken Ikeda was. It was difficult to tell. Probably thirty-ish — near Sean's age. That felt a little creepy to me, but in this world, lots of things felt that way.

"Sure, okay." The words just fell out of my mouth like liquid.

We walked up the creaky stairs, me behind him, as I watched the man in the tuxedo adeptly carry his instrument to the top. He stopped at the door with the gold letter "B" nailed to it, inserted the key, and stepped aside to invite me in. I crossed the threshold, and to my surprise, it was cozy, inviting even. I don't know what I expected. Shoji screens, with paper lamps hanging from the ceiling, and classic plum tree blossom lithographs above statues of Buddha? Instead, there was an eclectic combination of what appeared to be thrift store pieces coupled with sturdy, plump chairs and a John Singer Sargent watercolor replica above the couch. One of my favorites — *Gondoliers' Siesta*. I stopped to admire it.

Ken Ikeda pulled off his bow tie. "I'm going to change into something more casual, if you don't mind."

"Sure," I said, distracted, "if you don't mind me being overdressed at the café."

He walked toward the back of the apartment, presumably his bedroom, and then shouted, "We could stay here and have some wine, if you'd rather. I've got red or white."

Men have no idea the dilemma that kind of statement creates for a woman. I stood silent, pondering the pros and cons. If I said yes, he would surely think that meant, *I'll stay, stay.* If I said no, I would probably miss out on a great opportunity to discover who this Ken Ikeda is. How could I do this and still remain respectable?

I could see Ken Ikeda's reflection in the rain-spattered window, moving toward me — his young bare chest, with arms pulling a t-shirt over his head. I continued to stare at the painting.

"Have you been? To Venice?"

"Oh, no. I've always…" I realized what I was about to say might sound too regretful for a 26-year-old. "…I would like to someday."

Before I knew it, his body was next to mine, and I jumped a little when he said, "What do you think?"

He was dressed in tight-fitting Calvin Klein jeans and a black t-shirt, almost the color of his hair with the letters "PSO" on the front. I could see the outlines of his muscular body through the shirt.

"You look great," I answered, almost flustered.

"Thanks, but I was referring to whether you wanted to stay here or go down the street." His smile was meant to tease.

I could hear the rain pouring down outside, making the decision seem fairly practical.

"Sounds pretty treacherous out there. If you are okay with hanging out here, that works for me." *Was I crazy?* He didn't seem to think so. Still, I felt the need to explain myself – an old habit from my first life.

"Look," I said cautiously. "I hope you didn't think I was too forward when I asked you to grab a cup of coffee. I had no intention of ending up in your…"

He interrupted. "Kate…may I call you Kate?"

I smiled which he took as a yes.

"It's not very common for a beautiful woman to comment on my music, especially when we're not even the main event. And then to have that same beautiful woman, presumably single, want to buy me a cup of coffee? I mean, what guy would not go for that?"

"Did I say buy?" I teased. "I don't remember offering to *buy* you a cup of coffee. I merely said…"

"I know what you meant." He rescued me again with a sweet chuckle. "You could hardly believe you asked me to get a cup of coffee in the first place because that's not your style, but then to end up in my apartment tonight? That's really not who you are, so now you are wondering if I'm getting the wrong idea about you and that I might think you want something more. Does that sum it up?"

"Perfectly."

"Okay. So, let me be clear. You are beautiful, and I presume single. I am single and have not had anyone in my life for a while, so I was flattered you asked. I thought it would be a boring evening, and now I get to spend it with an interesting medical researcher who appreciates Handel, and presumably the cello, and maybe even the cellist. I think as boring Saturday evenings typically go, I hit the jackpot on this one, what do you think?"

For the first time since I encountered Ken Ikeda, I felt relaxed and back to my mature self.

"I think you are a very wise, and handsome, man who knows how to put a woman at ease when it is clear she is fumbling all over herself because she doesn't know how to date. She's always too busy to date. Not that this is a date or anything." My heart rate shot up again as I corrected my error.

"So, what if it was?" Ken Ikeda moved closer to me, his black eyes in a piercing, but confident, gaze. He took my hand, not taking his eyes from mine. "What do you say we walk down the street to the café? I've got an umbrella and we can get out of this confined space." Another rescue.

"I think that's a wonderful idea." If my grin was any indication of the wild excitement I felt inside, he would surely have me figured out in no time. At that moment, I didn't care. Ken Ikeda was amazingly perceptive and kind. That was all I needed to qualify him for a first date.

Café Pirog was nothing more than a deli, really, but with a more inviting atmosphere. We walked through the door, and a bell announced our arrival. It was clear Ken Ikeda had been there before, when a middle-aged plump man emerged from the kitchen and immediately lit up at the site of him.

"Kentaro!" He moved toward us and double-kissed Ken and took my hands in his. "And who have we here?"

"Jakub, this is my friend Kate," he said with ease.

"Welcome, welcome. What can I get for you two?" Jakub's belly shook as he chuckled with delight.

"I think we're going to just have a glass of wine and something to snack on."

"Perfect. I have a great Cab you might want to try. Just got it in from the old country. A Santa Stefano, 1987."

"Is red okay?" Ken Ikeda asked me, seeming a little embarrassed by Jakub's forwardness.

"Red is great."

"We'll have the Cab as you recommend, Mr. Kowalczyk."

"Mr. *Kowalczyk*? Since when?" Jakub walked off, happy to have someone familiar to serve, it seemed.

"Are you hungry?"

"Are you kidding? That dinner at the benefit was more than I needed. The wine will be fine, thank you."

"Well, those of us who were there to entertain did not get the benefit of eating," he replied while motioning Jakub to come back over.

"I'm so sorry. I didn't think of that. You are probably starving." I looked at my watch and it was nine o'clock.

Jakub returned to the table. "I've decided to eat something after all. How about the potato cheese pierogi?"

"Sure, and for you Miss Kate?"

"Oh, nothing for me. The wine will be great."

"Kentaro, I'll bring you a little something on the house for the lady." Jakub smiled big, winking at Ken.

"So, Kentaro is your given name?"

"Yes, Jakub knows a little about my history. My father is Japanese and my mother American, whose family is originally from Poland."

"I see." Now it made sense why I couldn't stop looking at him. His exotic Asian features were complemented by a European influence that made one question his heritage.

Ken continued. "Actually, my mother was born in Pennsylvania but raised in San Francisco. Her parents moved there after the 1906 earthquake – my grandfather was in the construction trade and they saw an opportunity to keep him working during the reconstruction period. So, my mother became an artist and still lives there, in fact. That's where I was raised as well."

I was watching Ken's eyes as he fiddled with the rolled silverware on the table. He seemed nervous talking about his roots.

"Ah, so you're a California boy, huh?"

"Yeah, but not the usual stereotype. I went to the San Francisco Conservatory and ended up getting a job here with the symphony. So, in a way, I've come back to my mother's roots, which is why Jakub is so enamored with me." He smiled and looked toward the kitchen, as if he was anxious to see what was delaying the wine.

"What about your dad? Was he born in Japan or the U.S.?"

"My father came here as a child in 1928, and his family was imprisoned in an internment camp in California during the war. He was 20 years old then and had two younger siblings. His father, my grandfather, died while in the camp, leaving my grandmother alone as a single parent. Eventually, my father attended and graduated from college and became an engineer. He met my mother, the artist, at a…" He paused and smiled widely. "At a benefit, actually."

"You're kidding. That's very…coincidental."

I realized how presumptuous that sounded and blushed.

"Yes, now that I think about it, it is," he responded without a hint of surprise.

Jakub interrupted with the wine.

"Here you go. Your pierogi will be out in a minute. Enjoy!" Jakub seemed way too anxious for us to have a good time. I was certain there was a story there that might be related

124

to an old girlfriend of Ken Ikeda's, but for now, it was clearly none of my business.

Ken raised his glass to me. "To new friendships."

"Yes, new friendships." We each sipped, locking eyes with one another.

"Sooooo, the benefit. Tell me more," I said eagerly.

"I don't know that much about it really. I think my mom had been commissioned to do some work that would hang in one of the buildings my father was helping to design and engineer. The benefit had to do with building preservation in the city or something like that and some of her pieces were on display there. All I know is, according to my dad, he was mesmerized by her artwork and they struck up a conversation about that and what he was doing, and the rest is history."

"What a great love story...abbreviated, but romantic."

"Well, I guess I never really asked much about the details, but the way my father looked at her said it all."

"So, your father lives in San Francisco as well?"

"No, he passed away a year ago. Cancer."

Jakub was suddenly at the table with the pierogi, and he placed a small plate of stuffed wild mushrooms in front of me, presumably for my enjoyment.

"Great, thanks Jakub." Ken unwrapped the silverware and put the napkin on his lap. "Is that enough for you? I feel bad that you are not eating anything."

"No go right ahead. I'm enjoying the story, so if you can eat and talk at the same time, I will be entertained. And these look delicious." I smiled, staring at the mushrooms approvingly.

Just then Jakub appeared again with a plate of meat and cheeses, what looked like Kielbasa and an aged cheddar.

"Here...more for you," Jakub declared.

125

"Oh, thank you so much," I said, feeling overwhelmed at the smell of the sausage. I sampled a piece of what looked and tasted like goat cheese. It was heavenly.

"So," I pressed, "your father had cancer."

"Yes, one of the reasons I was passionate about playing for the benefit tonight. It was leukemia. Acute. He found out about it one day and three weeks later, he was gone."

"How awful." I wished I could talk about my own personal experience with it but knew I couldn't. "I'm so sorry. I bet that was very difficult for your mother. He couldn't have been very old."

"He was only fifty-six. Way too young. So, it left my mom a young widow, but she is awesome and beautiful and will be fine. I miss her though. My sister and brother are still there, so she has plenty to keep her busy."

"Tell me about them…your siblings."

"Are you sure? I am doing all the talking here. Why don't you tell me about your life while I sample the pierogi?"

I felt the blood rise to my ears again, much like I did when in Ken's apartment. *Tell me about your life.* This is always a tricky ordeal. What I want to say is that I have two beautiful, awesome children, Deirdre and Sean. My daughter is getting married soon. I had breast cancer but survived. But none of that mattered in this life. This life.

"Okay, but I want to hear about your siblings before the night is out."

"Agreed." Ken alternated, with great fury, bites of pierogi, sips of wine, and dabbing the black cloth napkin to his lips.

"I grew up in the farmlands of Clearfield, Ohio. My dad a salesman, my mom stayed at home with my brother, Danny, and me. It was a pristine kind of childhood. Pretty sheltered, actually. Nothing very exciting about it, but I got to grow up near my grandparents, which was very special and enriching. I went to Harvard med school, interned at a research institute in Boston, and ended up with a residency here in Pittsburgh."

"Wow. That's a lot. You must have graduated high school early. You don't look a day over twenty-one." He grinned.

"Gee thanks. I'm twenty-six and I don't remember you telling me your age, Mr. Ikeda."

"Thirty-two, if you must know. But what's age got to do with it? I think it's about maturity, don't you?"

"Well, that depends. My parents would not have let me date a twenty-two-year-old when I was sixteen."

"Of course, but at this age, and with what you have already done with your life, I am probably the less mature one between us."

He had no idea.

"Well, that's to be seen." I said, slightly embarrassed, worried I might be too presumptuous again.

"So, go on," he said while finishing up the last of the dumplings.

"Well, there's nothing more to tell. Here I am. With you. Watching you eat and sharing a glass of wine."

He laughed. "Yes, ten years from now that will be the story, I suppose?"

Ten years from now. I felt both excited and concerned. He apparently read my face.

"Just kidding, Kate. You are quite sensitive about any hint of commitment, aren't you?" Ken Ikeda stated rhetorically, as if he was reporting the weather.

Did he just say that? It stung.

"Well, I don't know. I'm not sure how you came to that conclusion."

"Just observing, that's all. Yes, this is a date. If you don't want it to be, you can ignore my call tomorrow and we'll never see each other again. If we like each other and end up dating and even marrying at some point, we will, in fact, talk about my pigging out on pierogi while you watched and sipped wine. It's what we're both thinking, right? I'd much rather put it out there than dance around it."

Refreshing, but unnerving. I've never, *never*, had any man in my life who was willing to be that honest. It's a game, isn't it? Or maybe that's all I know. I've never had a man be so perceptive about what I'm thinking or feeling. Except for one. My thoughts reverted to the man with the soft round face. In his presence, I felt truly loved because I felt honestly known.

"Kate? Are you okay? Where'd you go?"

"Oh sorry. Just thinking about someone I used to know."

"Oh, no, here we go. Ghosts of the old boyfriend are returning?"

"No, nothing like that." I suddenly felt exhausted by the banter.

"So, you promised to tell me about your siblings."

"Okay, well, there's my sister Miya. She's two years younger. She's a patent lawyer in San Francisco, and then my little brother, Matsuo, or Matt, to the rest of the world. He lives in Silicon Valley and is a computer guy. Very smart and scary." Ken laughed, but with affection. "He's twenty-eight, but still acts sixteen."

"So, Ken and Matt. American names with Japanese roots."

"Yeah, my mother was adamant that we have names that could be shortened and Americanized."

"Oh, not like those outsourced tech guys in India," I joked without thinking. I feigned an Indian accent. "Hello, my name is Kevin…and you know his real name is something like Rajeesh." I laughed, expecting Ken to commiserate. Instead, he gave me a quizzical look, at which point I realized that I had been thinking about the wrong century.

"Never mind. An inside joke." I waved it off, but Ken looked offended. I tried to recover.

"Anyway, your siblings. Are either of them married or have children?"

"Matt? Never. I can't imagine that for him. Miya has a boyfriend. Has been with him for about five years now, but she is totally into her career, so I can't imagine marriage or children for her anytime soon."

"And you? Any heart-broken old girlfriends waiting for you to come to your senses?" I had been dying for an entry into this subject and was pleased I had finally found one.

"I wouldn't say that. But, unfortunately, I inherited my mother's artistic, romantic personality, and obviously my siblings took after my father's engineering mind. So, I've had more heartbreak, I think, because of that. They laugh at me…tell me I'm too sensitive and expect too much from a relationship. I disagree, of course."

This gave me more insight into Ken's need to jump to honesty right away. He wanted to know what he was dealing with up front to prevent the broken heart down the road. I understood that. Growing up with an alcoholic father made me ultrasensitive, not always in a good way, to those around me and what was really happening, or not. I felt a hint of compassion for Ken's need to control that somehow. Maybe this was a kindred spirit and that gave me a surge of confidence.

"So, what was her name?"

"Her name?"

"The one who broke your heart and makes you so anxious to call this a date and lay everything out on the table."

I could see that I had uncovered something in him. He answered humbly, but with grace.

"Well, Dr. Mulligan – psychiatry was your specialty, did you say?"

"Touché," I relented. "But I've been there myself and I can spot controlled desperation when I see it."

"Okay, fair enough, but it's probably not as deep as you may think. Her name was Barbara. I thought we really had something going. She was bright, beautiful, talented. We shared a lot of things in common. I was seriously thinking we might make it work long term. Then out of the blue, in this very place actually, she said she couldn't continue to be with me."

"I'm sorry. Does this place haunt you?"

"No, not really. Well, Jakub thinks it does, but do you wanna know her reason for breaking up?"

"I don't know, do I?"

"It's ridiculous. But ridiculously funny."

"Okay, make me laugh."

"My name."

"Your name?"

"Yes, Ken. And Barbara? Ken and Barbie? She said she just couldn't bear the jokes and snickers anymore. Oh, there's Ken and Barbie. Hey, should we invite Ken and Barbie to the party?" Ken began to laugh out loud, imitating Barbara's cries as she was sharing her concerns.

I laughed too. By then, the wine had begun to take effect and we were both laughing, mostly at ourselves.

eleven

1990

HER HAIR WAS IN AN UP-DO, WITH WISPS surrounding her angelic face. Her gown fit perfectly, accentuating a near-perfect size four, with just enough cleavage showing beyond the sweetheart neckline to be intriguing, but not revealing. The lace bodice was accented with tiny Swarovski crystals and the skirt flared out into a ruffled train. Her fiancé, Jake stood watching with anticipation and pride, as my sweet daughter walked down the aisle to meet her life partner, with Sam as her escort. I watched from the front row. I had never seen Sam look so proud and humbled at the same time. My eyes glistened with tears at the thought that we didn't make it long enough to see this moment, and other future moments, together as a married couple, giving our children some sort of hope. My eye caught Sam's and he smiled approvingly at me as if to say, "We did it. Despite our troubles, we produced this awesome child who is now an adult." I wanted to jump up and scream at him. "Why? Why did you have to ruin it for all of us?" Suddenly, everything went black. I began to cough, or sputter, or something.

"Kate! Kate!" I heard a voice, but I couldn't distinguish who it was. Then I opened my eyes to see Ken staring at me. He looked concerned.

"Hey," I said, confused and groggy. I had to reorient myself to the moment.

"Are you okay? You must have been dreaming," said Ken, who had the back of his hand stroking my cheek.

"I think so, why?"

"You were mumbling, well screaming, in your sleep."

"Oh." I didn't know what to say. I was still feeling angry and sad at the thought of Sam walking Deirdre down the aisle. An event I would never get to witness. But how could I ever explain that to Ken, a man I had learned to love and trust over these last few months?

"I'm okay. It was just a bad dream."

"Okay." He sounded groggy. "Can I get you anything?"

"No." I turned to look at the clock and it was two-forty-five. "Go back to sleep, I'm fine," I assured him.

He did, but I laid awake, wondering how it was possible to have such an amazing life with this new man, but not be able to reveal to him the most intimate details of my past that shaped who I am today.

Ken and I began dating steadily after our chance meeting at the benefit the year before. From the beginning, our connection was evident to both of us, although I think we were both equally scared about what that chemistry would mean long term. We had remained in our own apartments, although frequently spent the night at the others. Regardless, we learned how to ignore our relationship anxiety and make it through the holidays together with what appeared to everyone on the outside as a normal courting relationship. As much as I loved him, I had a very difficult time feeling innocent in love,

132

knowing I had lived nearly an entire lifetime without him. I had a past that I could never reveal to him. Two failed marriages. Two adult children. A tragic death and rebirth into this reincarnation of a life. The secret was sometimes unnerving. In his extremely perceptive moments, he would notice my preoccupation and ask what was wrong, like he did when he heard me screaming in the middle of the night. The answer was always the same. Nothing. It wasn't nothing, but there was no way to talk about the something without risking his perception of my sanity.

The first meeting with my parents was the real test of our relationship. He knew most of my history with them, in this life, but I was pretty sure there would be a culture clash when he was forced to be immersed in our world. My mother had invited us for Thanksgiving dinner. We drove from Pittsburgh on the Wednesday before, planning to stay through the Saturday after, but I warned him there would be no guarantees of that, depending on what drama we had to confront.

She had been hearing about Ken in bits and pieces from me, as I pretended it was simply a friendship and nothing more, even though my heart was totally enthralled. I never revealed to my parents that he was part Asian, and they never asked about his heritage. When we knocked on the door on that snowy November day, my mother's face was memorable – a cross between shock that I had not warned her and wonder about whether or not Ken knew what a Thanksgiving turkey was. He quickly charmed both of them and my dad, especially, seemed to be very interested in Ken's life journey from San Francisco to Pittsburgh. Daddy kept him talking while my mother stole quick moments of secrecy with me in the kitchen. "He's kind of short, but he has nice broad shoulders," she said as if I hadn't noticed all these months. My father was six-foot-two, so she was not used to "smaller" men. Ken was probably five-ten. I had never asked but given that I was five-five and he was still slightly taller than me in my four-inch heels, I was able to do the math.

"So, Ken, tell me about your family," Daddy said as he began passing the plate of turkey and mashed potatoes around the table. Ken talked while I sat silently wondering where Danny was. A place was set for him, but he was nowhere in the house that I could tell, and my parents were conspicuously silent on the matter. We said the perfunctory Thanksgiving prayer and began serving ourselves, but still no Danny. Finally, I broke in.

"Where's Danny? I'm assuming this is set for him. Where is he?"

Both of my parents looked as if I had asked for their right arm. As if I was stupid and should know the answer to this inquiry.

"He's been delayed," my mother said, unbelievably.

"He'll show up," Daddy said. "You know Daniel. He's unpredictable." He then resumed his conversation with Ken and my mother poked at her green bean casserole, obviously resenting that I had raised an unanswerable question.

I lost my appetite in that moment. I knew they were hiding something. Ken could sense my agitation and reached under the table to rub my knee, hoping I would calm with his touch. I kept silent out of respect for Ken and his desire to make a good impression on my parents, but everything inside me wanted to jump up and ask if anyone was going to acknowledge the elephant or if I had to sit under the weight of him all by myself. I stopped myself. I had learned early on to play the game, even if it felt crazy to do so. Ken understood and that was all that mattered.

After the pie and coffee, and the end of the televised football games, we retreated to my old room in the back of the house. Ken had offered to sleep on the couch, or in Danny's room if he was not coming home, but my parents would have none of that. They could see he was a respectable man and said they trusted him to be in the same room with me without any "hanky panky," as my father respectfully warned. We laughed and proceeded to memory lane. Not much had changed in the room I had grown up in, twice now. The first time, I had pink walls, a pink bedspread, pink stuffed toys, pink pillows, pink everything. The second time around, I had developed an appreciation for a more mature pallet, which drove my mother crazy. I wanted teal blues and sand browns to mimic the beach, and off-white furniture with accent pillows in yellow and coral – a shabby chic look that was a decade or two before its time. She interpreted my odd palette choice as rebellion and became more frustrated when we had a difficult time finding the colors I wanted, given they were not part of the 1970s décor of choice. Yet, once put together, I think she marveled at the look and said I might have an eye for design. She suggested I should consider that as a profession over something so male-dominated as medicine. I ignored her, knowing she had no idea what she was saying.

"Nice," Ken said as he eyed the little trophies on my shelf for first-place swim team and cheerleader of the year. "You were quite the athlete, huh?"

"Not really. I just happened to be in the right place at the right time."

"You're too modest," said the man who wouldn't brag on himself if his life depended on it. It's one of the traits I loved most about Ken. He was humble, to a fault sometimes, and did not place much importance on his own accomplishments. To him, rising to fourth chair in the symphony at such a young age was merely a result of his passion for music, not his ambition to reach that goal. His philosophy was to do what you love and whatever comes of that, money or recognition, was inconsequential to the fact that you lived your life doing what you loved to do. I tried to take the same attitude with my research at the university. I couldn't focus too much on the end result. I just had to stay passionate and hope that the passion would lead to cures that would extend the lives of humanity. Not a lofty goal at all! Truth be told, I had purely selfish reasons. I didn't want to face cancer again without the promise of a cure, nor did I want any other woman to face it as I had. It was a race against time, and I wanted to be part of something that might actually save this life I had embarked on for the second time, presumably with more grace and perfection.

"Your parents are delightful," said Ken, breaking my lofty thoughts about the human race.

"Yeah," I responded distractedly, while staring at a picture frame that was still on the bedside table of Lisa and me. Even though we were only sixteen in the photo, I could see a painful maturity in my eyes compared to hers. In moments like these, I still marveled at what I had done. *Was it courage or desperation?* Sometimes I wondered. "They are who they are," I finished my response.

"What?" he asked with concern, as he moved my hair off my shoulder, letting me know he got that I was agitated at dinner.

"I don't know. It's so obvious that they have no idea where Danny is. He is out there somewhere, with friends, or whatever you call those hoodlums he hangs with, and they act as if it is normal. It's not normal. It's Thanksgiving Day and my little brother is not where he should be. With family."

"Are you worried about him? Like you think he's in trouble?"

"That's the thing. We never know. We could get a call at two a.m telling us he's in jail and needs bailed out. Or he'll show up two days from now and be angry if anyone asks where he was on Thanksgiving Day, as if none of us has a right to know." What I couldn't tell Ken is that I fear that coming back to save him was a mistake. Maybe I should have let well enough alone. Playing God may have been a mistake on my part, and I was pissed off at myself and the man with the soft round face that I was led to believe I could make a difference this time around. But, of course, I couldn't say that to anyone. It was hard enough to say it to myself.

"Kate, we can't control what other people do, ya know?"

"I know. It's just that my parents don't deserve this. I know they had their issues, but I didn't go haywire because of it. What gives him the right?"

"You almost sound envious," Ken said with a smile.

"Yeah right. I would not change anything about my life right now. I've got you and that would not have happened if I had done anything differently. I was destined to find you." That I said with confidence. I felt I had been led to Ken for a reason. His confidence and sense of right and wrong, his character and integrity, and the whole package was almost unnervingly perfect. He would never attest to that, but I was constantly in awe of it. In one of our many conversations about religion, I shared that I had not grown up with any frame of reference for spirituality and religion, other than to say a rote prayer at bedtime or the dinner table, for good measure. I think my mother was sufficiently afraid of what might be that she ritualized certain prayers and holidays "just in case." But she certainly didn't live a life that indicated any dedication or commitment to a God or theological sway.

Ken's childhood was much different. His father's family embraced Shinto and Buddhism. His mother's family was staunch Catholic. Yet together, they taught their children to respect all religions and spiritual walks. When Ken was a young adult, he got involved with a local homeless mission in San Francisco and became a born-again Christian as a result, although he talked humbly about that conversion and chose to live the principles more than talk about them. The more I learned about him and got to know him, the more I began to feel that maybe I had missed something important the first time around. Slowly, he was beginning to show me the meaning of grace, which I had no real concept of in my first life. This second life seemed to be teaching me a lot about it.

I remember one night in particular when I was fretting about my job and the politics involved that were driving me crazy, he simply said, "Give it up, Kate. Just let God deal with it for you." He took me in his arms and quoted a verse from Psalm 37. *Do not fret because of those who are evil or be envious of those who do wrong; for like the grass they will soon wither, like green plants they will soon die away. Trust in the Lord and do good; dwell in the land and enjoy safe pasture. Take delight in the Lord, and he will give you the desires of your heart.* Spoken in his signature soft voice, I was instantly comforted and wanted desperately to believe it to be true. I remembered the green pasture of Quietude that the man with the soft round face showed me. It made all the cares of the day melt away. There was a place of safety awaiting me. For now, I had to go there in my mind only, especially when the reality of this second life felt barren and colorless.

twelve

1991

HE WAS STANDING AT THE FRONT DOOR WITH a backpack slung over his left shoulder. His face was gaunt and unshaven. His eyes were sunk into his sallow face. I hardly recognized him.

"Danny?"

He stood and stared, looking as if he wasn't sure this was the right house. We both hesitated and then I motioned for him to come in. *How had he found me?*

"How did you get here?" I looked around him to see if he was alone.

"A bus. I took a bus." He sighed awkwardly, as if not knowing what to do next.

I was shocked and excited at the same time.

"Come in, come in." It was the middle of winter and barely twenty degrees outside, but he only had on a light canvas jacket that smelled of weed, and a knit cap on his small head.

"Damn, it's cold out there," he said as if the last few years hadn't placed a wall between us.

"Yes, yes it is…" I was dumbstruck. Finally, I came to my senses. "Where the hell have you been? Do mom and dad know you're here?"

"Oh, yeah. I was having cocktails with them last night and happened to mention that I was going to Pittsburgh to visit my big sister," he said sarcastically. "No, and I don't want them to know."

"Okay, okay. It's just that…"

"That I've been a terrible son and only care about myself? I've already heard *that* speech."

"Well, I'm just glad you're here." I couldn't tell him that I was pissed off. Now. After all these years, he just showed up as if nothing has happened and expected me to not react.

"Thanks." He put the soiled backpack on the sofa. "You got a restroom I can use?"

"Sure, it's right down the hall." I reeled with a thousand emotions. It had been nearly four years since any of us had heard from Danny and I couldn't believe he was only a few feet away.

He emerged from the bathroom looking more relaxed.

"Nice place, sis. The big Harvard doc has a Pittsburgh apartment overlooking the city."

"Danny…" I sighed in frustration. In so many ways, he resembled our mother.

"What? It's true. Look at you. Not a hair outta place."

To my surprise he embraced me. His hair smelled of oil and smog, reminding me of the exhaust from the bus that had run me over years before. I squeezed him around the waist.

"I've missed you," I whispered to him.

He pulled away. "Really? You missed all the drama I create everywhere I go?"

"Surprisingly, yes. I'd rather deal with your drama than imagine your dead body in a ditch somewhere."

He sat down at the kitchen table, I moved my laptop and other items from the area where he was seated. I sat down next to him, eager to learn about his life.

"I'm sorry. It's true. I've been thinking more of myself, I guess, than what you or mom – or even dad, for that matter – might be feeling." He paused for a moment and then looked at me with a steely sadness. "It's just easier to think you might miss me than for you to know me and hate me."

"What does that mean? What does that fucking mean?" I felt the anger rise in my face. I got up from the table to retrieve two bottled waters from the fridge.

"Geez, Katie. Why don't ya just put it out there?"

"Well, that's a damned selfish thing to say." I mocked his statement. "*I'd rather you miss me than hate me.* Since when do any of us need to be perfect in order to be loved?" My own statement stuck to me like glue. "Do you have any idea how many sleepless nights I have had worrying about you and what tent you might be sleeping in or what crack house might burn down around you in the middle of the night?"

"See? That's what I mean! Even when you're missing me, you're hating me."

"Yeah, there's a fine line between worry and hate. I love you, so I worry, but I hate you for making me worry. Do you even get that?"

He hung his head and opened the bottle of water I had placed on the table.

"I don't know. I guess."

I regained my composure, trying to remind myself that Danny's life wasn't my business. I was glad to have him in my presence and know he was safe.

"Hey." I touched his arm to get eye contact. It felt bony, but warm. My heart melted. "Let's not do this. Not now. I'm glad you're here and that you're safe."

He nodded and took a big gulp of the water, followed by a hard swallow.

"Hey, you hungry? I have some vegetable soup in the fridge I can warm up."

"Ahhh…mom's famous veggie soup?"

"Yep. Secret family recipe. It always comforts on days like this."

"Sure, I'd love some."

I got up and rummaged through the cookware cabinet for an appropriate pan. I wanted to ask him if he'd like a shower because he looked wretched, but I thought we had had enough challenges for the moment. I looked over at the table and saw that Danny had walked into the dining room to check out my artwork.

"So, you live here alone?"

"Yeah…well, mostly. I have a boyfriend who stays here quite a bit." I didn't know why I felt the need to tell him that other than my instincts were telling me that his next question would be to ask if he could move in. I knew I could not consider such a thing,

"A boyfriend, huh? A doctor or lawyer or something'?"

"No, actually. Ken is a cellist with the PSO."

"Hmm…Ken." He was looking at the Picasso reproductions in the foyer. I felt a tinge of guilty distrust and wondered if I needed to worry about my valuables disappearing.

"I dated a lounge singer once, but she O.D.'d on meth. Sad," he said in a distracted tone.

"You are so full of it." I knew he was trying to get a rise out of me. "So, are you staying in town or just passing through? You're a long way from Clearfield."

"Yeah and I plan to stay a long way from there. Nothing there for me." He was back in the kitchen and began to look for the silverware drawer.

"Over there, next to the sink," I directed him to the drawer, and he retrieved two spoons. "Bowls are up there."

I remained shocked that he was actually in front of me and taking direction in the kitchen, which was a new side of him that I couldn't bring to memory. *Why couldn't he just be sweet like this all the time and put his mind to something productive?*

"I heard that Mr. Deitmeyer had a heart attack and croaked," he blurted out, like ten-year-old.

"Deitmeyer? I don't remember him."

"Eighth grade math...the guy was a real turd."

"Oh, is he the one who got you and Craig in trouble for vandalizing the school?"

"The one and only."

"Well, c'mon. He was only doing his job. You were an idiot for thinking you could get away with it."

"It was a Saturday afternoon, for God's sake. What was that guy doing there on the weekend?" Danny poured the soup into the bowls for me. The aroma took me back 20 years.

"Well, some people are dedicated like that, I guess." I wondered why we were talking about this guy. Danny got in trouble numerous times as a teen, so why did Mr. Deitmeyer's death mean anything to him?

"Like you? Bet you work weekends, too."

"Sometimes," I said softly and wondered why I felt uncomfortable admitting it.

"Speaking of work, what are you doing these days?" I could predict the answer but felt like I had an invitation to ask after his last comment.

He hesitated for a few seconds, I supposed to construct a lie, and then he answered.

"I'm between jobs but thought I might try to find something in Pittsburgh."

"Really?" I felt like he was testing me. "Why would you want to move back to the cold? Why not go somewhere fun like Florida or California?"

"Back?" His face flushed. He didn't know that I knew he had been in Texas for a while. That was the last address I had for him in the late 80s.

"Yeah, weren't you living in Houston a few years back?"

"There, among other places...what's the matter Katie? You afraid I'm going to try to move in with you?"

I knew that tone of voice – the I'm-gonna-pick-a-fight-with-you-so-you'll-ask-me-to-leave-and-then-I'll-have-an-excuse-to-blame-you-for-my-lack-of-success tone.

I stopped short of the next bite of soup and looked him in the eyes. "First of all, you will not be moving in with me. Secondly, when you're involved, I don't believe anything until I see it."

He looked stung by my honesty but recovered well.

"Fair enough, but this time I've got a buddy who has a warehouse job around here and he said there might be an opening for me."

Danny always had a "buddy" or knew a "guy" or had some scheme that never panned out. In true addict form, it merely served to provide a way of conversation to end any inquiries about his sense of responsibility.

Much to my surprise, I simply responded, "Cool."

144

I searched my heart for the frustrated sister who had a ready-made lecture and Harvard-inspired advice. She was either gone or had learned to erect a wall of protection by agreeing with the craziness living in those she loved. The latter seemed more plausible.

Danny fumbled with the paper napkin next to his bowl, not sure how to respond to my non-answer. Sadly, a warehouse job actually sounded like something he would be well-suited for. He had a lot of trouble in school and likely had dyslexia because he turned his letters and numbers around consistently. But there wasn't much support in the schools for that kind of thing in Danny's small-town elementary school. He then became labeled as a dumb kid and before long accepted that he was destined to be different. Then all it took was hooking up with other "different" kids who found solace in drugs and alcohol. That coupled with a family history of addiction stacked all the cards against him. Even though I knew all of that, I found myself wanting him to snap out of it and stop being so self-centered and juvenile. Mom and dad knew he was delayed, but they waved me off and said he would be fine every time I mentioned getting him help. He was never fine.

I couldn't help myself, as the advice-giver once again surfaced.

"Remember how you used to mix up your letters and numbers when reading?"

He looked at me like I was from another planet.

"I never did that," he denied. "And what does that have to do with anything?"

"Sure, you did. I remember you throwing your books across the room because you hated reading so much."

"So?" I could tell he was on the defense.

"So, I think you have something called dyslexia."

"Dis…what?"

"Dyslexia. It's very common, actually. A lot of people struggle with reading, but there are therapies now that can help you read productively…"

Danny interrupted, "Okay, okay. Here we go. I'm not with you 30 minutes and you've got some therapy that's gonna fix my sorry ass. For what? So, I can go to Harvard like you did?"

"Stop it. Can you blame me for wanting to help you get a leg up? You've had a lot of strikes against you and I think some of them can be fixed, whether you believe it or not."

"Well, I don't need fixin'. What's the matter? Don't want to admit your little bro might be a blue-collar worker? Sweating in a warehouse gig?"

"Yeah that's it. That's it completely. I can't stand the thought of my brother having a regular job and living in a lowly part of town. That would be horrible. Of course, I need him to be an Ivy League scholar." Sarcasm was always our best way of talking to one another, unfortunately. I stood at the sink fiercely scrubbing the inside of a clean coffee cup. "Wanna know the truth? I just want to know you can feed yourself and you have a bed to sleep in at night. Is that too much to ask?" I was banging the bowls around in the sink as I slung my words at him like darts. I looked back at the table and he was gone.

"Danny?" I wiped my wet hands on a dish towel and ran into the living room. His backpack was gone from the couch. I ran through the apartment and he was nowhere to be found. Danny was gone.

thirteen

1993

IT WAS MY SECOND THIRTIETH BIRTHDAY. February 2nd. Groundhog Day. I know. God has a stupid sense of humor.

As I showered to get ready for my date with Ken, my thoughts reverted to that first thirtieth birthday. I was married to Sam, and Deidre was seven. Sean was five. On that day in the first 1993, I was busy getting dinner on the table for the kids because Sam had promised when he got home from work that we would go to my favorite restaurant – Tanner's Steak House in downtown Clayton, a little town just east of Clearfield, where we both grew up. It would be an hour drive, but worth it. We had reservations for 8:00 pm. I got dinner on the table for the kids and Jenny, our sitter, had arrived by 6:30, as requested. Then there was no Sam. Seven came and then 7:30. There were no cell phones back then (at least not that we could afford), so I waited and worried. Finally, at 8:00 pm he walked in the door and apologized for being late, and said he got held up in a "meeting." According to the scent of Estee Lauder on his suit jacket, I knew the meeting had been more like a rendezvous and I ran to the bedroom and slammed the door like a teenager who'd just been dumped. Apparently, Jenny stuck around, because Sam stormed out – presumably to go back to the woman he had just left – and I stayed in my room until morning. I never asked Deirdre or Sean about that evening and they never mentioned it to me. I was fairly certain they knew mommy's birthday had not been a happy one, but they learned as small children, much like I had, to pretend that pain was normal.

I had blamed Sam's affairs on my weight, and back then, I attributed my weight issues on the last pregnancy, after giving birth to a nine-pound infant. Who could possibly get back to a normal body after that – five years later? In reality, I had a bad anxiety eating habit because I knew in my heart Sam was cheating, but I couldn't – or wouldn't – admit it. Admitting it would make it too real, and with two hungry mouths to feed and no training to do anything about that, I was totally dependent on the man who posed as my husband.

I stepped out of the shower and caught a glimpse of myself naked in front of a steam-framed mirror. I paused, dropping the towel, stunned by a perfect woman I hardly recognized. We stared at one another in awe. My fifty-year-old brain and thirty-year-old body were caught in a time warp. I stood motionless for a moment, not certain of where I was, who I was, or which life I was in. As I stared, still mesmerized at the figure looking back at me, I ran my finger down the middle of my breastbone, still warm and damp, and circled where I felt my heart beating. My nipples were dark and strong and pointed – untouched by infant lips, a cheating husband, or the devastation of cancer. I circled the full of my left breast, firm and confident, and proceeded around to the middle of my torso and down the flat and taut skin that enclosed my belly, once painted with stretch marks from the fullness of pregnancy. My fingers rolled over the indented button that had once attached me to my mother, and along the edge of pubic hair where a Caesarean scar, like a smile, used to itch and remind me of a painful birth. Now it was smooth and clean, without the red scarring that eventually had turned to white. My hand felt the inside of my thigh, muscular and undimpled by cellulite, and then it reached around to the firmness of my buttocks that I worked on relentlessly in my second life because I was well aware that it was a problem area in my first one. I felt a strong sense of futility as I grabbed the flesh that made up my behind. It was exactly what I had wished for before. The right shape, the right texture, the right size. I had it all. I squeezed hard. I had the perfect body – the one I longed for at age fifty when it seemed I could not capture the attention of a man without promising to lose most of myself. The blood rushed to my behind as I scraped it with my nails, trying desperately to make a mark to feel alive and significant. I looked at my face and was surprised to find I was crying and thinking about Sean and Deidre, who would be in their forties. *Where are they? Do I have grandchildren? Why did I do this? So what? I have a freaking perfect body this time. So what?* I fell to the floor and pounded my fist into the damp carpet. I felt ashamed, and stupid, and cowardly.

The phone rang, startling me out of my parallel universe. It was Ken. He was going to be a few minutes late, which was a blessing given my present state of mind.

"You okay?" he asked. "You sound distant."

"Oh yeah, sure. Just stepped out of the shower and heard the phone ringing." I noticed I was a little out of breath.

"Wish I could see that," he joked.

I didn't reply, creating an awkward silence.

"Okay, sounds like you're distracted. I'll be there around 7:00."

"Sounds good." I hung up and felt guilty for thinking, *Oh sure, seven. That's what they all say.* I think it was more like anger for not being able to tell Ken about my former life and what Sam had done to blow up our marriage and how sometimes I struggle with trust, even with him. And how I wish I could tell him about my children and how much my heart aches for them.

"Do you want children?" I asked pointedly while Ken poured the bottle of Pinot the waiter had just delivered to our table.

He choked a little. "Where did that come from?"

"I don't know. We don't ever talk about the future. I'm thirty now, and you know, the clock is ticking, as they say."

"Well, sure, but it's pretty common for someone your age with a career to wait, don't you think? I mean, the work you are doing is amazing. Is there room for kids?"

"Well, someday, I hope."

Ken put the bottle back on ice and took my hand in his. It was warm and gentle.

"Listen, Kate. I know you well and this is not you, so spill your guts. Where is this coming from?"

You don't know me. That's the problem!

"I guess I don't want to miss out. On anything. I want it all, Ken. I want the career and a life with you and the house in the country and the white picket fence, two dogs, four kids. You know. The whole thing, but it seems that no matter how someone's life plays out, they end up missing out on something."

"I know. I get it. If we were only cats – with nine lives, we could really have it all." He looked intently at the menu.

I chuckled at the irony of that statement. Little did he know that I have already figured out that two lives are definitely not enough.

150

"That's the smile I want to see," he said and kissed me lightly and lovingly on the lips. "What would you like to eat birthday girl? You can have whatever you want."

We were at a swanky restaurant called The Riverfront Grill, overlooking the Ohio River, with British Chef Jeffrey Carson at the helm. The menu was an eclectic mix of seafood, choice cuts of beef, and unique creations that were satisfying just to say their names. Chicken L'Orange with capers, atop wild rice and shallots. Chef Carson's famous prosciutto wrapped tenderloin with grilled shitake mushroom and burgundy Boulaise sauce. And even a treat for the kids – Chef Jeff's gourmet burger topped with gouda cheese served with house-fried potato chips.

"I'd like the veal...Veal Cotoletta?" I struggled to pronounce its name.

"That surprises me. You know veal is baby cow, right?"

I laughed. "Yes. I grew up on a farm, remember?"

"Okay, it's just that with all this talk about babies..."

I shot him a disapproving gaze. "One has nothing to do with the other."

Our waiter, who had introduced himself as Franklin, returned to the table to take our order. He gave Ken a look of approval that was so obvious, that I almost laughed out loud because it probably meant Ken had ordered a cupcake with a candle on it. The minute Franklin walked away, Ken returned to our former conversation – a characteristic of his that I found to be priceless.

"So, let's get back to the idea of children. I didn't answer you because it really threw me off."

"Why?" I felt a hint of defensiveness rising in me. "Is it so unusual for a thirty-year-old woman to talk about children with the guy she's been dating for years?"

"No…but…" he moved off of his chair and to the floor. On one knee. My mind started to race. *He must have dropped something.* He grabbed my left hand. Suddenly, it seemed that everyone in the restaurant was staring at him. And me.

"I was kind of thinking the same thing."

My heart raced along with my thoughts.

"We've been together for what? Four years now? And I couldn't be more certain about who I want to spend the rest of my life with and who I would want to mother my children."

For the second time today, my eyes filled with tears. He reached into his suitcoat pocket and pulled out a brown velvet box.

"Katherine Mulligan…will you agree to be my wife?"

"What?" The shock of it had washed over me and I felt the need to clarify.

"Will you marry me?" he nearly shouted.

I swallowed hard. "Yes, of course, yes!" I took the box from his hand and gently opened it, as if it were breakable. It was the most unique ring I had ever seen. The band appeared to be a swirled mix of white and yellow gold, with a rich layered design, and an emerald-cut diamond, rather large, in its center. It was obviously an antique. I was speechless.

"I hope you like it. It belonged to my grandmother, given to her by my grandfather in 1935."

"It's…amazing." I was still having trouble with words.

Ken's face gleamed with pride. He kept talking in absence of my ability to speak.

"I know it's rather different, but it's called Mokume Gane, a traditional Japanese method of laminating various colors of metals together to look like wood patterns, like they used to decorate Samurai swords. This one is platinum and yellow gold.

It would be an honor if you would wear it…at least while we are engaged and then if you want something different later…"

"It's perfect," I interrupted and placed my fingers over his mouth. I had never heard him talk so fast and nervously. He took the ring from the center of the box and placed it on my left ring finger. I could barely see it through the tears, which I had noticed were now falling onto the black napkin on my lap. I blinked a few times to bring it into clear view. In the distance I heard clapping, presumably from the restaurant patrons who had just witnessed the proposal, but the noises were muffled compared to the voice in my head, which was loud and clear.

Kate, I am with you. I have you in the palm of my hand. Do not fear. Your children are safe. Live this life without regret. Learn your lessons. Be content. Be at peace.

I reached toward Ken and put my arms around him and began to sob.

"Hey, hey. It's okay. I hope these are happy tears." He sounded worried.

"Yes, yes they are. You have no idea what this means. You have no idea."

fourteen

June 12, 1994

THE WEDDING DAY WAS AMAZING. THE choice of 1990s dress styles, though, was hideous. For all these years, the image of Deirdre as she had posed in front of the mirror at the bridal shop was imbedded in my brain. She had chosen a classic fit and flare gown, with a lace and beaded bodice, dropped waist and full tulle skirt. It had a plunging V-neck with capped sleeves that went into a deep V-shape in the back. She looked absolutely stunning in it and the minute I laid eyes on her, I was overwhelmed with pride and love and awe. Awe that my little girl, whose resemblance remained in this beautiful bride-to-be's angelic face, could possibly be old enough to get married.

Those memories were hard to shake as I walked down the aisle to meet Ken in my A-line taffeta gown, which I thought was elegant, but agreeably plain for the times. I just couldn't abide the big veils (that were created to complement the big hair) or the long laced-sleeves and necklines, akin to Princess Diana's trousseau. My mother was not too satisfied with my choice (of gowns, that is) and said I looked like I was going to a

154

dinner party instead of walking down the aisle, but she had grown to love Ken, which had nothing to do with her and everything to do with his ability to calm anyone he met. And if anyone responded to a dose of calm, it was my mother, given her history with mood altering drugs. My dad had liked him from the beginning, I believe, because he saw how happy I was with him, which was a stark contrast to my marriage to Sam. On that wedding day, my dad had leaned in to whisper in my ear during the father-daughter dance.

"He better treat you right or he'll have me to answer to."

I remember silently smiling at the suggestion but feeling uneasy at the hint of things that were likely to come. I knew Sam's integrity was shaky and that trust might be an issue, but I wanted to be married and probably thought he was the best I could get at the time. How stupid of me, I thought, as I approached the altar and saw Ken – more kind, more intelligent, more worldly, more spiritual, than I could ever be – beaming with pride and excitement to be joining his life with me. Me. I was amazed and proud of myself. Amazed that I had the good fortune and blessing to meet him. Proud that I made a good choice this time. *This one I will not regret.*

After the short, but sweet, ceremonial vows, we were received by family and friends in the tiny church's reception hall. Lisa served as my matron of honor and Ken's best man was his friend, Jon, an old college roommate who he had remained close friends with through the years. So many friends and family members on both sides chose to spend the day with us, which amazed me. I think in my marriage to Sam I was so young that the guests reflected more of our parents' choosing rather than those who knew us personally or wanted to actually celebrate our union. It felt more like an excuse for a party than a wedding. This time, it felt different. This time, I looked around and everyone I saw was someone who thought highly of either Ken or me, or us as a couple. That made the day more meaningful...more understandable. There was a sense of responsibility to it. These people are here to witness our vows, to hold us to them, to support what we have together. I felt like everyone there wanted us to succeed. Or was that just wishful thinking? Whatever it was, it made the day seem necessary to our future. The beginning of commitment for life that I don't think I really made to Sam, in all honesty. I think I knew even back then that if Sam didn't behave, it wouldn't last, and I was willing to take that chance. This time, there was no question in my mind that Ken would be faithful, supportive and dedicated to me and the family we might create. For the first time in either of my lives, I wondered if I was the last one to know this was how marriage was supposed to start. Maybe this is how everyone feels, or is supposed to feel, when they meet their soon-to-be spouse at the altar. I felt juvenile and naïve for realizing it for the first time at nearly 31 years old (68 if I wanted to get technical).

I visited with so many people that day, including Mr. and Mrs. Corbin, our neighbors who lived down the lane from us when I was growing up. I was fascinated to talk to Mr. Corbin, since in my first life, he had died in 1985 in a farm tractor accident one hot June afternoon. His two daughters didn't know how lucky they were to still have him around. I marveled at what my return may have changed in a minute way to keep him from the same fate. Or were there other people in this life who were in my position? Had others been given a second chance at life and were able to change the course of events in a small way? It boggled my mind to think about it. Distracted by my thoughts, I failed to notice Ken approaching with a man I didn't know.

"Excuse me for interrupting, but I wanted you to meet my cousin, Tai. He flew here with my mother from San Francisco."

"Oh, yes, Ken has said so many good things about you. Pleased to finally meet you." I saw Mr. and Mrs. Corbin walk away out of the corner of my eye and I felt weirdly anxious about it.

"Thank you so much for inviting me to your special day. Ken is a lucky guy to have such a beautiful wife."

"Aw, you are so kind, but I think I am the lucky one." I smiled at Ken and he reached for my hand and squeezed it gently.

"Let's get a refill on the champagne," suggested Ken. He motioned for Tai to walk to the drink table with us. As I stood waiting for my husband to make another private toast "to us," a wave of unexpected guilt washed over me. Guilt that I was so happy. Guilt that Sam had died in the car crash, but Mr. Corbin got to live. Guilt that my friend Lisa looked so worn out from her weighted down life. Guilt that I had succeeded at the expense of others. Fear that I did not deserve this day with this man.

"To you, my love," Ken finished the toast and pressed his warm, moist lips to mine, making the guilt fade away for the moment. I smiled, knowing I had to make the best of what I had created for myself in this life, despite what I knew about the other one.

Just then, I heard the room become eerily silent. All eyes were turned toward the door where a bearded man, disheveled and wobbling, stood and smiled. My uncle Charlie walked toward him to presumably let him know he was in the wrong place, but I recognized that smile. It was Danny.

"Wait!" I think I yelled, but maybe it was in my head. "Danny?" I ran toward him, pulling up the edges of my gown so I wouldn't trip.

"Hey, Katie," he said with a slur.

"How...how did you know?"

"Oh, word travels, I guess." He stepped toward me and put his hands out to reach for me. His fingernails were black underneath and his faded green canvas coat was soiled at the cuffs.

"You look beautiful, Katie," he said, as he grabbed my hands. His were rough and thin...and hot.

Ken came closer. He had never met Danny but knew about him from the many conversations I forced upon him. I felt his reassuring hand on the small of my back.

"I'm so glad you are here," I said softly.

"Really?" he chuckled sarcastically. "I bet you're the only one." He looked over toward my parents, who were horrified and dumbstruck. He waved at them and smiled. "How's it goin' mom and pop?" His teeth were brownish, and his breath had a metallic odor.

"Danny, come sit down and I'll get you something to eat and drink." I led him by the arm to the nearest empty seat. Ken followed reluctantly, but dutifully.

He pulled away and seemed annoyed by my mothering gesture.

"I'm here for you, Katie. I'm sorry I missed the part where you said, 'I do'." He looked at Ken. "This must be the guy – the musician. That's cool, man."

Ken reached out to shake his hand. My brother looked surprised but reciprocated.

"Glad to finally meet you..."

158

"Yeah, I know, you've heard a lot about me." He laughed nervously and leaned back in his chair, nearly slipping off of it. I noticed sweat beads on his forehead.

"Danny, you look ill. Let's get your coat off."

"Nah, I'm fine…just need something to drink. Ya got any Vodka?"

As I helped him with his coat, my hand brushed his cheek and it was burning up.

"You've got a fever." I turned and asked Ken to get a glass of water. Danny's pupils were dilated, and his lids were half-mast. Ken returned with a cup of water and I put it to Danny's lips. "Here drink this."

He put his hands to it and they were shaking. I heard my mother behind me.

"Kate, what's wrong? Is he okay?"

No, he's not okay, Mom. He's probably got an infection from a bad needle and his immune system sucks because he doesn't eat anything to support it.

"No, I think we might need to call an ambulance. Dad, could you get that done?" I felt the adrenaline flow through my veins. I wanted to be angry that Danny would do this on my wedding day, but I went into crisis mode instead, as all good physicians are trained to do.

Danny's head hung as he tried to sip more of the water. He was obviously delirious, high, or both.

"I don't need an ambulance." His words were slow and labored. "I just need you to tell me you still love me. Do you, Katie? Do you still love me?"

"Of course, I do." I looked at Ken with my best *I'm sorry* face and asked him to find some blankets.

"I need to get him on the floor, so he doesn't fall off of this chair until the paramedics get here."

Ken ordered his cousin Tai to do that and he and Joe instantly took over the labor of getting my brother off of the chair and walked him out into the foyer of the reception hall. I was thankful he did since I didn't have the strength or the ability in my tight wedding gown to do it with grace.

"Thank you," I said breathlessly. I heard a quiet murmur around the room. I looked up and felt helpless. How to make this right? Then I heard Ken's voice, as he returned from the foyer. It was that reassuring calmness that made me love him more than I thought I ever could.

"Okay, everyone. Danny is going to be fine, but we need to wait for the ambulance to be sure he gets the help he needs. Continue eating and drinking and we will return to you as soon as he gets situated and is off to the hospital. Thank you so much for your patience."

He walked back to the foyer where Danny was lying on the bright orange carpet. I turned and walked toward my dad and noticed my mother had left him to talk to Danny.

"Dad, please go with Mom. I've got to stay here with my guests."

"She can go to the hospital with him if she wants. I've had it with that kid. Who does he think he is barging in like this? On *your* day! I'm ashamed...embarrassed."

He shook his head in disgust and drank down his half-glass of rum and Coke in one gulp. I noticed his hands were shaking, too.

"I know..." I was at a loss for words and put my hand on his shoulder. I sighed and looked away to avoid seeing the anguish in his face.

Lisa came across the room with a worried look.

"Kate, I am so sorry. Is he going to be okay?"

"Yes, it seems Danny has nine lives. He'll be fine once they get some antibiotics in him and a couple of decent meals. I'm more worried about Ken. Talk about a damper on the day."

She smiled. "He's the last one you need to worry about. That man…" she looked toward the foyer. "That man would go to the ends of the earth for you. Did you see how calm he was? I'm telling you, hold on to him for dear life, Kate. He's definitely a keeper."

I hugged her and thanked her for being so caring.

"What a day, huh? I didn't think it would end like this."

"It's not over yet," she said with a sparkle in her eye. "You've got tonight and the honeymoon to look forward to. I hope you won't let your brother's return throw that off. You and Ken deserve to enjoy this. Let your parents deal with Danny. He's their problem now, not yours."

"Yeah, I guess you're right," is what I said but didn't feel. She didn't know that Danny *was* my problem. I created this problem, but now I couldn't fix it. The loneliness in that moment was almost surreal. A hundred people were in that room to celebrate with me and I felt like a doll in a china shop – high on a shelf for everyone to admire, but not to touch. I was not real. This life was not real. I created the cast of characters but had no control of the plot or the setting. It was madness, pure madness.

୭

Ken and I visited Danny the day after our wedding, before we departed for our week-long honeymoon to Hawaii. Danny was his usual self and so were my parents. I couldn't wait to escape with my new husband.

"You scared us, Danny," I heard my mother say when I first walked into his room. My father was sitting in a chair, reading the Post-Gazette. I walked over to kiss my dad on the top of his head and saw why he was glued to the paper. The story had just broken that Nicole Brown Simpson had been murdered. Chills went down my back and into my legs, weakening my knees a little.

"Oh my," I said. I was not as shocked by the news as I was that I now knew why I had been hesitant when Ken suggested we get married on June 12th. There was something about that date that seemed ominous, but I just couldn't put my finger on it when he brought it up. Now, it made sense. I got married on the day she got murdered, which led to the trial of the century and a lot of racial tension.

"Yeah, can you believe it? That's O.J.'s ex-wife. Poor guy. I wonder what she was doing whoring around with some young kid anyway?"

"Dad…" I stopped myself since he would see the footage later of O.J. and the white Ford Bronco. Then his O.J. world can start falling apart. There was nothing I could say.

I looked at my mom, who had warmed up to Danny and was stroking his hair. He was sucking it in like fresh milk.

"So, how's everything this morning, little brother?" I realized there was some sarcasm in my tone. Ken remained silent, "Just great, thanks to my super smart sister. Gee, if it wasn't for you, I'd probably be dead by now."

"Danny," my mother chided. "We were all worried about you and Katie was right in getting some help to you."

"Thanks," he acquiesced, "but I missed out on all the good food at your reception, and the champagne, for sure. They won't even give me a pain pill in this place."

"Are you in pain?" asked my mother.

162

"Yeah, I fell in the gutter the other day and I think I bruised by bottom." He laughed, but no one else did. I felt Ken fidgeting beside me.

"So, what did the doc say? I guessed it was a dirty needle stick by the swelling in your right forearm." I knew I sounded superior, but I didn't care. He had ruined my wedding day and I was not going to sugar coat any of it.

"None of your damn business, so why don't you just back off, bitch?"

Ken left my side and addressed Danny directly.

"Alright, that's it."

"Who the hell do you think you are? You've been part of this family, like, what? Five minutes?"

"I know enough to know that you barged into my wedding reception and upset my wife, who's done nothing but save you time and time again." Ken's face had a reddish tint that I had never seen before.

He doesn't even know about the biggest save.

"So shut your sorry-ass mouth and have a little respect for these two women who are likely the only ones in this world that give a damn about you." He then turned to my father. "I'm sorry, Mr. Mulligan, but I must defend my wife."

My dad smiled and got up from his chair, laying the paper aside.

"No, no…you're fine. This kid needs someone other than me to put him in his place, so I rather enjoyed that."

"Geez," Danny sighed. "Well, I'm glad to see you married somebody with some balls, Katie." He looked at Ken with a patronizing glare. "Please forgive me, *Kentaro*, for offending your wife. Can you please ask my sister to talk to some of her doctor friends and arrange for a release? It's getting way too stuffy in here."

"Thank you, *Daniel.* Apology accepted. Let's see what we can do to get you out of here." Ken left the room to either talk to a nurse or to shed the trash he had just collected. Ashamed didn't even begin to describe how I felt.

"I like him," Danny said, and shook his head in approval.

"Listen Danny. We're going on our honeymoon for a week. Where will you go?"

"Far from here, that's for sure."

"Danny...," the only word it seemed my mother could utter.

"I don't know what the big deal is. I came back to see my sister get married. Okay, I kind of missed the wedding, but at least I tried. I didn't mean any harm, but once again, Danny's the problem."

"Don't play victim with me," I began to lecture. "I don't know how you found out about my wedding, but I've been worried about you since the day you disappeared from my apartment like a gust of wind. You think you can just come and go as you please, hurting everyone in your path, and then blame us when things don't go your way? It's so damned selfish. I'm going to leave some money with Mom and Dad to get you some help. When I get back, I hope to see you taking advantage of that opportunity. If you don't, that's your choice, but don't ever show up unannounced in my life again. The next time you want to see me, you call me like normal people do and respect my time and my life, and then maybe...just maybe...I can learn to respect yours." I turned and left the room.

I heard my mother utter, "Katie..." and my dad's footsteps were right behind mine.

"Hey..." he shouted to me. I stopped and turned around. By this time the tears were flowing. My father embraced me.

164

"Katie...my sweet Katie. I'm sorry your brother is who he is. It's a lot my fault, you know."

"No, it's not..." I knew better.

"Well, it's complicated. He will always have this problem, you know? I hate him for it, but at the same time, he's my son."

"I'm going to leave a check for you and Mom and the name and number of a place in California that will treat him..."

"No, Kate...it won't work. Did you hear him in there? He's the victim. We are the enemies. All we can do is wait for him to figure it out on his own."

"But he could be dead before that ever happens."

My dad simply shrugged his shoulders. I was amazed at how calm he was when just last night he was shooting daggered looks at Danny and downing his liquor to forget.

"How can you just sit back and watch him self-destruct?"

"I don't know, honey." He lifted my chin with his fingers. "Look at me." I did.

"We live in a flawed world. It is imperfect and stained and toxic."

I gasped. "What did you just say?"

"What?"

"About the world being imperfect and flawed.

"Yes, that's what I said. You'll just have to trust me, Kate. I love Danny, but I can't control him. I can only love him."

You live in a flawed world. It is imperfect and stained and toxic. You will just have to trust me.

Those were the words of the man with the soft round face when I asked him why people...why I...had to suffer. My heart stopped beating for a moment. I hugged my father tighter than I had ever before. He hugged me back with purpose, whispering words of comfort in my ear.

"It's okay, Kate. Leave Danny to your mother and I. We'll be fine, I promise. Go enjoy your honeymoon with Ken. You deserve it." His hand was rubbing circles on my back.

I squeezed my eyes shut and whispered *thank you*, to both of my fathers.

I saw Ken rounding the corner from the nurse's station.

"Okay, I just talked to the doctor and Danny's release papers should be ready in 30 minutes." He saw my face stained with tears and looked concerned.

"Hey, are you okay?" He took over the back rub for my dad.

"Yes, I'm fine. My dad was just telling me to get out of here and enjoy my honeymoon. I think that's the best advice I've heard in a long time."

"I'm good with that. Tell Mrs. Mulligan goodbye for us?"

"Sure, get out of here," my dad waved us away.

An instant relief enveloped me as we practically ran out of the hospital into the parking garage. All the way to the airport, I couldn't shake the words of my father that so closely mirrored the words I had heard so many years ago. All I could do was see it as another sign that I had to trust. I had to have faith that this choice I had made would not be totally in vain.

166

fifteen

1996

IT HAD BEEN TWENTY YEARS SINCE I BEGAN my second chance at life. Twenty years, but it seemed like yesterday. I should have had the face and body of a seventy-year-old. Instead, I was blessed with more knowledge and wisdom I could possibly have at the ripe young age of thirty-three. *Then why did I still feel inept at dealing with life?*

Ken and I tried for two years to get pregnant, but to no avail. We began the long and arduous process of fertility testing and just last week, we discovered that the problem did not lie with me. It was Ken. For some reason unknown to him or anyone, he was, by technical definition, sterile. The doctor did not say that he could not produce a child, *per se* (I have come to hate that phrase), but that he produced such a small quantity of sperm that it was unlikely there were enough strong ones to make the journey to the coveted egg. As we sat there listening to the specialist explain the problem in technical terms, I watched Ken's face fall and his eyes dim. That pained me more than the prospect of not having a child. I already had children and missed them terribly, but I knew the love of parenthood. He did not and likely would never – at least not from his own flesh and blood. It was devastating news. Yet, as we walked out of the office to our car, he found it in himself to comfort me. He apologized and said he didn't know, and probably should have checked into it before asking me to marry him. I stopped in my tracks.

"No, don't do that. I didn't marry you for your sperm count. I married you because of this. Because this is how you deal with life. You take responsibility for it, you make sure I am okay, no matter what, and then you process it for yourself. You don't blame, you don't wallow, you don't hate. That is why I love you and *exactly* why I married you." He gave me a half-smile, but I could see his eyes brimming with tears.

"Are you okay?"

"I'm okay. I never thought I would find a woman deserving enough to have children with anyway, so when I did, it made sense to have a family. But all I really need is you. Besides, it sounds like having kids for us will take a lot of practice. What did Dr. Goldstein say? It's a numbers game and since my numbers are down, it will require more *attempts*."

I chuckled, remembering the doctor's scientific description of making love. "C'mon then…we took the day off, so let's get some lunch and go home and make some attempts." I took his arm and felt a strong sense that everything would be all right, whether we could make babies together or not.

Later on, after Ken and I had an afternoon of tender lovemaking, I lay awake, listening to his steady breathing and I felt a wave of panic. Followed by disappointment. Followed by guilt. Followed by sadness. Once again, life felt unfair and I wasn't sure how much I was to blame. How is it that a man like Ken, who would be the best father any child could ever have, would be denied the pleasure of parenting, while a man like

Sam, who had no interest in family could produce children by just thinking about sex? One of the things I dreamed about in my second life is the joy of having children with someone who wanted to be my partner in life. Now, it seemed that dream was shattered, and I didn't know what I was supposed to learn from it. All it did was make me feel sad that I walked away from the children I did have and that the man I was deeply in love with would not be given a chance to feel the joy of fatherhood. There was something in this world to be cursed. I just didn't know what it was.

◦

"Are you serious?" I cautiously inquired of my colleague Dr. Renfroe, who nonchalantly reported that scientists at Johns Hopkins had identified a second breast cancer gene – the BRCA2. "How did they happen upon that?"

I knew there was a second gene, but I didn't remember how it had come about.

"By chance, actually," he replied while peering into his TEM microscope. "They discovered a small piece of DNA was missing from a pancreatic cancer cell, and it turned out to be the BRCA2 they were searching for. Very cool."

"So, what will that mean for us?" I asked with obvious enthusiasm. My heart was pounding since I knew this would be a chance to go further. Clinical trials were underway, and FDA approval around the corner for the drug tamoxifen, and I happened to know some of what could come next if Renfroe would play in the sandbox with me.

"Don't get too excited, Mulligan. I know what you are thinking, but there's a long path between here and where you'd like to go."

"Of course." I tried to match his nonchalance but couldn't contain myself completely. If only I had been permitted to go back to gather some documents and Google the research before starting this life, I wouldn't have had to reinvent the wheel. I had studied cancer research only as a patient, not a scientist. I knew the breakthroughs but very little about how they got there.

"So, when will they be publishing their findings? Can't wait to get my hands on that baby," I said while disinfecting a glass beaker.

Renfroe looked up from his instrument and smiled.

"Have you taken any days off lately?"

I ignored the question, but he stood upright and went on, facing me this time.

"I admire your passion. I do. But you know what they say about all work and no play?"

I decided to look at him out of respect, chuckling at the same time. Dr. Renfroe was in his early sixties, married, with two grown children and a grandchild on the way. But he lived his life in the lab just like I did.

"No, what do *they* say? Since you're the expert on that," I said sarcastically,

He got a kick out of my comment.

"Okay, okay. I know I'm the pot calling the kettle black, but you've got a lot more going for you than this lab. That talented husband of yours – shouldn't you two be taking a trip to Japan soon? Or traveling somewhere in the world? Live it up. Have some fun."

"Are you trying to get rid of me?" I asked with feigned disappointment.

"Of course not, but take it from me. Margo and I didn't do enough of that when we were young, and now…"

I knew what he was going to say, and I interrupted him before he had to say it.

"How *is* Margo? Any of the new therapies working for her?" She had just been diagnosed with multiple sclerosis.

"Has her good days and bad, I guess. There's just not much out there for the pain."

I wanted to encourage him...tell him to hang in there a little longer because amazing drugs would be introduced for that in a few years. A few decades.

"I saw how you changed the subject there, Mulligan," he said, while peering through the microscope.

I hesitated because all I could think about was the news we received from the infertility doctor. That's not something one shares with a male colleague. But it had put a damper on our marital bliss, that's for sure.

"Yeah, well. We do need to plan a trip of some sort. I'll think about it. Thank you, Dr. Renfroe."

"Just trying to keep it fresh around here," he mumbled, distracted by the cells on the specimen slides. I would have taken that comment wrong if I didn't know him better. In some ways, he represented a father-figure to me that truly appreciated what I was doing. My own father struggled with my career because he didn't understand why I would spend seven years at Harvard only to work in a lab.

"What is it exactly that you are doing?" my father asked me at the New Year's Eve party Ken and I last attended at their house.

"Daddy, just tell your friends I'm doing cancer research. That's all."

"But I thought you went to medical school to be a doctor, not a lab scientist."

"I *am* a doctor, Dad. I just don't have a waiting room and cranky patients and late-night hospital visits."

"Oh," he said with a disappointed tone. "If that's what you enjoy…" And then he poured himself another glass of scotch and went back to the drunken guests. He meant well.

৯

That evening, I took Dr. Renfroe's advice and told Ken about our earlier conversation. Ken found it as humorous as I did.

"That guy has a lot of nerve," he said while tossing the salad.

"Yeah, but he's right, ya know? You are so patient with my work and the hours I put in." I stopped grating the cheese and grabbed a dish towel to wipe my hands. I walked up behind him and put my harms around his waist. I could feel his shoulders relax and he sighed. He turned around to meet my gaze and brushed my hair away from my shoulders. In true Ken-fashion, he looked directly into my eyes as if there was nothing more important in the world than what I was about to say.

"If everyone in the world cared as much as you do about fighting this deadly disease, the fight would be over. You are the embodiment of passion and compassion. How can I argue with that?"

"I know but that's such a lofty goal. And I'm not single. I can't do whatever I want without considering your feelings. I don't want this to get in the way. Of us." I laid my head on his chest and he squeezed me tight.

After a few seconds, he grabbed my shoulders and pulled me back to look at him.

"Where is this coming from? This doubt? About us?"

172

"I don't know." I did, but I couldn't say. I couldn't tell him that things never work out for me. In 50 years of trying, it didn't work out for me. That I'm a relationship fool. I have never done it right and don't expect to do it right even when I have a second chance at it. Instead, I apologized. Something else I learned to do.

"I'm sorry. I didn't mean to turn our evening into a downer. Let's eat." I pulled away from Ken, but he wouldn't let me go. He pulled me closer and kissed me with a deep passion. He then spoke softly.

"There's an old Japanese saying my mother used to tell me when I would do what you are doing now – this self-doubt."

"What's that?"

"Saru mo ki kara ochimasu."

"What does it mean?"

"Even monkeys fall from trees."

"What?" I laughed at the reference.

Ken smiled mischievously.

"Are you calling me a monkey?" I pulled away and slapped him lightly on the shoulder, in jest. I grabbed the grater again to finish my work.

"Of course not." He laughed, faking surprise at my gesture. "It's the literal meaning of the words. The figurative meaning is nobody's perfect. I don't want a perfect wife. I want you."

He kissed me on the back of the neck, and I felt my eyes well with tears. One dropped into the cheese.

If I have done nothing else right in this life, I at least found this man. Or he was found for me.

ॐ

In July, we travelled to Atlanta to meet a couple of Ken's cousins who were coming from Japan for the 1996 Summer Olympics. When Ken first told me about the trip, I was excited but nervous. I wracked my brain, trying to remember when the infamous Olympic bombing took place that year. Was it at the beginning or near the end of the games? I remembered that it had happened at the Olympic Park but didn't know if we could avoid that or not. I had only been to Atlanta once before for a research conference, so I had no idea about the logistics. Where was the Google crystal ball when you needed it?

As it turned out, we weren't scheduled to go until August 31st, four days after the bombing, which I learned about through CNN on the day it happened. Ken's cousins called that evening, expressing fear about making the trip. Ken convinced them that security would be better than ever, and we were likely safer now than if it hadn't happened. He had a way of making everyone feel protected.

Reika, Ken's 24-year-old cousin and her newlywed husband, Tomo, were delightful. To his dismay, it seemed, Tomo was labeled *Tom* by the Americanized Ikeda family, but I tried to be respectful and called him Tomo when I had the chance. Ken, on the other hand, seemed to get some pleasure out of referring to him as Tom whenever possible. *Hey, Tom, can I get you a drink? What do you think about this, Tom?* – emphasizing the name for effect. Ken came from a close-knit family and I got the impression that no outsider was good enough for the females in the family until they passed muster. They had to take a silent test and a year of marriage was obviously not enough to pass. I wondered how Ken would be with our own daughter if we were lucky enough to have one.

Thankfully, Reika and Tomo spoke very good English, although with a little alcohol, Ken and Tomo lapsed into

Japanese, reminding me that there was a side to Ken that I was not privy to, nor could I culturally understand. We were equals in that regard. There was a whole life of mine he was not allowed to know about, and in some weird way, it assuaged some of my guilt.

Ken and I entertained our Japanese guests to the best of our ability, despite not knowing much about Atlanta. On the first night there, we made our way to the bar at the Omni Hotel downtown where we were staying. CNN was silently on the overhead screen, with words flashing across that reported the Olympic bomber had been identified – Richard Jewell – a 33-year-old police officer. A memory flashed back to my time with the man in Quietude. *You will be tempted to tell others what you know,* and it was no truer than it was at that moment. I wanted to yell, scream, stand up in the bar and tell everyone, "He didn't do it!" But I knew it would be another decade before they would hear from the real killer, Eric Rudolph, who was by now in hiding and wouldn't be found for years.

I wondered if there was a way for me to surreptitiously lend a hand, give the FBI some sort of clue, lead them to the truth. But I couldn't think of anything that wouldn't make me sound like a crazy lady trying to get attention. Another glass of Merlot and I resolved that I really couldn't save the world, least of all Richard Jewell.

Even so, I had trouble staying in the moment. It was if the clash between these two worlds was exploding in my head. My own personal bombing, of sorts. I felt short of breath, and out of my body, as if I were a mermaid watching the action above from under the sea, wanting to swim away because I knew I couldn't be in it. I watched Ken leave a tip on the bar and heard muffled laughter between Tomo and him, playing in this underworld world I knew too much of and they knew nothing about. Reika made unintelligible conversation as we walked out of the revolving doors and down the street toward our dinner destination. I pretended to listen, but my feet felt like fins, and before I could steady myself, I was on the ground – faint and unable to speak. This was a good thing because I wanted to say things that would get me in trouble. I wanted to tell Ken. I wanted to stop the chatter in my head so I could go back to my old life where I knew nothing of the future. The words of the man with the soft round face reverberated in my head. *You will be tempted…you will be tempted.* I lost consciousness.

When I awoke, I was in a hospital room and Ken was holding my hand. My mouth felt dry.

"Hey there, sweetheart," Ken said lovingly. "How are you feeling?"

"I'm thirsty," is all I could muster.

He poured some water from a pitcher and I took a sip with his help.

"What happened? What time is it?"

"Well, you fainted. On the street. I'm just glad you didn't hit your head."

Ken was smiling with a childish grin, which annoyed me.

"What? Why are you laughing at me?" I noticed I was still slurring my words a little.

"I'm not laughing, but I do know something you don't know that's pretty incredible."

"Like?"

"Like the reason you fainted is because you're pregnant."

"What? Did you say I'm pregnant?"

"Yep, that's exactly what I said." He squeezed my hand and I could feel his joy seeping into my body.

"Oh my God." I took a deep breath. I could feel the tears coming. I was blown away by the news and the irony. The last thing I thought before I fainted is that I couldn't bear this life any longer, only to awake with never wanting it to end.

"Oh no," I said, worried.

"What? What's wrong?" Ken's joy turned to concern.

"The wine. I had two glasses on an empty stomach. The baby."

"Oh, you're fine. I don't think that matters until later anyway."

I knew better, but I wasn't going down that path again. Not now. Not after this news.

"If you say so, love."

"Hey, we're having a baby," Ken spoke as if he just wanted to hear his words out loud.

An hour ago, I wanted to shout it from the roof tops that Richard Jewell was innocent. Now there was something else to shout out. Something much more in my control.

"We're having a baby." I smiled from ear to ear. "And a strong one at that – those little swimmers were determined little buggers."

Ken kissed me and nothing else around me mattered but our little world.

sixteen

1997

NINETEEN-NINETY-SEVEN BEGAN WITH A hard-core depression. Two weeks after returning from the Olympics in August, I suffered a miscarriage. I tried to be strong by throwing myself into my work, but by the holidays it had caught up with me, and by January, I was in full-blown shut down mode. Ken had a more difficult time with it at first, so I did my best to comfort him, but when it seemed he was handling it better, maybe I thought it was my turn to feel. I don't know. My pregnancies with Deirdre and Sean were so simple that I never imagined something like this would happen. But I was younger when I had them and maybe this was a sign of my age. Ken tried to understand my silence and my irritable moods, but eventually, he began to show signs of wear and tear due to my inability to deal with our fate.

"Maybe you should see a therapist," he said one morning as he was pouring my coffee.

"Okay, like I have time to do that."

"I'm just saying…"

"I know what you are saying. You want me to get back to the way things were and talking to somebody might help me to do that. How? What can I possibly say or a therapist possibly do to reverse time? That's what I need you to know. I need to go back and not drink that wine and not make this happen." I began to sob uncontrollably.

"Hey, hey..." Ken set the coffee in front of me and knelt down where I was sitting at the breakfast table to console me.

"Remember? We talked to the OB and he said it had nothing to do with the wine. You didn't do anything wrong, baby. It's not your fault, so why do you keep dwelling on that?"

"I don't know. This never happened before."

"Of course, it hasn't. You've never been pregnant before." He paused for a few seconds. "Have you?"

I was sorry I had said it like that. In my weakest moments it was hard to separate my two lives.

"No...I just meant I've never been through a miscarriage. I've had friends go through it, but I always thought it was just the end of something they never had to begin with. Now I see how it's a real death. The grief. It's real."

"I know. I'm going through it, too." He had felt the sting of my words.

"Oh, God." I felt like such a selfish little girl. "I'm sorry." I grabbed a napkin from the table to blow my nose. "You know what I mean. We just do it differently. Men and women, I mean. We just handle it differently." It's all I could think to say.

What I couldn't express was everything else I was feeling that I couldn't tell one single soul, not even a therapist.

"Think about seeing someone, okay? Not because I think you're unstable. I just think there are things you might need to tell someone that you can't tell me."

"Don't ever say that, okay? There's nothing I can't tell you. Nothing." I knew I was lying but needed to delineate in my mind that as far as this world was concerned, we had no secrets. The secrets from the old world belonged only to me and the man with the soft round face. The only man who could get me through this. And he did.

ॐ

The year that started out with sadness and anger for both Ken and me, transformed us in a way we could not have imagined. Our differences manifested in unique ways. He used his artistry to process the emotions; I used my brain-led research to control mine. Together, we found some sense of peace through it all.

While I was spending time at the lab, Ken spent time in his studio writing the most beautiful piece for cello that I believe was ever written. The first time I listened to it, I was instantly moved to tears by the emotion it expressed.

"I'm calling it Two Seasons," he said with a contemplative gaze, as if he wasn't sure and was still mulling it over in his heart.

"Okay. May I ask why or is too personal?"

He chuckled in a "you're silly" way.

"Please ask. I'm dying to tell you." He patted the hearth near the fireplace where he was sitting with a glass of Chardonnay. "Come, sit."

I was in my work clothes and wanted to change into something comfortable, but something told me that Ken needed me to sit and hear him. So, I did.

"The first season," he began to explain as he pointed to the printed score, "is our meeting at the dinner. It's formal and predictable. Then it moves into something less so, with lighter tones and a strong tempo."

I loved his little boy emotion as he was excitedly sharing his creative process, explaining every detail to a novice who only understood music from the emotion it invoked. He continued.

"When you hear the tempo begin to slow and it deepens to almost a nocturne-like piece, that's our first time making love. It's sultry and darker, but not depressed."

I smiled and he looked perplexed.

"Am I losing you with the musical jargon?"

"No more than I lose you when I talk about genetic mutations and heterozygous alleles."

"Yeah…" He nodded in agreement.

"Go on. I'm fascinated. Please…"

"The point is, there's a definite movement of emotion as I interpret our lives in this piece. I've written a violin movement over the cello that represents our different voices, but rarely competing. Mostly in harmony. But by the second season – the loss of the baby, there are some competing harmonies that almost clash, but quickly resolve into a deep tone – the cello goes higher and the violin reaches lower. It's really rather beautiful, if I must say so myself."

He blushed, I assumed, because he was uncomfortable bragging. But I was moved in ways he couldn't imagine.

"I wish I could play the violin. Who do you have in mind for the piece?"

"I don't want to assume we will perform it. It's rare that we get that opportunity. But I've asked Elizabeth Kurz to play it with me so I can actually hear the sound that's in my head. We're rehearsing tomorrow."

"That's amazing. I'm so proud of you." He was deep in concentration as he looked over the score, but I pulled his face toward me as he always does when I'm distant, to remind him how much he meant to me. "*You* are amazing." I kissed him and ran my fingers through his thick, black hair. He smiled.

"Thanks," he said modestly and with appreciation for my rare gesture of romantic approval.

"So, have you spoken to the meister yet?" That was an inside joke between us. Dr. Schmidt, the symphony conductor, referred to himself as the Kapellmeister, an old German reference for conductor, which we shortened to the "meister," especially when Ken was not feeling so warm toward him.

"No, I want to play with Liz first and do a re-write until I feel it's meister-worthy."

"That makes sense." I got up to make my way toward the bedroom to change into something that smelled less clinical. "Can I get you anything?"

"No, I'm good. Hurry back." He winked at me. "I want to hear about your day."

I never got tired of hearing that phrase. *I want to hear about your day.* Where did he learn this stuff? I thought of calling his mother to thank her for raising her kid right, but I had a feeling she had little to do with it. This was deep within him. It was just him.

෴

The time came when Ken did, in fact, perform his cello and violin piece at the concert hall. I hurried in that night, after a long day at the lab. I, too, was immersed in my own solo composition, not of the creative type, but the scientific variety. We were close to linking BRCA2 to a unique form of breast cancer that could lead to a new understanding of how to fight and cure it. But that had to wait, for tonight was my lover's moment in the spotlight.

"Kate, so good to see you," the meister, Dr. Schmidt, said to me as I rounded the corner near the backstage door. He was smoking outside minutes before the show started.

"Hello, Dr. Schmidt. Good to see you as well. I am so excited to hear Ken's work tonight."

"As are we," he said proudly. "It's absolutely phenomenal. Borne of lots of emotion that I'm sure you had something to do with." He smiled, while stamping out the butt on the ground.

"Well, I don't know about that. He's a musical genius in my book."

"I'll give you that."

"Good luck tonight."

"Thank you. Enjoy the show."

I was glad the conversation was short, as I was late and didn't want the curtain to open before I was safely in my seat. Ken told me they were opening with his piece and I had to be there at the start.

I made my way to my regular seat, row four, seat 27. I sat, smoothed my silk skirt, and looked at the program. There he was, front and center. His photo featured with a caption, Kentaro Ikeda to perform his work "Two Seasons."

The curtain opened and my heart was racing. This was his night. I had to remind myself this was akin to me being recognized for some monumental lab discovery. This was his night.

He was so handsome and so serious. Dr. Schmidt lifted his hands in a gesture to begin. And then the spotlight was on Ken and Ken alone. Just like he had described to me, he began with a somewhat predictable tune, and then I remembered, this was an adaptation of the Handel piece I first heard him play when I caught a glimpse of him at the benefit dinner. I felt chills run up my bare arms and I took a deep breath. His strong, but tender hands, moved the bow effortlessly across the strings with precision and passion. For the untrained eye, there was no way to know how he knew where to place it in order to make the desired sounds, but he knew. It was magical. It was how he made love to me. With precise understanding, but no comprehensible way of knowing how it was done. It was intuitive for Ken, like this feeling he used to play his cello.

The piece then moved into a light movement, followed by the nocturnal one that he said had represented our first time together. I watched his face. I couldn't tell if it was pained or simply intense, but he was definitely in a world all of his own, despite hundreds of admiring ears in the audience. What came as a surprise, and I'm assuming the part that outlined the second season, was something I had not heard when he had played it for me privately at home. This was different, maybe something he and Liz had added. The spotlight came upon her and she began to work her violin with intensity, but with alacrity. It was beautiful and strong, but cheerful. It made me bubble with anticipation. Then the fall. This was the part that I knew would be hard to hear. The morose let down. The depression. I had not realized it but Ken had felt what I had felt, but much earlier. Much sooner after the death of our unborn child. I felt guilty, again, that I had not been more present for him. That I had simply disappeared into my work.

His face became strained and sad, but then a slight smile. I watched his left hand command the notes, while his right drew the bow perfectly across the deeply-toned strings. This felt like contentment, and peace. Acceptance. The lump in my throat was growing and I didn't know how to resolve it but to allow the tears to flow. It was so beautiful, so real. So Ken. By the last few notes, it was clear he was exhausted with the emotion and so was I. Elizabeth prompted him with a few high notes and he answered with a beautiful sequence of tenor bravado. It was finished.

The crowd rose to their feet and applauded for what seemed like forever. I had never felt so proud and so undone in all my life. Nothing in my first life had ever compared to this moment – this sense of knowing and being known by a man who loved me with his entire heart. I was completely spent.

I heard the rest of the concert, but I did not listen. I couldn't help replaying in my head the sounds of Ken's heart. The literal story of our lives in a five-minute score. After the show, I met him backstage and he was giddy with relief and pride. His fellow musicians were clearly proud of him, and when I walked through the door, they all greeted me as the muse – the inspiration for the creator. Their beloved Kentaro. I'll never forget that night as long as I live, no matter how many lives I live. No amount of personal success could match the beauty of what Ken had just accomplished for himself and for us.

I had no idea mine was on its way.

৵

"Come here," I demanded with urgency, to my lab assistant, Jodi. I wanted her to see what I saw through the tiny microscopic lens. I pulled away from the instrument and she peered through it.

"I see a cancer cell duplicating," she said with eyes transfixed on the slide. "Wait, but now it's…now it's…what is it doing?" She was hyper-focused. "It appears to be attaching to a healthy cell, and it's...it's being obliterated." She looked up, perplexed. "What's happening to it?"

I grinned like a Cheshire cat.

"It's being shut down. That duplication is being shut down."

"No kidding, but by what? Is this a healthy patient's sample?" She peered back into the lens.

"It's being shut down by the patient's own antibodies and you are wrong," I said emphatically and began dancing around the crowded lab. "You are wrong, wrong, wrong, my friend! This dude is about as sick as they come."

Jodi dropped her hands and was stunned at my performance. "What are you talking about? Please...spill the beans or I'm going to have to tackle you!"

"Okay," I said, sitting back down at the table, excitedly. "Advanced cancer cells are able to attack the checkpoint protein sites, right? PD-1 and CLTA-4 – the ones that keep the body from attacking its own healthy cells?"

"Yes, go on..."

"Typically, once the cancer army takes over the checkpoint proteins – the gate guards, so to speak – it confuses the immune system and opens the door to the cancer to attack the healthy cells. The defense is gone, and the war of malignancy is on."

"So, what did I see happen on that slide?"

"What you saw is an engineered antibody – I took two antibodies, one that typically attaches to a cancer cell and one that attaches to an immune cell and combined it into one – a double-duty antibody, so to speak. So, no matter where it is – even at the checkpoint sites – it gets ambushed by the immune system. A sort of double agent spy fools the cancer into trusting him and then boom! It pulls a fast one and the immune cell shows up with an MK47 and obliterates it."

Jodi seemed a little confused by the military analogy.

"In more simple terms, when I introduced it into the blood, one part of the antibody attached to the cancer cell and the other attached to an immune cell, bringing the two together. Once merged, the cancer had no chance and the immune cell dominated! If you introduce enough of these buggers into the system, in theory – and that's a great big in theory – they should each seek out a cancer cell and introduce it to an immune cell for a match made in heaven!"

She seemed to get the dating reference. Jodi had had her share of questionable relationships before meeting Trent.

"Talk about a wolf in sheep's clothing, Jodi. I've been waiting all my life to double-cross this son of a bitch and here it is. Right before my eyes." I felt sadness along with the elation, as I thought about Cherry and the others who couldn't hang on for a cure. "Here it is."

I sat back down and was exhausted at the thought.

"Does Renfroe know about this?" Jodi asked eagerly.

"No, but he is about to find out." I thought about the possible reprimand I might be facing.

"You mean you've been working on this solo? You know that goes against protocol."

"I know, I know…but when I first brought up the idea to him a few months ago, he scoffed at it. He said I was playing God with the human body and asked if I thought I was in a science-fiction movie or something. Of course, my smart-ass response was that our lab's middle name was God, to which he took offense and the conversation fell apart and never came up again. I think he thought I was crazy."

I was speaking a mile a minute and I could tell Jodi was overwhelmed by my mania.

"What do you think he'll say when you tell him?"

"I don't care what he says. Protocol, schmotocol…he can fire me if he wants, but this is big Jodi. Really big!" I got up and grabbed her by the arms and twirled her around with me. She laughed out loud and hugged me tight, obviously delighted at the great ending to an otherwise boring day.

"So, what now?" she said with anticipation.

"You've got to keep this quiet for a few days, okay? I need to run some more tests and be sure I'm seeing what I really think I'm seeing. Then we'll both talk to Renfroe."

"Both? I shouldn't be there when you break the news."

"What do you mean? You don't want to be part of this? I won't get you in trouble, I promise. I'll tell him you knew nothing about it. But just so he doesn't think I'm stark-raving mad, I need you as a witness. You saw it, right?"

"Yes, I saw it and I'm amazed…it's just that…"

"What? What is it?"

"Kate this is your baby. You deserve all the credit. It doesn't feel right to be sitting there when you tell Renfroe."

"Listen, Jodi." I grabbed her hand and she seemed surprised. This wasn't usual lab behavior, but I didn't care. "I'm no prima donna. I'm not like most of these guys around here who are waiting to be courted by the drug companies and make their millions. Hell, I don't even care if they put my name on it. In my heart," I grabbed at my lab coat near my chest. "In my heart, I just want this damn disease to go away."

Jodi's eyes welled up with tears and she patted the top of my hand that was holding hers.

"Okay...okay. You're a saint and I couldn't be prouder of you. I'll lead and then we'll shout it from the damn mountain tops if you want!"

I started to cry, too, but quickly recovered at the thought of going home to tell Ken.

"Okay, the first step is you're going to go to Kroger with me, we'll buy some Champagne, and we're going to my place to break the news to Ken."

"I thought we had to keep this quiet?"

"Well, yes, we'll keep it from everyone around here, but there is no way I am going home tonight and being silent with Ken — and you need to celebrate with us."

"You got it...give me a minute to call Trent and let him know I'll be late."

"But don't tell Trent our secret, okay?"

"Don't worry...I'll tell him you're pregnant or something," she said with a smile.

That stung, but Jodi had no idea about the miscarriage. I went to my desk to get my purse and wished both secrets were true.

seventeen

2000

"KATE, LET'S GO. IT'S ALMOST FIVE-THRITY!"
Ken was yelling through the bathroom door, while I fussed
with my up-do. I've never been good at getting the hair right
when I really needed it to be. Somehow, on random days when
absolutely no one but lab rats would see me, I would have the
best hair days.

"I'm coming," I said frustrated.

"I'm sure you are stunning, Sweetie. And you know how
traffic can be into the city this time of day."

I was surprised that he sounded as nervous as I was. He
was right. I was being ridiculous. But how often does someone
get honored for their cancer research discoveries? Like never.
This was the biggest night of my life. THIS. *This.* It made the
whole crazy do-over journey worth every minute, despite what
I gave up to do it. This was my higher calling and I answered it.
Finally. No more regrets. No more wondering why I was given
the opportunity to return. I came back and I nailed it. I took
one last look in the mirror and finger-curled a wisp in front of
my ear.

"You rock, Kate Mulligan. You freaking rock this time around." I smiled confidently and opened the door. Ken was standing in the kitchen, looking over the front page of the Pittsburgh Post-Gazette.

"I still can't get over this article about you." He smiled, grabbing his coat from the back of the counter stool. "Next you'll be on the cover of TIME."

"Yeah, right. I think that's reserved for the really important people, like celebrities and politicians."

"Well, tonight you *are* a celebrity." He gestured for me to go before him.

"Beauty before beast, and you are gorgeous, my dear."

"Why thank you, my prince." I feigned a British accent. "You are looking quite dapper yourself tonight."

And off we went to the annual Pittsburgh Cancer Research Institute's dinner and award ceremony at the swanky William Penn Hotel.

I hadn't been to the hotel for some time and forgot how stunning the lobby was. The marble floors and crystal chandeliers shone like diamonds in the early evening light. I spotted Dr. Renfroe and his wife, Camille, standing at the elevators. He looked up and smiled like a proud father. He held out his arms for me.

"Kate...this is your night." He gave me a heart-felt hug and then let go to extend a hand to Ken. "Ken. Good to see you again."

"Likewise," Ken replied.

Camille and I exchanged hugs, as well. She was looking particularly frail, which hurt my heart.

"There are rumors of a big grant coming from the National Cancer Institute to fund the double-blind clinical trials we've been asking for," Renfroe said after we were safely in the elevator. "And I mean really big. Huge."

"Really? I thought that was put on hold until we gave them more data." I wondered what *really big* meant.

"Lucky for us, it's an election year. According to the big guns, President Clinton wants to capitalize on this before he leaves office, and at the same time, give Gore a leg-up, if possible, by claiming the cancer cure for the Democrats."

"Great. I'm a political pawn now. And, oh yeah, we need that cure by...um...yesterday, please?"

"Yeah, I know. There's a price to pay for the money. But you're in the thick of it now. You know what they say in this business, Kate. Just take the money when you can get it and don't ask too many questions. And we're talking huge...a half billion dollars huge"

"Wow." I gulped at the number but wished Renfroe hadn't ruined my pre-dinner experience with thoughts of my impending political prostitution. Yes, half a billion would be amazing, but I never liked the politics of how we got the money and who and what had to be bought and sold to get it. Dealing with the drug companies was bad enough, but now we've got Clinton, Gore and Bush battling for votes. Great. The Republicans ruled the Senate and House, so any pre-election vote for that kind of federal funding would likely get bogged down in congress anyway. I had visions of being invited to speak at a congressional meeting of some sort, when the elevator doors opened and I saw Jodi standing there nursing a glass of champagne with her husband, Tom.

"There she is," exclaimed Jodi, reaching out to hug me. "You look gorgeous."

"Why thank you. You look..." I glanced at her chest. "...voluptuous." I was shocked to see her showing so much cleavage. Lab coats generally covered up anything that indicated gender. Trent blushed with pride and took a long sip of what looked like a whiskey and Coke.

"I know. Hey, if ya got it flaunt it, isn't that what they say?" The champagne had taken hold. She grabbed my arm to lead me into the event area. Ken followed dutifully behind, exchanging mundane courtesies with Tom.

The Grand Ballroom was captivating. The ornate golden-railed balcony above, that surrounded the room, was highlighted with huge arched inset windows covered in red velvet and lace draperies. A magnificent crystal chandelier hung from the intricately tiled circular inlay that was the centerpiece of the ceiling and the room. Three sets of French doors on each of the four walls gave it a Parisian feel. I felt like a queen just entering the space, wondering what it would mean by the end of the night. I felt surprisingly uneasy, I guess because I was never one to think too highly of myself. There was a part of me that just wanted to accept the plaque without the fanfare and go home with Ken to our modest little apartment. My heart raced with anxious anticipation.

"Kate, my dear," I heard our CEO, Dr. David Chandler, proclaim behind me. I turned around to his professional smile.

"Dr. Chandler," I said while extending my hand. "So good to see you."

"No, the pleasure is mine." He bypassed the handshake and went for a hug. I wasn't sure what to do with that, so I managed a side squeeze.

"This is my husband, Ken," I gestured away from the hug. "Ken, this is Dr. Chandler, our CEO."

In these kinds of moments, I was always so proud to be with Ken. He had an innate sense of knowing how to read people and give them what they expected. Always the gentlemen, always the right look and attitude.

"Good to finally meet you, Dr. Chandler. How proud you must be tonight."

"Proud of this young lady," he said while lightly patting me on the arm. "She's taken us into the 21st century, that's for sure."

"We are all very proud," said Ken, while smiling lovingly at me. He placed his hand on my lower back to assure me he was in control of the situation. I took a deep breath and finally relaxed. We were escorted to our seats with Dr. Chandler and his wife, Rita, as well as Jodi and Tom. I felt prouder to be with Jodi than the CEO. She was the one who hung in there with me when everyone else thought I was absolutely mad. I glanced at her with affection and she returned it knowingly. This was *our* moment."

After a mundane meal of baked chicken and green beans, I turned to Ken and reminded him of the night we met.

"Does this feel familiar?"

"How so?" He took a sip of his Merlot and patted my thigh.

"The benefit where we met." I tilted my head and shot him a *don't you remember* glance

"Well, familiar to you, yes. I was over in the corner playing the cello, longing for the whole thing to come to an end so I could meet you and hopefully get something to eat. God, I was starving that night when the dinner was finally over."

"Oh, so you were waiting to meet me, huh? That's not how I remember it."

"Well, okay. Maybe I didn't realize I was going to meet anyone that night. I just wanted to get paid and get out of there. But the stars aligned, and I got more than I bargained for. I got to meet you and get something to eat." He smiled affectionately and took his last sip of wine.

"That was a magical night. It changed everything for me, ya know."

"Yeah?" Ken put his arm around my shoulder and pulled me closer. I saw Chandler look at us with envy.

"Yeah. Everything."

Ken kissed my forehead, as if he understood. He whispered in my ear. "What feels familiar is wanting to get you outta here and get you home."

I whispered back. "Not so fast, I've got an award to receive first."

"Oh, yeah. That." He feigned disappointment, but it was clear he was as anxious as I was.

The music stopped and Dr. Chandler got up from the table and moved toward the podium. This was the moment.

"Good evening, esteemed colleagues and guests. I am delighted to be here tonight for our annual awards gala and couldn't be prouder of the work the Pittsburgh Cancer Institute has done in the past year to further cancer research and usher us into the 21st century."

After a few ice-breaker jokes and introductions of key executives and donors, he proceeded with the awards announcements.

"Lastly, but definitely most importantly, I am proud and honored to award the Jan B. Fox Memorial Award for Excellence in Cancer Research for the year 2000 to a colleague, friend and woman, whom without her ingenuity, tenacity and ability to inspire a team, we would not be leading the cancer research industry today. It is my pleasure and honor to give this award to Dr. Katherine Mulligan."

I heard my name, but it didn't sound real. Dr. Katherine Mulligan. *Hey, that's me.* Ken nudged me to get up and I dutifully did so, but my body did not feel real. I was reminded of the day I left my old life and moved into the new one. The surreal feeling of watching myself from a distance returned and suddenly, I was transported to the stage, where I found myself in front of a microphone, holding the engraved crystal award that Dr. Chandler had just handed to me. It took a few seconds for my brain to catch up with reality.

"Thank you, Dr. Chandler," I heard myself say. "I am touched and honored to be receiving this award. But it is not mine alone to claim." I began, as planned, to name the team members who had been by my side and performed tasks they did not always understand as we forged toward the discovery of immune therapies. I had been asked to talk a little about the ground-breaking work I did, but not to the point of boring the guests with medical jargon, so I did my best to explain how the body's own immune system is the best army to fight cancer and we were simply discovering ways to equip the body with the right tools to go to battle. Ken had helped me with the speech, encouraging me to use military analogies. I saw the delight on the faces of the audience, so I knew his idea had worked beautifully to explain our work. Before I knew it, the 20 minutes I had been allotted passed and I was leaving the podium to a standing ovation, feeling higher than I had felt since the day Deidre was born. Both days were full of miraculous triumph. This day was all mine.

On the drive home, Ken was beaming with pride and said he couldn't wait to get me home and show me how much he loved me. We sat in blissful silence, holding hands in the car, knowing exactly what we would do as soon as we were alone.

A little light-headed from the champagne, I watched as he turned the key in the door and opened it to our private space. The one just he and I shared. No one else was allowed to be part of it. The world disappeared the minute we entered and thoughts of anything else but us were left at the door.

He shut the door behind him, locked the deadbolt, grabbed me by the shoulders, and kissed me passionately. I could feel the warmth of his mouth and tongue, swollen with excitement and a slight taste of the alcohol he had consumed. When Ken and I kissed, we truly felt like one being. He was entering my world and I, his. We exchanged knowing without speaking. We each knew exactly what the other wanted just by tasting. I cupped his neck in my hands and he pushed back the hair from my forehead. He pulled away and looked into my eyes and then resumed the kiss, more forcefully this time. He wanted me to know that he was yearning for more than a kiss.

He bent down and lifted me up into his arms, cradling me and my black dress like a priceless porcelain doll. He carried me into the bedroom, managing to turn on the soft light of the lamp. He gently laid me on the bed and said, "You are beautiful." I said nothing. Speechless. I felt my eyes well with tears at the beauty of the moment. He gently turned me to the side and unzipped the back of the lace dress. I could feel his fingers slowly following my spine under the zipper. When he reached the end, he continued on, caressing my bottom with his hand. He moaned. I turned over and pulled the dress from my shoulders, revealing my push-up bra and protruding cleavage. I felt as if my heart was visibly pounding. With both hands, he pulled down the bra straps and revealed my modest breasts and nipples that had hardened with excitement. He reached around and unsnapped the back of the bra, freeing me from all inhibitions. I moaned this time at the thought of being taken by my lover.

I arched my hips and he slid the dress and bra off of my body, leaving me completely naked and free. He kissed me again, passionately, and I reached for him. He was fully engorged and ready. He moaned again and I unclasped his belt and unzipped his pants. He hurriedly did the rest, until he, too, was naked and free. In one fell swoop, he shoved the many pillows off of the bed, with a laugh (indicating how ridiculous they were in times like this) and we both pulled at the down comforter to reveal the crisp white sheets. This was our domain. This was sacred. This was our martial bed where we shared everything and anything. My feet were cold, but his arms were hot around me. The contrast was mesmerizing. I felt his lips on my breasts and I shuddered. He knew me. Unlike any other man had ever known me. He knew me, he loved me, he felt me, he conquered me. Time stopped and nothing else mattered but this man. This moment. This knowing.

Slowly and gently, he entered me. We were one flesh, moving in rhythm like he played his cello. So beautifully, so masterfully. Seamless. Then the crescendo. I began to cry out and he followed. We were screaming for the world to hear us say, "This is it! This is the reason we live!" Then the collapse. The fall. The resolve. The melody fades. Our eyes closed. Together. It's finished. It was amazing. Then quiet. A long quiet.

"Are you hungry?" he said at last.

I thought for a moment about what had just happened and said, "Yes. Actually, I am." I chuckled at the contrast of the two hungers. One purely spiritual, the other uniquely physical.

"I'll be right back," he said as he got out of bed and pulled on a pair of sweats that had been draped over a nearby chair.

We ate cheese and crackers and Ken seemed quiet. I didn't think anything of it until the next morning at breakfast when he sat down with two cups of coffee and said we needed to talk.

"What? What is it?" I could tell by his face that something was gravely wrong.

He grabbed my hand across the sunny breakfast nook.

"A lump. I felt a lump last night."

"What are you talking about?" I struggled to understand the reference, like hearing a foreign language without any gesturing toward the thing one is speaking of.

"Let me show you." He cupped his hand over my left breast and then encircled my nipple and said, "There."

He took my hand and guided it to the anomaly.

I gasped. He was right. A lump. I looked away — out of the breakfast nook window where I saw a couple jogging on the street below, as if there were no cares at all in the world. Like we felt last night. But now, there is today and a cruel need to care.

eighteen

2001

TWO THOUSAND ONE. THE YEAR I LOST BOTH breasts and the twin towers came down. In that order. A strange parallel since both were traumatizing and out of my control. Both were the result of terror – against body and country. Both cancer and Al-Qaeda had invaded my first life, but this time both were more terrifyingly real.

After my second round of chemo, I asked Ken to take me to the beach. I hadn't been in a long time and it seemed the only place I could feel insignificant, like I needed to when the world was pressing down on me.

"I want to go to Alabama," I said emphatically one evening and without warning, cross-legged with an oversized couch pillow on my lap.

"What?" Ken looked surprised since I had never mentioned a desire to go there.

"Alabama. Gulf Shores."

"That's random. Where did that come from?"

I stared motionless at a television commercial about Viagra, the newest drug craze for middle-aged men (and women, I suppose). Chemo had zapped all of my energy, including my libido, so I wondered if Viagra might work for me.

"Sweetie?" Ken snapped me out of the trance. "Why Alabama? Do you know someone there?" he continued while flipping through his latest copy of *Symphony Magazine*.

I thought about it for a few seconds.

"My dad took us there when I was about five years old. He had a work thing in Mobile and thought we might like to tag along for a mini vacation. I don't remember much about it, other than we helped him catch a ton of crab and mom made this really awesome soup."

I could almost taste the saltiness of it with the memory.

"Mostly I remember watching the eight-millimeter movies that my dad loved to narrate over the years."

I could still hear my giggle as I jumped into his arms with total trust, while my mom amateurishly pointed the out-of-focus movie camera toward us.

"It's also where he taught me how to swim."

"In the ocean?"

"No, at the pool. We stayed at a Best Western efficiency unit about a block from the beach, and after crabbing and slurping soup, we would go to the pool and Danny and I would splash around and vie for my parents' attention. Danny was too young to swim, but not me. It's one of the few memories I have of my dad basking in the joys of having a family."

"Sounds nostalgic," Ken noted and put the magazine down, looking at me more intently.

I couldn't tell him, like I couldn't tell him a million things, that I wished Danny had become a better swimmer. That if he had been a better swimmer, then…

"Kate," Ken spoke in a near whisper. "You okay?"

"Yeah, why?"

"I don't know. You look strange, like you're a million miles away."

That's about right.

"We'll go to Alabama," he said affirmingly. "Gulf Shores, you say?"

"Yeah," I replied without looking at him. The commercial had changed to Jif peanut butter.

"I'll make some calls tomorrow." He patted my hand like I was a demented old woman.

Resentment welled up in me. I wasn't sure for what or why. Just something confusing that was swirling around in my soul. I hated Ken for not knowing the truth about me and hated myself more for not telling. There was no way to escape who and what I was – a fool for thinking I could beat myself at my own game. A fool.

§

We decided to wait until schools were back in session in order to hit the Alabama Gulf coast. Less kids, less crowds, less tourist mania. Ken had rented a cute little beach bungalow for a week over the Labor Day holiday. We would leave on Sunday the second and return on Saturday the eighth. The closer it got to Tuesday, September 11th, the more anxious I became. Ken just thought it was my anxiety about finishing up chemo right before the trip. He had no idea I was grappling with what I should do...and if I should tell someone. But who?

I toyed with the idea of sending an anonymous letter to President Bush, but feared I would be tracked down by the CIA. I thought I should at least call American and United

Airlines and ask them to ground flights 11, 93 and 175. But I knew they would either call me crazy or arrest me for being part of a terrorist operation. In the end, I settled on praying to the man with the soft round face and ask that something I did or said would change the course of history so that 9/11 would not have to happen. My prayers got more desperate as the day grew closer and I became more unhinged.

On Friday the seventh, our last night at the gulf, I woke up around midnight in the middle of a horrifying nightmare. I couldn't recall the details, but I knew it was related to the impending attack. We had left the window open and the cool and balmy breeze was coming in off the ocean and drawing me out to it. I rose gently from the bed, leaving Ken to his soft snore, and put on a pair of shorts and t-shirt, grabbed a hoodie and flip-flops, and headed out to the moonlit surf.

It was dark and calm, and the tide was low, just lapping against the beach with an occasional crashing wave. The moon was waning, about 80 percent full, but the intermittent clouds obscured it. If I squinted, I could see white foam now and then on an incoming wave, but mostly everything was black and mysterious – like my life.

I made my way to the damp sand near the surf and sat, with my hood over my head and my knees to my chest. There was a chill in the air, and goosebumps formed on my thighs. I was overcome by peace as I typically am when alone with only the steady sound of waves gently breaking at the shore. Peace that tells me I am like one of these grains of sand – insignificant as one, but massive along with others like me. Peace that assures me I can't do any of this alone. I am part of a bigger world. Peace that shows me I am totally and unequivocally out of control and have been in both of my lives. So what was I thinking?

I could feel the sadness welling up with the peace. It became overwhelming as I thought about not only my own pathetic tries and fails at life, but all those who were about to lose theirs for no reason. No reason. And there wasn't a damn thing I could do about it. Why? *Why?* I heard my voice screaming into the ocean air.

I felt a wave come up and soak my shorts and then another. Soon, the waves were strong enough to lift me up and set me back. Then up and then back. Eventually, I felt my body being taken in by the surf, with attempts to return me, but with each wave, I drifted further out. By this time, I was sobbing uncontrollably, loudly and guttural. Panic had set in, but my body would not respond to survive. I felt emotionally distraught but physically resigned. I didn't deserve to live. I discovered an amazing cancer treatment only to be told it wouldn't work for me. *Damn you, God, or whoever the hell you are!* I saved my brother from drowning, only to watch him self-destruct. *What the hell, Jesus?* I know that three thousand people are about to die by the hands of pure evil and I can't tell anyone. You pathetic little poor excuse for a human being. *I hate you! I hate you! I hate you!*

This went on for what felt like a long time, although it likely only lasted a few minutes. I went completely under a couple of times, but my natural instinct to breathe kicked in. Yet, with each sob, I took the salted water into my mouth only to spit it out with another scream.

Then I felt something like an arm come up under my back, and then another over my chest. At first, I wondered if a shark was clamping down on my weightless body, but it wasn't painful. It was buoyant. Soon it became clear that it was indeed a pair of arms.

"It's okay, Sweetie. It's okay!" Ken was yelling over me and the dark expanse of the ocean.

I was confused at first. Maybe I was dreaming. How did Ken get here? Then I heard him sobbing through the words.

"C'mon, Kate. C'mon. It's okay. I swear, we're going to make it...I swear. Do you hear me? I swear."

I'd never heard him like that. My heart ached and it was my fault.

He pulled me out of the surf and on to the beach and gently laid me on the sand. I was still disoriented and crying. He put his head on my chest and let out a guttural scream.

"Don't ever do that again, you hear me? Don't ever...don't ever." Exhausted, he kept his head there trying to catch his breath.

"I'm sorry," is all I could say through the gasps. "I'm sorry."

☙

I slept for twelve hours that night. Things were awkward between us when I got up the next morning. Ken had been up for hours and wasn't sure how to respond when I emerged from the bedroom, looking like I had died and gone to hell.

"Coffee is still hot," he said almost apologetically like he should have put the world on hold until I woke to greet it.

"My head hurts," is all I could think to say. I looked for my purse to find some Advil.

Ken got up from the couch where he was watching CNN and grabbed my hand.

"You okay?" he asked gently, as if I was breakable. Maybe I was.

"Yeah, I'm…yeah…" I rubbed my forehead and then tried to wipe the tired out from under my eyes. "I'm sorry about last night."

"I'd like to talk about it, if you think you can. I mean, you scared me to death." He led me to the couch, which was bright with a seahorse and starfish motif. I hadn't noticed before, but there was a big wooden whimsical sign over the television that said, "What happens at the beach stays at the beach."

I sighed, at a loss for words and still wondering how to interpret the goofy sign over the TV.

"I can't really explain it. I had this nightmare and couldn't get back to sleep so I just decided to go sit by the water. Then I just got so sad. And then I can't really remember the rest."

"Kate, you could have drowned. You were going under and crying, and it didn't look like you were even trying to swim."

I could hear the terror in his voice, and it crushed me that I put him through that.

"How did you know I was out there?"

"Uh…window was open…I heard loud screaming. I get up…you're nowhere to be found. I grabbed a flashlight and went toward the noise." His voice started to shake. "Were you trying to…"

"Kill myself?" I paused but knew the answer. "No! Of course not. I don't know what happened. Maybe it's the anti-depressant stuff they have me on. I think it might be messing with my head."

Ken looked relieved, but not convinced. I moved closer to him and wrapped my arms around his waist. He folded his arms around me tightly.

"I'm better now, okay? I just got caught up in the moment. Thinking about stuff."

"Like the cancer? The doctors say this chemo thing is just a precautionary measure and they doubt you'll have any recurrence at all. We're past the bad stuff, right? Or is there something you're not telling me?"

"What?" My heart sunk. "No, no. I guess it just does a number on you. I've lost my breasts, I've lost my hair. I've lost so much."

He lifted my chin with his hand and looked at me in a way that only Ken can do.

"We have each other and that's what matters, right?"

"Of course."

He pulled me closer, and we stayed that way for a number of minutes, like it was the only thing either of us had to hold on to. For me, it was absolutely true.

nineteen

September 10, 2001

KEN BENT TO KISS ME AT THE BREAKFAST table where I was staring at the front page of the Pittsburgh Post-Gazette's morning edition. Front page news was conspicuously uneventful – at least to me. The headline read, "Depression in the family shortens lifespan." Below that, an article about small farms not getting aid from the government. How I wished this was all we had to worry about.

"You okay, babe?" Ken asked with concern.

"Uh, yeah," I said, distracted and barely kissing back.

He poured himself a cup of coffee and sat down next to me.

"Wild beasts almost ran over me last night."

"Uh-uh," I said staring at the paper, while rubbing my chin with one hand and squeezing the knee I had raised to my chest with the other.

"Okay, okay, I know that look. What's going on?"

I was busted.

"Nothing. Nothing…I mean, it's…nothing."

"That's bull," he said, while pulling the paper toward him to see what I was looking at. "Depression? Is that what's got you worried?"

"No, of course not. Well, kind of. I talked to my dad yesterday and he said mom has sunk to a new low again. All the stuff with Danny. God, Danny."

I was fairly sure I had diverted the conversation to something Ken could understand.

"Well, we've talked about this before. A hundred times before. I don't think Danny is going to get better and neither is your mom. In some ways, they feed off of each other. It's almost like a game, with each of them daring the other to just try and get better."

"So, are you saying depression is something you can just get better at — or even addiction?" I was surprised by my defensiveness.

"No, no, of course not." Now Ken was defensive. "I'm just saying that they are toxic to each other. Without each other, they couldn't justify their bizarre behavior."

I took the silent approach because I knew he was right but didn't have the energy to argue this point because, quite frankly, I was more concerned about something and someone way bigger.

"C'mon, Kate. Surely you can see that neither your mom or Danny has to act the way they do, depression or addiction, or not. I don't know how your dad puts up with it."

"You're right." I looked at him lovingly.

"What? You wanna repeat that?" he said with a smile.

"I said, you're right. I don't really want to talk about this right now, if you don't mind."

"I'm sorry, I know it's a tough subject for you."

I reached over and kissed him more passionately to show I was fine. He accepted.

"Well, I better take off," he said while getting up from the table. We've got some early meetings this morning and a mad rehearsal getting ready for the fall series. You'll be able to come for the opener on Friday, right?"

"Of course," I said with feigned confidence. *Who knows what anyone will feel like doing by Friday evening?*

Ken grabbed his satchel and gave me another quick kiss before heading out.

"Love you," he said, as he walked out the front door.

"Love you, too." For a second, I felt like a total hypocrite. *Who says that and keeps the kind of secret I have inside me?*

I grappled all day with the nagging sense of duty versus self-protection that weighed on my heart and soul. I still had another week before I was to return to work after my last round of chemo and I desperately wished I could be in the lab to distract my mind from this boulder hanging around my neck. During the course of the day, I picked up the phone a couple of times to dial 911, but then thought better of it. I sat down at my computer and wrote a draft of an email that I thought might sound sane and innocent but ended up trashing it and watching daytime television instead. I watched *Good Morning America, The View*, even an episode of *All My Children* and was surprised I hadn't missed much since college. I took a long walk through town. The weather was cloudy and drizzly at times, but I knew it would be gorgeous on Tuesday morning shortly after 9:00 am on September 11th. Not a cloud in the sky, but the shadow of a giant airliner crashing into thousands of unsuspecting victims.

I cried off and on throughout the day and a couple of times screamed and punched whatever pillow happened to be nearby. Nothing helped. Nothing. I made a light dinner, not wanting to eat too heavily, since there was a strong possibility that I would be ill in the next 12 hours. Ken was fine with that since he went for a run when he got home and said it was too late for a big meal anyway.

He wanted to make love that night, but I couldn't find it in my heart to seek pleasure. It didn't seem right. I blamed it on the chemo, and he was content with just holding me, although I could tell he was disappointed.

I was in the stairwell of the first tower. Lights were flickering off and on and firemen were screaming for us to keep running down. A man was on one of the landings, holding his hand to his chest. I reached down to help, and a fireman screamed at me to keep going. "But I have to help him," I tried to say, but nothing would come out. "I have to help him." I looked back as I descended the stairs and he was desperate with fear. I walked back up to him and realized it was my father's face. "Help me, help me," he was saying. "I can't daddy, they won't let me," I again tried to say, but only a squeak would emerge from my parched lips. One of the firemen grabbed my arm and said there was no time and that we had to get out of the building because it was about to collapse. "I can't leave him behind. That's my dad! He's my dad!" No one believed me and even if they did, it seemed they didn't care. The stairs went on and on forever, but I couldn't stop thinking about leaving my dad behind to die. The heat became more intense until at some point, it rose up behind me and I screamed out in pain.

Then I heard a muffled voice calling my name and thought it was my dad.

"Kate...Kate..."

I'm sorry daddy, I'm sorry...

"Kate...wake up. Baby, it's okay." It was Ken.

My eyes popped open and I was sobbing. My t-shirt was completely soaked with sweat. The heat was unbearable, and I threw off the sheet and comforter with an angry vengeance.

Ken began rubbing my back, but I pushed him away, not able to bear his warm touch against my flaming skin.

It took me a minute or so to regain some sense of time and composure.

"Jesus, it's hot in here."

"You're soaked. Let me get you a towel and something else to put on."

"Okay," I sighed and pulled off my underwear and top. The fan going above felt good and cool against my naked, damp skin.

"Maybe you should talk to the doc about this medication they have you on – the anti-depressant?" Ken said while handing me the towel and an old ratty night gown he fished out of the closet. I almost laughed, but it was too sweet.

"Yeah, maybe." I couldn't concentrate on anything but saving my dad from certain doom.

"Can I get you some ice water or something?"

"Yes, that would be awesome. Maybe an ice bag or two just to get cooled down."

"Sure, I'll be back in a minute."

While Ken was gone, I felt a strange sense of peace. It came from absolutely nowhere but felt familiar. I took a couple of deep breaths and remembered that it was exactly how I felt in my first life when I was on the bathroom floor, sick after my chemo treatments. It was the warmth that came over me when I prayed – the time the man with the soft round face reminded me that it was him.

Ken returned with the water and a couple of frozen bags of peas and carrots to cool the bed.

"Thanks, sweetie. You're the best."

"I wish I could make this all go away, you know that, right?"

"This is exactly what I need. It's all you can do."

He kissed me on the forehead and pulled me into his arms. I clutched the bag of peas and carrots I had wrapped inside the corner of the bedsheet.

"Thank you, sweet man," I said to Ken out loud, but also to the man with the soft round face.

twenty

September 11, 2001

ONLY A BENADRYL WAS RESPONSIBLE FOR ME getting any sleep at all. I sat up in bed with a start around 5:30 am, glad to see the world outside my window still dark and still at peace. Ken was sound asleep, so I tiptoed out of the room, grabbing my favorite microfiber robe out of the closet and wrapped it around the ugly cotton nightgown I ended up wearing after my sweatfest in the middle of the night. I flipped the coffee maker to "on" since the timer wasn't set to start until six. My nerves were jumping like splashes of water on a hard pavement. The combination of a groggy post-Benadryl fog and the clarity of what the morning held were two feelings I couldn't seem to support at one time. My thoughts went back and forth in a perpetual ricochet of emotion. I've never had a heart attack, but I've had my heart broken. I don't think either could describe what I was experiencing this morning. My heart just ached.

I took a seat on the couch and covered my legs with a brown and turquoise throw Ken's grandmother had crocheted for us as a wedding gift. I stared at the intricate waffle pattern of the stitches softened by the little bit of light that was coming

214

from the kitchen and marveled at the redundancy and minutiae. Thousands of stitches to make this wonderful work of art. My thoughts reverted to the peace I felt while nodding off to sleep the night before and the realization about where it had come from.

Words from over a quarter century ago were still seared into my memory.

You'll be with me, right?

Like I always have.

And he was. So many times, I knew it was him showing up when I was about to give up. It was uncanny, really. But in a bizarre way, it didn't feel unusual or strange. Was it possible that someone else was in control? The man with the soft round face. Was he what some people called God, Allah, Jesus Christ? I wasn't raised in any kind of religion and, quite frankly, I knew a lot of so-called "Christians" who were not people I wanted to imitate. And these crazy terror attacks – all done in the name of a faith that was so radical, so destructive. My logical, scientific mind resisted believing in anything that couldn't be explained by molecules and carbon dating. But even my fellow physicians agree that some people miraculously defy the odds of science. For no explainable reason, cancers are cured, tumors disappear, paralysis is overcome, and when you try to find an explanation for it, the families are no longer interested in the science. They are happy to accept that a higher power was in control, which has always baffled me. Yet, here I am, more than twenty-five years into a second chance at life – a completely fucked-up idea at the very least – and I stay silent through it all in total faith of a deal offered to me by some fat bald guy, so I could gain entrance to a place that looked like a haven for hippies on LSD. Go figure. So, who am I to judge those who choose to believe they are simply passing through a world knitted together by an all-knowing being who is creating a giant tapestry of beauty that is greater than anything we could imagine?

I looked down at the stitches on the throw again. Maybe I'm just one of them. And together with the others, we have our place but it's not our choice where we are situated and how we connect with the others. We're just here. *Oh, God, if there is one, help me to believe that's all I am. I don't want to have a choice today.*

I heard Ken stirring in the bathroom. I looked at the clock, ticking softly and steadily toward 9:10 am, as if it was just another day. It was 6:12. Ken walked into the living room, looking a little worn from the night.

"Hey beautiful. Did you get any sleep?"

"Yeah, I took a Benadryl and that helped a little."

He sat on the couch next to me and pulled a piece of the throw over his lap. We sat and stared for a minute.

"What's on your agenda for today?" I asked, wanting him to say he was staying home to be with me.

"Nothing too important. I'm meeting with that new intern, Gabriella, at the studio at 9:00 to work on some of the movements in that new piece I helped her compose. You?"

"I'm really going to take it easy today. Just stick around here." I realized that he would be in studio when all the events of the morning unfolded, which gave me an uneasy feeling. I wanted to be there for him. I was mentally prepared. He would be totally caught off guard and I remember how that felt.

"You grew up kind of confused about religion, right?" I asked Ken out of the blue. He turned toward me with a quizzical look.

"Yeah, I guess you could say that. Growing up with parents who were Shinto, Buddhist and Catholic offered a

216

variety of options, that's for sure." He laughed, waiting for a smart-ass response, but I remained silent.

"We haven't talked about this in a long time. If I remember correctly, you didn't want me to...."

"Talk about religion, I know, I know. It's just that..."

There was silence again.

"That?" He waited patiently.

"I don't know. Maybe it's because I'm getting older and having gone through this cancer scare. I guess I just want to believe there is something out there bigger than me. Bigger than us, ya know?"

"Yes, I absolutely know. And there is. I know that for a fact."

"When I see you reading your Bible and know that you are praying when you go on your morning run, I'm envious."

"Really?" He asked with a smile. "That's a new one. My impression was that you thought I was drinking the proverbial Kool-Aid of the masses." I could tell he was enjoying my humility.

"Don't get me wrong. I'm not ready to raise my hands in church or anything, but I don't think I've ever made fun of you, have I? I mean, I've always respected your need to believe and be around others who do, haven't I?"

He put his arm around me and pulled me into him.

"Yes, you have, and I appreciated that, just like I tried to respect your need to come to whatever conclusions you came to on your own. Actually, I've been praying that this temporary insanity of chemotherapy would bring you into a better understanding of your need to believe and..."

Ken's voice cracked. I sat up and saw that his eyes were glistening. He wiped them and went on.

"…and give you some peace. Calm that tortured soul of yours."

Tortured soul. He nailed it. And I *was* coming to something monumental, but not for the reasons he thought or could ever understand. But maybe it was simpler than I was willing to give credit for. Who knows? Maybe Ken was one of the stitches entwined in this intricate life that I'm just supposed to hang on to without questioning. That thing he calls faith.

"Thanks. I do feel calmer." I kissed his cheek and could tell he felt some peace as well, like maybe he could relax and not worry about me so much.

"I'm gonna shower. Do you need anything?"

"This tortured soul? Nah. I'm good," I said with a smile and got up to get another cup of coffee. Ken shook his head as he walked back toward the bedroom. He knew he could only count on a few moments of spiritual introspection from me every few years or so.

After Ken left for the studio, I went into a cleaning frenzy. I began organizing kitchen drawers and cabinets, emptied old cleaning liquids that had been around for years, started a recycle bag and a Goodwill box, and threw myself into total distraction mode. At about 8:30, I became somewhat unglued. My heart was racing as I was mopping the kitchen floor. I knew the first plane would hit at 8:46 am and the second at 9:03, the one that would seal everyone's fear of the enemy. Shaking with trepidation, I turned on the TV at 8:47. There was a commercial. A commercial? Tide and it's new stain-resistant ingredient. Bryant Gumbel of The Early Show was supposed to be interviewing a witness to the first crash. I remember that day. I was in the breakroom at Schuster and Bates, getting my second cup of coffee, or maybe a third. Heather, one of our receptionists, had the TV on and told me some idiot had run his plane into the side of the North Tower. I proceeded to add two sugars and a Cremora pack to my cup, when she yelped.

"Another plane. Oh my God. Another plane!"

I sat down next to her and fixed my eyes on the TV newscast for about 20 minutes before getting up to call my parents to make sure they were okay, since by then I was pretty sure we were under attack. My second thought was that Sean was a teenager. Would there be a draft? Would my son be going off to war? I had a perpetual lump in my throat the entire day. Little by little the break room filled with employees until about noon when everyone was allowed to leave and pick up their children at school and go home to be with their families. It was clear no advertising work was going to be done on Tuesday, or the rest of the week, for that matter.

I switched from ABC to CBS, and then NBC. Nothing. *Oh, God. Maybe it's not going to happen. Maybe.* I sat mesmerized by the mundane nature of morning television, switching back and forth between stations, frantically hoping for nothing to happen. I prayed but had already resolved in my head that this wasn't about me or about my prayers. This was about one of those stitches in the big throw of life. One very painful stitch.

At 9:14, after an agonizing 30 minutes of near elation and joy, the report came on. A plane had hit the North Tower. Why the delay? What was different? I cried, then sobbed, as I knew what would come next.

My phone rang 42 minutes later.

"Did you hear?" Ken's voice was shaky.

"I did. You okay?"

"I guess. It's devastating. What can anyone say?"

"I know."

"No one is able to do much around here. We'll probably all head home soon."

Silence.

"That's good. When do you think you'll be home?"

"Soon. I'll be home soon."

I hated the devastation in his voice.

"Okay. Love you."

"Love you, too."

I remembered that feeling so vividly when I was first confronted with the prospect of war on our turf. I wished I could tell him that all would be okay, but I really couldn't. It would take a long time for things to be okay.

I knew I had an hour or so to scream, yell, shake my fists at God, or do whatever I needed to do in order to play the part when Ken returned. He was going to need me to sit and watch with him like everyone else in the world was doing. I wasn't sure how I was going to do it again. All these years later. But I would. There was no choice. I made this ridiculous decision to live my life over and this was part of my payback. I understood. Begrudgingly. I understood. I took a deep breath, decided to do some yoga to relax, and then wait with loving arms for Ken to come back home.

By 12:30, I was concerned. We had talked around 9:25, and it was three hours later. Where could he be? Maybe he got sidetracked by listening to the newscasts with the others at the studio. I finally broke down and called his cell. He didn't answer. *What the...?*

At 2:10 pm, I had visitors. The officer shifted his weight on his feet, while mine went numb. The words ran together like ice tumbling into a glass. *Your husband. Accident. I'm sorry.* I wanted to throw the cold, hard words back at him. *Could I come to the morgue?* He wouldn't take them back. They stuck together stubbornly, melting this reconstituted life away with them.

twenty-one

September 15, 2001

KEN'S FUNERAL WAS NOTHING LESS THAN inspirational and celebratory, or so I'm told. The days ran together. Somehow my colleagues at work found out since they were in attendance. Jodi came by the evening of the accident to sit with me, but honestly, I don't really remember much about it. She brought me something – Xanax or Klonapin. Whatever it was, I had relaxed into a state of not caring about anything, including the funeral. My dad showed up the next day to relieve Jodi. Mom was too upset to come, which wasn't surprising, nor did I care about that either. My world was destroyed so the decisions about what to do next seemed to have little consequence. In a twisted way, I was proud of myself for not caring. My former self would have been worried about the details of the funeral, what to serve at the wake, and what others thought of me and how I was handling the tragedy. It was a poor consolation prize, but it was one, nonetheless – maybe I had finally given up managing everyone else's feelings.

Many who came to the service told me how beautiful it was. The music, the pastor's kind words, the eulogies, were all superb. I later thanked Jodi who had planned it all while I just nodded in agreement, or not, to every empty question. Burial or cremation? Plot or mausoleum? This urn or that? Video? *No. No video.* Life insurance? A will? We'd never talked about it. Who talks about it? When it happens, you don't care about it anyway. The only ones who care are those who are trying to help you get through the week. With every question, I was reminded he was gone, so I finally asked Jodi to stop asking. She must have talked to my dad because then he started asking. He was sweetly frustrated when I gave no answers.

"Sweetheart, I just want you to think about what Ken would have wanted, that's all. This is a time to honor his memory. Do you understand?"

"No, dad, I don't understand! I don't understand why he's not here, why that woman didn't see him in the street, why I came back to save Danny only to have this happen, and where the hell is mom?"

The moment I spoke about Danny, I knew the drugs were talking and my dad would be confused, but again, I didn't care.

"Really, Dad? She's too upset to be here? *She's* too upset?"

If I had the energy, I would have put my hand through a wall, but I was too exhausted to get off the bed.

He patted my thigh in silence.

"I know, Baby, I know. With everything going on in the world that day, I think she wasn't in her best state of mind."

I wasn't sure if he was talking about my mother or the lady who slammed into my husband and crushed our lives. I actually felt more sympathy for the accident-prone stranger.

On the day of the funeral, I dressed in a black sleeveless shift with a dainty string of pearls and wore Donna Karan sunglasses. While in the car on the way to the service, I took the sunglasses off and stared at the DKNY symbol, wondering where I'd bought them. I had no memory of them and haven't seen them since, although the dress is still hanging in my closet next to Ken's tuxedos, but the pearls are gone. I suppose they belonged to Jodi, as well as the sunglasses. She must have bought the dress, hoping it would fit, or maybe it was hers, too, but she couldn't bear to take it back.

Ken's colleagues performed a haunting and mesmerizing piece he had written to open the service, which moved me to pride in his accomplishments and who he was as an artist apart from me, but it also sickened me. Who was he with me? Did I add anything to his life? I remembered our last conversation about faith and cringed. He must have thought of me as so weak. Everyone said how strong his faith was and how sure they are that he is in a *good* place. Like Quietude? I couldn't picture it. All I could think of was the man with the soft round face and how he gave me a second chance, but not Ken? Or did he? The knot in my stomach began to churn as I sat in the pew waiting for the song to come to a thankful end.

"Some things in life are simply unexplainable," the minister spoke as he looked past me, out into the congregation, who waited hungrily for words of wisdom and comfort.

"We will not know until we have come to the end of our own lives why someone like Ken, who had so much yet to give the world, would be taken from us so randomly – on a day, when so many lives were blotted out uselessly and intentionally in service of evil. None of it makes sense. That's where our faith comes in."

He paused as if to either clear the lump in his throat or refrain from giving in to his own rising anger.

"What we can be sure of is that he was a godly man and loved his family, especially his wife, Kate."

He smiled pitifully while nodding my way.

"We know he is with our loving Father now and is at peace. In our hurt and pain, we must think of his peace and let that be our guide and comfort in this world."

I stopped listening. I couldn't concentrate. My stomach churned again, and I wondered if I was going to have to get up to find a bathroom. What kind of a mess must I have been that I had to do this whole thing over to find some peace? For the first time, I felt angry at Ken. How does he get a pass? That quickly turned to guilt, as I knew what he had endured as a child. My childhood was a cakewalk compared to his. He never let that dictate who he was. I did and was now paying the price. *Get over yourself.*

None of the minister's words helped me understand why Ken wasn't sitting beside me right now, holding my hand and telling me everything would be fine. He had died while walking across the street from his studio to the parking garage on the morning of September 11th. I suppose everyone driving that day was in a hurry, thinking about their loved ones, and probably struggled to concentrate on driving and walking. The irony was not lost on me as I considered how even in death Ken and I were joined by experiences. I died on the street going through a life I dreaded, and he, coming from the one he loved. It was a perfect metaphor for how we both lived. Apparently, an elderly woman had been hurrying home to find out what her family knew about her son, who worked in the South Tower. She ran the red light where Ken was crossing, and he had nowhere to go but up and over the front of her Cadillac's hood. He was barely recognizable when they asked me to identify him at the morgue. My Ken, my rock, was gone. Erlene, the woman who hit him, was not physically hurt, but she attended the funeral against her attorney's advice because she knew what I must be feeling. She had lost someone that day, too, in New York. I had no intention of suing her. She couldn't give Ken back to me and I certainly didn't want to take whatever life she had left from her. We embraced after the service, said a few appropriate words, and then I was glad she was gone. Nine eleven forever connected us, but we were not going to be friends – the guilt-gilded souls would be too thick to penetrate.

My mother remained too ill to make the trip to the service and of course, Danny was nowhere to be found, which wasn't any more shocking than my mother failing to attend. I would have liked to hear him say that he cared, though. To hear him just be a brother for once in his life. But there was an undeniable silence that sat aching in the void. No one asked where he was and sadly, many people there were unaware he existed. Big family secret kept. Safe and sound.

Ken would have said, "That's just Danny. Don't take it personal. He doesn't know how selfish he's being. He's just trying to survive." Just thinking of that made me want to scream as I walked out of the chapel toward the hearse and funeral cars, where I would be in the front vehicle to lead everyone to my husband's final resting place. As I neared the exit door, I noticed a young, dark-haired woman loitering near the back of the chapel. Alone. Something made me walk toward her.

"Hi, I don't think we've met," I said as I extended a hand to her. "I'm Ken's...wife...Kate."

"Oh, yes, I'm pleased to meet you," she said with a slight Hispanic accent. Dried tear stains streaked her olive skin.

"How did you know him?"

"Uh...through the symphony. He was a good...friend." She looked down. I wasn't sure if she hesitated because of guilt or I was feeling paranoid in my weakened state.

"You were *friends*?" My sideways glance must have given me away.

"Oh, no, not like that." She smiled sheepishly. "He was a mentor. I'm an intern from U of P. He was such an amazing musician, but even more an amazing human being." She hesitated again gazing at the torn Kleenex in her hands. "But you know that, Mrs. Ikeda."

"Call me Kate," I said with a hint of annoyance.

"Of course." When she looked up, I saw the liquid blue in her eyes that felt vaguely familiar. The pale blue eyes and dark hair were an engaging combination.

"What is you name again?"

"Oh, Gabriella...everyone calls me Gabby."

"Oh yes, I think I remember Ken mentioning you." I said somewhat condescendingly. I wasn't sure where the skepticism was coming from.

"Will you be coming to the gravesite?"

"Oh, no...I don't think so. That's for family and those who were way closer to him than I was." She hesitated, looking toward the door. "I guess I'm having a difficult time thinking of him as gone, you know?"

"I know."

"Of course you do." She recoiled in embarrassment. "I'm so sorry. What a stupid thing to say. Please forgive me."

"No apology needed." I was warming up to her with this newfound humility. Jodi touched my arm from behind.

"Kate, the driver is waiting," she reminded softly and apologetically.

I turned and answered that I would be there in a second.

"Well, I should be getting in the car."

"Yes, I am sorry to delay you."

"Thank you for coming to pay your respects. I am sure Ken is touched to know you were here."

I turned to walk away, and Gabby spoke again.

"Kate?"

I turned toward her.

"You were a very lucky woman to have known him so well and to have him love you. He talked about you all the time. He loved you with all his heart. He had so much more to do in this world. But there was something about him that makes me think he was ready to go. He knew where he was going and why. He was ready, Kate."

The way she spoke my name was so personal, so knowing. I noticed her tone changed from the schoolgirl with a crush to a wiser, much more sophisticated woman who had a message for me. I turned to walk away with Jodi, but my curiosity wouldn't let me continue. I looked back over my shoulder and she was gone. I hadn't seen her in the church before this moment, and now she had disappeared in a split second. I drew in a deep breath and my insides changed as if the tide had gone from high to low.

Thank you, I whispered for the familiar assurance.

twenty-two

2003-04

THEY SAY THE GRIEF PROCESS TAKES ABOUT two years to get through, but in my case, I was grieving for two lifetimes, not just the untimely death of the love of my life – both lives. So, I gave myself a little extra time to resolve the depression, but eventually my friends and co-workers grew impatient with me and my refusal to engage in something remotely relaxing or fun. I felt guilty doing anything frivolous without Ken. I became, as if I wasn't already, an unreasonable workaholic, determined to find a cure for every cancer out there, and maybe a few other diseases while I was at it. Turning 40 didn't help either. I questioned the decisions I had made, the lack of friends I had acquired, and the dichotomous way in which I spent my time – in bed or at work. I had 27 years in this new existence and questioned if I'd accomplished what I set out to do. My brother was a mess, my mother was a worse mess, and my poor father had to live with both of them, while I got to live my dream, sort of. It's not exactly what I had envisioned. Even though I had been duly warned, I was disappointed to find that I was still me. You can take the girl out of the screwed-up life, but you can't take the screw-up out of the girl. Why was my perfect husband taken away? Why couldn't I stay pregnant? What was the purpose of life anyway? When I would say things like that to Jodi, she would read me the riot act.

"Okay, Kate, if I hear that one more time, I'm done hanging out with you," she warned, as we sat one day after work at our favorite downtown sidewalk cafe. "You exhaust me. Do you have any idea how many women would die for what you have accomplished? You went to Harvard medical school, for God's sake, and probably made the most significant cancer treatment discovery of the century. You had a really hot, sensitive, creative husband, who did die too young, I'll give you that, but still! It wasn't your fault. I'll never understand why you label yourself a screw-up. What did your mother do to you?"

She took a long sip of her Riesling and looked out onto the busy street, seeming proud of herself. A city bus whirred by and I shivered as I always did at the sound.

"You have no idea," I returned, with my own sip of wine and thoughtful gaze into the sea of pedestrians leaving their workdays behind. There was a temporary tension between us, but I knew we would move on to the next topic in a minute or two.

Jodi was a good friend, but no one could be a truly good friend if you were living a lie in front of them, as I most certainly was. Or was I? I regretted that I had not confided in Ken about all of it. But would he have understood? Or would he have wanted to find some medication to calm the voices in my head? I always came to the same conclusion to protect myself as well as everyone around me. *Jodi* is exhausted with me? *Try being me.*

Jodi dug in her purse. Pulled out a brochure and slid it across the table.

"What's this?"

"Read it." The mood had changed as I predicted. She seemed pleased with herself, like a child who had stolen our favorite candy.

"Partners for Professionals? A dating service?"

I slid it back across to her, declining the idea.

"Yeah," she slid it back unfazed by my rejection. "You know, it's like those new dating websites – Match.com? But this is for, you know, educated people. You meet with a consultant and they find a guy who matches your interests and you go out and see if it works."

"God, you must really think I'm a loser that I can't do this on my own. A consultant? To find a date?"

"Not that you can't do it yourself, but that you won't...or you're afraid."

"Afraid? Of what?"

"Dating. Betraying Ken. Seeing if you still got it goin' on." She tapped her shoe on my leg and smiled mischievously.

"I don't know, Jodi. It's a little...desperate, don't you think?" I rolled my eyes.

"That's one way to look at it if you're prone to desperation, which you're *not*. I think it's more about being willing to see what's out there. Like, who are you going to meet with your eyes glued to a microscope 20 hours a day? No one! So, what's the harm?"

"Oh, I don't know," I said sarcastically. "Possible humiliation, finding out there's no one to match me, or *danger*? What if I go out with some guy who's a serial killer?"

"You didn't know Ken wasn't a serial killer and you trusted him, right?"

I hesitated.

"Right?" she insisted.

"C'mon. You're the best friend a girl could have. Really. But I don't need you to manage my love life. I'm just not ready. Okay? I'm not." I took another sip and gaze, while Jodi sighed in disappointment.

"Well, I better get home to the kiddos." She pointed to the brochure and smiled with a slight air of pity. "I'll leave that with you. Think about it, okay?"

"Sure," I said to accommodate. I watched her walk away with a confidence I envied and ordered another glass of wine. It was rare for me to linger when the pull of the lab was calling me back. Surprisingly, I drank, and leisurely watched the not-so-happy workers dart across streets in front of buses and cars, anxious to get home to their expectant families. *That was me once.* I marveled at the irony and just sat. The happy, beautiful couple stared up at me from the brochure and for a second, I was tempted to read it. Instead I stuffed it into my purse, determined to throw it away.

꿍

I don't remember much about 2003. I recall it generally as a *nothing* year since it didn't hold any distinct memories, which is a little unsettling. When you can't identify a year as having any significance, it feels like time lost. When someone mentions something that happened in that year, or a song on the radio is identified as being from 2003, I strain to remember holidays, activities, events, what happened, who was I then? But nothing comes to mind. It's as if I didn't live through it or in it. Yes, unsettling. I guess I was just learning how to live without Ken, which was eventful enough. Even so, it felt like nothing. Some say I should welcome the uneventful times in my life since they can be regenerating. For me, though, uneventful means I'm not doing enough. I'm not good enough. All of that changed in January. Nothing turned into something. I'll never forget the voicemail.

"Ah, yes, Dr. Mulligan...this is Justin Gonzales, assistant to Dr. Marshall Ohlin from the National Institutes of Health in Washington, DC. Dr. Ohlin will be traveling to Pittsburgh with Secretary Gauvain next week and would like to schedule a time to meet with you – maybe for dinner? Please call me back at your earliest convenience so we can schedule a date and time."

I kept that message on my phone and eventually recorded it onto my laptop so that I had a constant reminder that maybe I had done something important in my life. The call led to dinner at the elegant Grand Concourse restaurant downtown, which became, in essence, a job interview for the directorship of the National Cancer Institute, a division of the NIH.

I was clad in the most impressive business navy blue suit I could find – an Anne Klein from Bloomingdales, paired with six-inch Michael Kors pumps and a lacey camisole under a crisp linen collared ecru button-down. I finished it with a simple diamond solitaire necklace and earrings set Ken had given me one Christmas. I even added an American flag lapel pin, which was in vogue at the time for government officials. I was, as they say, *put together.*

Ultimately, my fashion ensemble mattered little as a first impression. Ohlin was a balding 70-something married man who didn't seem to notice anything I was wearing except the dot of remoulade sauce he pointed out on my upper lip halfway into our dinner. He and Secretary Gauvain, also an all-business kind of guy, were more appropriately interested in my knowledge and experience than my visual presentation. I laughed later when I realized how ridiculous I had been in my tailored preparation. It had been two and a half years since anyone acknowledged I didn't look like death warmed over, which drove me to the brink of female desperation.

"So, Dr. Mulligan..."

"Call me Kate, please," I said as I motioned for the waiter to refill my Pellegrino.

"Kate," Secretary Gauvain corrected with a smile. "What are your thoughts about the directorship? I've spoken to the President and he is anxious to get a replacement appointed and discuss the future of cancer research. You know there's not much time, with Director Williams leaving at the end of this month."

The President? The President! In that moment, I couldn't have felt more inadequate, more undeserving, more thankful, more lonely for Ken. I fought to swallow the lump in my throat, thinking how awesome it would have been for Ken to be sitting there with us.

"I'm intrigued and honored," I said, not as confidently as I would have liked. *Intrigued?* What did that mean?

"We've been following your work," Ohlin interjected, "and we can't think of a better candidate. You check off all of the boxes. And you're a woman," he finished, raising his glass, as if that was the last triumphant word. His eyes were glassy, indicating he had had one too many Manhattans.

"What he means," Gauvain attempted to recover. "is this administration has been working to develop diversity among our leadership and we're delighted to appoint a female with your credentials to the directorship. We just need to know you are willing to move to Rockville and take on this enormous task."

I thought I noticed a few beads of sweat on his brow, but it may have been the way the light was reflecting off his forehead.

Move to Maryland? I hadn't even considered that, but it made sense. I couldn't stay in Pittsburgh. In a split second, I considered a dozen different variables. My dad. Jodi. My townhouse. Memories of Ken. The opportunity to escape, which seemed powerful and necessary. I said yes.

"If that is an offer, Secretary Gauvain, I accept!" I smiled larger than I had intended because I was still slightly annoyed by Ohlin's reference to tokenism. Yet I couldn't hold back the excitement.

Gauvain raised his martini and I my pinot grigio to Ohlin's third Manhattan. The out-of-tune clash of the odd-shaped glasses began an equally odd partnership among the three of us. I smiled in grateful disbelief. They smiled like a couple of cats cornering a mouse.

twenty-three

2005

I SPENT THE FIRST MONTH IN ROCKVILLE in a hotel on Shady Grove Road, a few minutes from the NCI campus. As much as I hate hotels, the room service and nightly turndowns were a welcome reprieve during those first weeks of constant meetings and late nights. A meeting with the President, I was told, was on the horizon but I was also warned not to hold my breath. NCI was a priority, but we were still in the midst of the war on terror – to destroy the axis of evil – so the terror of cancer would have to be dealt with by using the resources currently allocated, which weren't enough for those of us who had dragons to slay in the field. Nevertheless, the work went on despite my disappointment in not being invited to the White House. I quickly learned how not to get thrown from the political rollercoaster that began ascending the day I assumed my position as director. That didn't make the ride less bumpy, though.

Thankfully, Jodi visited in that first month to help me look for a more permanent place to live. The real estate prices were much higher than in Pittsburgh, but I also didn't need much to live on my own, according to me. Of course, Jodi talked me into something more than I needed – banking on Mr. Right showing up at some point. I explained that I had already found the Holy Grail of husbands in Ken, so how could I possibly accept anything less? She waved that off as an excuse and proceeded to talk as if he was right around the corner and needed to be considered in my home purchase.

"What do I need three bedrooms for?" I complained.

"He might have kids," she replied. "Or what about grandkids someday?"

"Grandkids? I'm forty-two years old. I've gotta have a child first before the grands come along." I laughed at her ridiculousness. But then thought more deeply about it. I was actually seventy-nine if you counted both lives. A twinge of pain and regret shot through me as I wondered if Sean or Deirdre had children now. Would I ever meet them? *They* might even be grandparents. The thought was mind boggling and I felt dizzy.

"You okay?" Jodi touched my arm and I flinched.

"Yeah, yeah." I paused to get back in the moment. "I think I need to sit down."

"Hey, I'm sorry," she whispered apologetically. "I know this has to be hard without Ken. Maybe we should take a break. Do this tomorrow?"

I waved for her to go on so I could have a moment.

She was wrong, I wasn't thinking about Ken, but she wasn't too far off. My thoughts always seemed to turn to what might have been. I lowered myself into an accent chair in the master bedroom we were viewing. Everything seemed foreign. I recovered in 30 seconds and rose to look for Jodi, who was checking out the shower and advising the Realtor it needed some updating.

"Everything alright?" She mouthed with her back to the Realtor.

"I'm fine," I mouthed back.

She moved closer to whisper. I began to feel embarrassed.

"Seriously, we can resume this tomorrow," she almost begged.

"No, it's okay. I think I might need to eat something, though. Let's get some lunch."

౭

Three days later, I made an offer on a quaint little bungalow on a quiet street about five miles from the campus. I moved in within a few weeks. It had been built in the 1940s and the street was lined with leafy poplars and cars that wouldn't fit in tiny garages. It was quite a diversion from the city life Ken and I had in Pittsburgh. But a pleasant one. I felt as mature as the rhododendrons that bloomed without care along the front of the house and as old as the sweet neighbors next to me who had lived in their home from the day it was built. She was eighty-seven and he eighty-six. I marveled that in all my years of living, I had not achieved what they had, which was acceptance and contentment. I once asked Mrs. Goldstein what she and Irwin talked about on their morning walks – both in their New Balance athletic shoes, holding hands like they were on a first date.

"Oh, we don't talk, dear," she said as if my question was naïve. "What is there left to say? We've already said everything important to each other." She looked up from the rose bush she was pruning. "When you're our age, it's enough to just to be in the same room together. Ha! To be able to walk!"

With that, she gathered the spent buds from the ground in her gloved hands, tossed them into a plastic bucket, and walked away, bidding me a good afternoon. As she walked, she held her head high, despite her slightly curved spine. In an odd way, she reminded me of Jodi – her confidence and lack of care about anything but the simple joys in life and relationship. I felt desperate to trade places with her. To grow old with Ken. To just be, without caring to become.

᠙

The National Cancer Institute was buzzing with young, energetic med school grads who I was surprised to learn knew who I was and admired my work. Several articles had been published in journals such as the *Journal of Clinical Oncology* and *The International Journal of Cancer*, as well as several chapters in edited monographs and volumes about immunotherapies. To me, all of that was simply journaling my day-to-day, year-by-year work that I didn't view as a whole. I was uncomfortable with the praise and I mostly enjoyed interacting with the researchers who were building on my work and hearing the stories of how clinical trials were making a real difference in people's lives. I thought of Cherry and people like her who might have a fighting chance with these new, more natural, therapies that wouldn't reduce a cancer patient to resemble the walking dead.

The political rollercoaster I was on had little to do with my passion for the work. Against my nature and will, the major pharmaceutical companies unfortunately became a major focus of our organization. How the NCI interacted with them and disseminated information to them surprisingly took center stage, relegating the needs of dying patients to the peripheral. I tried as much as I could to focus on the job I was appointed to do, but it was impossible for me to avoid getting sucked into the vortex of political wrangling in Washington. I was not only expected to take part, but also show my political leaning, which I refused to do. It came to a head when Dr. Ohlin and I were summoned to a meeting with Senators Davee and Parr, republicans who sat on the Committee on Health, Education, Labor and Pensions. They were proposing a bill to require the FDA to regulate how big pharma interact with the NCI and how their researchers interact with ours. I had read some recent articles in *The Hill* that criticized Davee and Parr's efforts to protect their pharmaceutical interests at the expense of other smaller companies who were not as politically connected. Senator Chambers, a democrat from Ohio, opposed what he termed "courting" of the NCI, suggesting our organization was catering to certain pharmaceutical executives, which was nothing but a lie. I took that personally. As far as I was concerned, everyone including someone's sick grandmother should have all the information we had available, but I also knew how dangerous it was to provide incomplete details regarding scientifically complicated data.

I called a staff meeting to be sure I was well-versed in the protocols before I faced-off with Davee and Parr. I had barely convened my staff for the meeting when my assistant interrupted with a look that told me I would want to be interrupted. Shawna was a 40-something, tall and slender brunette who wasn't easily manipulated. She protected my calendar and screened calls in a way that I would trust her to protect Fort Knox. When Shawna interrupted, it was urgent.

"What is it?" I whispered with the conference room door half shut behind me.

"It's Danny." She pursed her lips and seemed as put off as I was at the timing. I saw the call-waiting light flashing on her phone and wished it to stop.

"I'll take it in my office."

twenty-four

2006

THE LEAVES HAD FALLEN FROM THE POPLARS which left the street in front of my bungalow exposed to the November sun. But there was nothing to grow. Nothing to sprout. Just the pavement and the sidewalk to absorb and waste the nurturing rays. It was an unusually warm day for this time of year – the mid-sixties – but a welcome warmth, given the chilly events of the last couple of months.

Danny had been admitted to a treatment program in Denver after his overdose in the Spring. He was to stay for ninety days, but as usual, he checked himself out after thirty and went missing for the summer. He showed up at my parents' home in September, expecting money. They offered him room and board instead, with my dad putting tight reigns on the cash flow. Shortly after his arrival, and his realization that they were not going to fund his drug habit, he got arrested for kiting checks and stealing money from the offering plate at the local Methodist church's Sunday morning service. The pastor didn't press charges and simply asked Danny to return the money. He returned the checks, but the cash had been spent and shot up his arm. Dad paid the church, plus a little

242

extra for the stolen bills as gratitude for their benevolence, but he insisted on leaving Danny in jail to await his hearing. Mom made her usual threats if Dad didn't bond him out, so Dad accommodated. And they returned to their dysfunctional triangulated balance once again. His hearing was set for the end of this month, and I had contemplated going, but couldn't imagine taking time off work with all we had going on. I knew it was an excuse to stay away from the family drama, but a damn good one, nevertheless. It wasn't something I wanted to think about when I had the opportunity to relax for a change.

I made some coffee and decided to spend this Saturday afternoon with a book, since I had nothing on the agenda and everyone at the office thought I was at a meeting in Seattle, which got cancelled at the last minute without their knowledge. There was an exhilarating sense of privacy about being secretly at home. I curled up in the wicker settee on my screened-in side porch, with a copy of the latest Harlan Coben mystery. My cat, Peaches, named after a friend of mine in Georgia, crawled into my lap. I met Brandi in undergrad and she was a die-hard animal rescuer who would save a pet over a human any day.

"You need a cat," she had said matter-of-factly, after she heard about Ken's accident and my move to Rockville.

"What am I going to do with a cat?"

"It's not something you *do*," she replied indignantly. "It's something you love...and they love you back."

That part of me had changed in this life. Many things had changed in me in this go around that weren't necessarily desirable. Why wasn't I more open to pets? Memories of my chow Max surfaced, and for a moment, I tried to grasp the feeling, but it escaped me. Before Max, in my first life, there was my beloved terrier, Bugles. Not his real name (I think we originally named him Spot or something), but he was so obsessed with those triangular-shaped corn snacks, that my dad and I started calling him Bugles. I was in high school when he passed away and thought I would never have another dog because it would never be like Bugles. I tried to warm up to the cocker spaniel mix my dad got after Bugles died, but I just couldn't feel the same way. My mother would get angry with me if I didn't snuggle with him like she wanted me to, but it always felt like I was betraying Bugles somehow. The same feelings were not there and, honestly, I never wanted another animal after that. Deirdre and Sean had their share of animals, from hamsters, to lizards, to stray cats and dogs, but nothing like Bugles or Max. I marveled at how animals were not part of my childhood or my adulthood the second time around. What had changed? Maybe I was so focused on keeping Danny out of trouble, I couldn't muster devotion to anything else. Ken was allergic to certain pet dander, so we didn't risk it. Somehow, I had lost my connection with the four-leggeds who gave me so much joy before.

I grabbed the afghan Ken's grandmother had made for us and laid it over Peaches and me for an extra layer of warmth in the cool afternoon. I ran my hand across her smooth coat and could feel the purr beneath her skin. It was comforting, but not demanding. Peaches enjoyed quiet and independence as much as I did. The afghan reminded me of Ken and his protection, which brought me comfort in every room of the house. I made a habit of dragging it around like an insecure toddler. I might have also sucked my thumb when I clung to it, but I refrained only because I didn't like the taste.

I nodded off without realizing it because when I awoke, Peaches was gone, and the book had fallen to the floor. I looked at the clock and it was 3:05 pm. Two hours had passed that felt like two minutes – an indication I slept deeply, which was something that didn't occur much lately. My phone was ringing with the tone that indicated it was family.

"Katie," my mother slurred. "We need you."

"Mom, what are you talking about?"

"We... need you...here."

I was annoyed at knowing the Xanax was talking.

"Is Dad there? Let me talk to him."

"He's not here. He's...he's..."

"He's what, Mom?" I wasn't hiding the annoyance.

"He's with Danny."

"Where? Where are they?"

"I don't know, Katie." I heard her swallow hard.

"Never mind. I'll call dad on his cell."

I hung up and dialed my father's number and saw my mother's number come up again. She was trying to call me back.

"Hello?" His voice sounded frail.

"Hey, Dad. Um, Mom just called and sounded..."

"Loopy?" He was annoyed, too.

"Yeah, slightly. She said, 'we need you'. What's going on?"

He sighed heavily and I knew what was coming would not be good.

"Danny's gone missing again."

I wanted to say, "Is that all? Mom interrupted my perfectly good nap to tell me something that has happened a dozen times?" But I didn't. I've learned some things aren't worth saying.

"She said you were with him."

"No, I wish. I have no idea where he is. He left two days ago after he and your mother got into it, and we haven't heard from him. She probably thinks I'm out looking for him, but I don't have the energy anymore."

"I hear that. Are you okay?"

"Sure...sure. I'm more worried about your mother than him, actually. He'll show up – or he better when it comes time for his hearing. But when he does this, she goes into a tailspin and there's nothing I can do."

"Where are you?"

"I'm at the club."

"Drinking?"

"Just a beer, Kate. Just a beer."

I knew that was code for five or six, but there was something in me that justified he deserved it.

"Well, take a cab home, will you?"

"Yeah, I'll be okay. Stan will drive me home if I need him to."

That didn't make me feel better since Stan would probably be as lit up as my dad before the afternoon turned to evening. I hung up with a surprising sense of indifference. My family, who once held so much of my heart and soul, were now more like nuisance plants in a garden I was too tired to weed. They lay dormant for weeks and then would sprout up larger than life as if to say, "I'm here. Just try to ignore me," and suck the beauty away from all I was trying to cultivate. Fatigue let them live one more day until I could muster the energy to pluck them away from the good growth and put them in their rightful place. Today was not the day.

I picked up Coben again, but after the call, I was too antsy to read – sitting still and concentrating on something other than work or family issues was never natural for me. I went in the house and thought about how I could be productive on this unexpected weekend at home. The dining room was lined with boxes from the move that still needed emptying and decisions made about what to throw away and what to keep. They were all labeled "Office," which meant sorting through the tediousness of tax returns, personal papers, notebooks from numerous conferences I had attended, and whatever else I kept that I thought needed a file cabinet. I knew part of the reason I had not opened any of them was fear of finding cards and letters from Ken that would unearth emotion I wanted to remain buried. What was the point of reexperiencing it? I had someone suggest to me that as part of my grief, I should create a scrapbook and a memory box of all of the things that represented good memories of him. That way he was honored, not just relegated to a box, and I could keep his memory alive by having something organized that was easy to return to when I needed to connect with him. That made a lot of sense to me at the time, but the thought of trying to put it together seemed overwhelming. I decided that might be something Jodi and I could do together the next time she came to town for a visit.

I started with a box that seemed safe, as it was mostly work-related articles and papers that needed sorting. Partway through the first pile, a brochure fell to the floor. I knelt to pick it up, and there was that beautiful couple staring up at me again. *Partners for Professionals.* I smiled as I thought of Jodi and her relentless quest to convince me I needed romance in my life. Cats, men...my friends were not okay with me being alone. I set it aside, but then picked it back up, reading the tagline. *Where the Cream of the Crop Fall in Love.* Remembering my advertising days, I scoffed at the corniness. I could hear Fletcher's words. "Go back to the drawing board. That's the worst idea I've ever heard," he would say, staring at his computer as if you weren't in the same room with him.

I got through a couple of boxes and took a break, turned on the television, and as if the dating gods were speaking, a commercial blared out a catchy jingle that ended with "creamofthecrop.com." With that, I grabbed my laptop off of the kitchen counter and searched Cream of the Crop. The first reference that came up was for the meaning of the idiom. I never knew where that phrase came from, so I distracted myself by reading that it had its origins in the 1700s and represented the best of the best – as in several European languages, the cream was seen as the most excellent part. Amused, I went back to my search and found the dating web site. I clicked on the link and I was quickly taken to a page that was plastered with photos of professional looking men and women who I thought couldn't possibly be single and if they are, there has to be something seriously wrong with them. Narcissistic? Greedy? Emotionally unstable? Crazy ex-wife? Out of control children? Why aren't these people already married or with a significant other? *Maybe they're widows like you, Kate*, I scolded myself for being so judgmental. For a second, I thought about searching for a site called widows dot com or something that might be more my speed. Unsuccessful with that, I returned to Cream of the Crop. After learning the protocol, I realized the photos on the home page were probably advertising models, not real people. I would not get access to real photos until I had an interview with Lorna Cunningham, the creator and guru of the business. Once approved, and I paid the "processing" fee, the matchmaking would begin. I clicked on "contact us" and began an email to Lorna, but halfway through, I chickened out and thought better of it. Who was I kidding? No one would ever match up to Ken, so how would that be fair to anyone?

Until Ken, Bugles and Max were the only loves I had in either life that felt completely unconditional. It would be tempting fate to ask for it again, wouldn't it?

As if the gods needed to complete the lining up of the stars for me, Jodi called to check in and ask the usual questions. Was I getting out and having a good time, *ever*? How was the job going? Had I met the President yet? Were the politicians in Washington as crooked as everyone says they are? We talked for about thirty minutes and I never mentioned my almost-foray into the assisted dating world. I resolved to call Lorna Cunningham that week, if for no other reason, to prove to Jodi that I still saw myself as a desirable forty-something – the new thirties, she would remind me.

❧

"So, Katherine...or do you prefer Kate?"

"Kate is fine. That's what I would prefer a...friend call me." I hesitated on the word *friend* since it felt awkward and weird to think of anyone as a boyfriend at this stage of my life. Lorna Cunningham seemed to detect my nervousness. She smiled and went on without acknowledging it, as if to indicate it was no big deal.

"You were widowed five years ago? Is that right?"

"Yes, actually on 9/11."

"On the actual day?"

"Yes, unfortunately."

"Was he..."

"Killed by the terrorists? No, it was a freak pedestrian accident."

"Oh, I am so sorry. That sounds horrible."

"Yes, not the best day of my life, or anyone else's for that matter."

"Have you dated much since then?"

I wasn't sure how to answer that. I didn't want to sound completely unsocial and admit that I hadn't gone out with a soul, but I supposed I needed to tell the truth if she was going to help me.

"Not really. Well, not at all." I looked at the photos on her credenza. They were of her and a handsome man and two children. What did she know about tragedy?

"It's okay. Losing someone is really hard. I've been there."

"Really?" *Guilty again.* I reminded myself again to not be so quick to judge.

"Yes, my first husband died in Iraq on his second tour. We had just gotten married. It was terrible. Even when someone would say that he died honorably, I would still want to hit them, ya know?"

"I know!" I was shocked at my insistence.

"But I'm remarried now, and he has two beautiful daughters. We're hoping to have a child of our own soon."

I smiled, not sure where this was all leading.

"Do you have children?" she asked as if I would say yes. It was a question I always had so much trouble with in this second life. I do, damn it, I do. They're just somewhere else. To keep it simple, I would always say no with a certain amount of guilt for being disloyal to Deirdre and Sean.

"I don't. My husband and I were pregnant once, but I lost the baby. He died before we could get..." I choked at that and Lorna went on without seeming to notice.

"Kate, do you feel ready to date again? I mean, it's okay if you don't. Everyone is different in the amount of time they need after losing a spouse."

"Yes, I think so. I haven't dated because I have been consumed with my work these last few years."

"I understand. Work is a great distraction when you're grieving, isn't it?"

A distraction? I was slightly annoyed with her assumptions. She seemed to be minimizing my job, but she had no idea who I was and how much my work demanded of me. After my extended silence, she spoke again.

"You know, I did an internet search on you – I do with all of our potential clients – and your career path has been quite impressive." *Nailed me again.*

"Oh, thank you." I hesitated. "Am I unique?" I must have looked skeptical about her qualifications because she interjected quickly.

"No, no, you are perfect for this service. A lot of our clients are high-powered Washington folk. Some very handsome ones, in fact." She smiled mischievously and I wasn't sure how to take that. Something about this exchange felt like she was a madame and I, one of the girls. I continued so she understood my position.

"My new duties as the NCI director are demanding, so we will have to talk about how to fit in these meetings I'm supposed to be having with you and your staff and, well, the men you will be assigning to me."

Lorna smiled as I stumbled on the language.

"It's okay, Kate. In some ways, it will feel like business transactions as you vet them, and they vet you. But I prefer to use more personal language – like dates and matches."

"Of course. I'm sorry. This is just so new."

She nodded in understanding.

"Also, as the contract states, we keep everything confidential, meaning no one will know that you have accessed our service. Even if someone were to hack our records, you are referenced as a seven-digit number, cross-referenced and encrypted with your personal information. You don't have to worry about your employer or your colleagues finding out. We also ask that our clients keep their dating partners' information confidential. Of course, we cannot ensure that, so you take a risk by what you decide to tell those you meet, but I have found because we are working with the Cream of the Crop, that has not been a problem so far."

Lorna seemed proud of herself for plugging the company's tagline.

"That's good to know," I said, thinking instead about how Jodi might use her skills to get information from these people.

"So, do you think you're ready to sign on for this adventure?" She smiled big with pen in hand.

I sighed, I'm sure with visible trepidation.

"Why not?" I giggled nervously and took the pen from her hand to scrawl Katherine Mulligan across the page, regretting it before the ink dried.

"You won't regret it. We have an eighty-five percent satisfaction rate. Have you read our web reviews?"

I hadn't, but instantly worried about them wanting me to write such a review and who might read that.

"Okay, here we go." She turned around and put the signed paper under the glass of her desktop copier. When my copy spit out, she placed it in a folder and handed it to me.

"You might want to look over the documents in the folder when you have a free minute. There are dating tips and things you might consider before we set you up with your first match. I'll be in touch after we have gone over the results of your assessment and think we have someone in mind for you. Do you have any questions?"

Why did this sound like I was scheduling a colonoscopy or some sort of surgical procedure? Of course, I had questions.

"No, I think I'm good for now," I lied.

Lorna smiled, shook my hand, and I left the building hoping she would never call me.

Two days later, she called.

twenty-five

2008

IT WOULD BE A LIE TO SAY THAT ALL WAS well in my world. All seemed that way on the exterior, but internally, I was coming apart at the seams. The job was unbelievably frustrating. The familiar idea that those who love the field die a slow death behind a desk is truly a reality. I wanted to be on a research team more than in countless meetings with pompous politicians and heads of departments who had never set foot in a lab in their entire careers. I wanted to be staring through a microscope looking at cancer cells more than wining and dining in the finest restaurants, which seemed like a total waste of my talents. I wanted to make a difference.

As far as the assisted dating, it had been eighteen months since I met Lorna, and I had been matched with seven different men – all who were either too old, too rich, too arrogant, or too something. I never got the hang of what always felt like a job interview and not the kind of encounter in which it's clear that something else was at work (fate or divine intervention) that convinced me I was meeting my future and second soul mate. I finally told Lorna I was resigning from the position of available widow and resolved to live life singly and without unnecessary and exhausting reminders that I was not a good match for the cream of the crop. I was still a country girl from small town Ohio who had lived two lives in order to achieve more than what most people do in one. I was, I had concluded, too wise and too old for the fantasy everyone else called love. It was a lonely place of acceptance, but tolerable.

The one thing I could count on for sure was my brother making everyone's life a living hell. And the irony of him was definitely not lost on me. He was a living, breathing, walking example of it, and the guilt I lived with in this life was almost worse than the first time around. At least now I knew something I didn't know before, but that didn't matter to those whose lives were constantly being torn apart because of his inability to be a decent human being. Yes, well, okay, the addiction thing. It's a disease and all that. But there was obviously something else going on in the heavenly realm when Daniel was mercifully plucked from this world as he sunk to his death in the serenity of the Mulligan family pond. Of course, that is something I couldn't have known, but am convinced now it's what I was supposed to learn. All this...for that.

"Okay, okay!" I often looked up to the heavens when taking my early morning walk. "I get it. So now what?" Most often there was silence. Sometimes I felt comforted. By what and whom, I can't say. Despite my failed attempts to right something in both lives, and the resulting despair at the thought, I was usually able to calm myself in these moments and think of what was accomplished in both lives, although separately and literally as two different versions of myself.

This year was particularly difficult because I didn't feel I had much of a purpose to go on living. My work was not what

I expected, but how could I outdo what I had already accomplished in the field? I missed Dierdre and Sean terribly. That never went away, much to my surprise. I had erroneously thought with time and the distractions of a better, more fulfilling life, I would learn to accept not having them in my life. Sometimes it was unbearable, especially when I was also missing Ken. I had recurring dreams of all of them. Mostly they were beautiful, but sometimes disturbing. Sometimes they were each calling out to me to wake up. Other times it was clear they were angry or confused at my not being there. I dreamt of Deirdre's wedding more than once – and I was always late. I also dreamt of Sean's baby boy, even though I have no idea if he ever married or fathered a child. But the face of the boy – my grandson – was so clear. So real. I woke up crying from those dreams and hoped they were messages from the man with the soft round face who might want to assure me that all was well in their world. But I could never be sure.

Weirdly, I thought often and randomly about my old job, my insecure co-workers, the cut-throat drama of the corporate world. I almost craved the simplicity of that, even though when I was in it, it seemed complicated. I had no idea what complicated was until I became embroiled in Washington politics.

It's not surprising, then, that I struggled with depression, which led to a dark place of self-loathing as I began to see myself as more like my mother. That was an all-time low. Then, as usual, a chance encounter reminded me I was not.

&

Of all places, it happened at the grocery store. I was giving a cantaloupe the proverbial squeeze and out of the blue, a tall, dark handsome man appeared next to me, also squeezing.

"You look like you know what you're doing," he said. "I just squeeze 'cause that's what everyone else does."

I smiled dismissively, but he kept on.

"Is it firmness or softness that you're testing?"

"For me, it's firmness, but I guess it's a personal thing. I don't like mine too ripe."

"I see. That makes a lot of sense. What happens when it's too soft...ripe, I mean?" He corrected as if he knew I'd take it the wrong way.

"I think it changes the taste. I prefer mild and sweet...less juicy, I guess."

He smiled like the Cheshire cat who had managed to get me to play. His expression changed when I didn't alter mine.

"Like a first kiss," I continued with a grin to not seem prudish. The smile returned to his face, only this time it indicated a touché. He took that as permission to continue.

"So, do you live around here?"

"Yes, actually. About a mile or so down the road. You?"

"No, I'm on a business trip, but so tired of eating out. I thought I'd find a grocery and get some fruits and veggies to take back to the hotel."

He put his cantaloupe back and I noticed his left ring finger was bare.

"You know they have the ones that are already sliced in a package...I mean, you know, if you don't have utensils to cut..." I trailed off, realizing he wasn't needing my help in that department, nor was he interested in the packaged fruits. Several options ran through my head in about three seconds. Walk away and say, "Good luck with your business trip." Lame. "Hey, you're hot, do you want to have dinner?"

Desperate. Or, "What kind of work do you do?" I settled on the latter.

"Pharmaceutical sales. What about you?"

What to say? Who am I? Do I cut right to the chase or just play it cool? Again, I chose the latter.

"I work for the National Cancer Institute."

"Really?" He paused pensively. "I'm so fascinated with all of the new research lately." He paused again nervously, like a boy ready to ask me to the senior prom. He was not so subtle in looking at my ring finger.

"Yes, I spent a lot of my career in the lab. In some ways, I wish I still was."

"I know what you mean. I used to be more out in the field until I took a regional manager's job. It's not as fun as it used to be. You have probably guessed. I'm a people person. I hope I wasn't too forward talking about cantaloupe. I just like to talk I guess."

"No, no, of course not. I sometimes don't notice people like I should. I get too wrapped up in what I'm doing and block out everyone around me."

"That's the researcher in you, huh?"

"I suppose. But it's not very social sometimes." I smiled and looked into his eyes. They were a deep brown that melted into the black of the pupil.

"Well, I was always told I should be more focused, so we all have our stuff, right?"

"That's for sure." I noticed I was still holding the cantaloupe for security. There was a lull in the conversation but neither of us seemed to want to walk away. I placed the melon in my cart, not knowing what to do next. Mr. Tall Dark and Handsome must have taken that as my departure move.

"Hey, uh, would you like to grab a bite to eat sometime while I'm here? I'll be in this area for a few more days, so..."

"Uh, I...well, yeah, I guess that might work. Wait..." I laughed apprehensively. "Did you tell me your name?"

"Oh, of course." He eagerly reached into his trouser pocket and pulled out a business card.

"I'm free tomorrow night if that works for you."

I stared at the business card as if I'd never seen one.

"Sure..." I said distracted. "Where and what time?"

I couldn't believe I was considering this.

"Well, since this isn't my neck of the woods, why don't you suggest the place and I'll be there, maybe around seven...ish?"

"Where are you staying?"

"At the Hyatt on Shady Grove Road."

The same hotel where I lived the first month I was in Rockville.

"Yes, I know it well. There's a great little Thai place only a mile from there, that is, if you like Thai."

"Love it."

"I could make reservations and call you to confirm?"

What am I doing?

"That would be awesome. My cell is on the card. You can text me if you like."

I reread the card trying to appear nonchalant despite the anxiety about not having any idea who this guy was.

"Okay, it's a date..." I looked at the card again, "Mike." He returned my smile.

"I'm glad we ran into each other." He chuckled. "I look forward to tomorrow night." He touched my upper arm, waiting for my response.

"Me, too." I nodded and turned toward my shopping cart since I was sure he could see my heart pounding through my chest.

He put his hands in his pockets and turned to walk away, but then stopped and turned back to me.

"Your name? That might be helpful," he laughed uneasily.

I laughed, too, and was glad to see he was as nervous as I was.

"Kate. Kate Mulligan. I'm sorry I don't have a card with me." I was suddenly aware that I was in yoga pants and a grungy Harvard t-shirt.

"That's fine. I'll see ya tomorrow, Kate." He pulled his right hand out of his pocket and waved, a sheepish grin covering his face.

I watched him leave the grocery store, without making a purchase. He had apparently changed his mind about all that eating out. I wanted to kick myself for giving him my full name. All he had to do was search the NCI site. But there was no reason to delay the inevitable. *I had a date. Oh, God. I had a date.*

௸

What to wear? I spent the morning trying on twenty different combinations. Sexy or conservative? Cute dress or casual pants? Bright or muted? Heels or flats? Hair up or down? I called Jodi three times. Despite her giddiness, she advised me to be practical, but not too boring. Unassuming, yet bold. Pretty, not cute. None of that helped.

"When should I call him?" I asked Jodi like a scared schoolgirl. "I don't want to seem too anxious, but then again, I don't want to wait to the last minute. That would be rude."

"Girl, you are way overthinking this," she replied. "Call him around lunchtime. The restaurant probably doesn't open earlier than that anyway, right?"

"I suppose. Ughhh. I hate this."

"You love it. I haven't heard you this excited since..." Her voice trailed off, but I knew what she was about to say, before she caught herself.

"Since I met Ken?"

"Well, in a long time, that's for sure. Just enjoy it, okay? Promise?"

"I'll try."

Too nervous to wait, I called the restaurant right at noon and made the reservation. Soon after I called my prospective date, secretly hoping he wouldn't answer or that he would tell me he had an unexpected emergency and wouldn't be able to meet me after all. That wasn't in the cards.

"Mike?" I asked as if someone else might be answering his phone.

"Yes, is this Kate?" He said jokingly. I laughed, slightly embarrassed.

"I made a reservation for 7:00 tonight at Chakkri Curry, the Thai place I mentioned. Do you think you can find it?"

"I'm sure I can."

There was a long silence I couldn't abide.

"Okay, well, I'll meet you there." I said, too abruptly.

"Thanks. It sounds nice."

I obsessed over my wardrobe a little more after lunch, but eventually, I ran out of time and settled on the black leggings, medium heels, and a top that only hinted at cleavage. A mint green that complimented my eyes, I thought.

By the time I left the house at 6:30, I was exhausted and needed a nap. Off and on all afternoon, I had thought of Ken and it continued in the car on the way to the restaurant. I talked out loud to him once, half hoping he would answer in a whisper or a booming voice or something. There was nothing other than my memory of how he always responded to my anxiety. He would say, *It will be fine. Just be yourself. I want you to be happy.* He really did want my happiness. He would not want me to sit at home when I could be out enjoying the evening. But with another man? I never witnessed any jealousy in Ken, although at times, I wished he would have shown a little of that to balance my insecurities. Instead, he was ultra-protective, especially when it came to my family. But jealous? Never. He had a quiet confidence about him. He knew he was a catch but didn't flaunt it. Much to my chagrin, if he were sitting in the passenger seat next to me, he would likely laugh and say something silly like, "I'm dead, Kate, so go talk to someone who can dance!" That put it in perspective and got me to the parking lot of Chakkri Curry.

This was the most awkward part. Opening the door to the restaurant, I wasn't sure if Mike would be waiting at the hostess station or already seated, or worse yet, late. When my eyes finally adjusted to the dim light, I saw him wave from a booth in the back of the room. He was smiling and stood as I made my way toward him. I must say he was better looking amidst the muted tones of this décor than among the bananas and melons at the florescent-lit grocery.

"Wow, you look great," he said as he moved forward to hug me. I returned the gesture, being careful not to linger.

"Thanks, so do you." We sounded like third-cousins who hadn't seen each other since the family reunion two decades ago.

Mike sat, folded his hands on the table and leaned forward intently.

"*Director* of the National Cancer Institute?"

"You Googled me," I said with disappointment.

"Well, yeah...why wouldn't you want me to know that?"

"It's not that I didn't want you to know. It just sounds so pretentious when I say it."

"Whatever. I almost called you and cancelled, thinking you were way out of my league."

"Stop. I don't think of it that way. Don't get me wrong, I am proud of what I've accomplished, but like I said earlier, I have more respect for the people in the lab than the job I do."

"Well, regardless. I'm impressed and shocked that you're single. Lucky me." He smiled, but quickly detected my discomfort.

"Sorry, did I say something wrong?"

"No, I just hate that word *single*. It sounds so wild. Maybe because of my age."

"C'mon, you can't be a day over thirty-nine."

I blushed.

"You are a charmer. Try forty-five."

"Now I'm doubly impressed. I'm behind you a couple of years, but age doesn't matter, right?"

"A couple?"

"Well four to be exact."

"Okay." I replied tentatively. I wasn't sure how to feel about dating anyone younger than me. I instantly thought of what Jodi would say, which amused me.

"How long have you been single?"

"I lost my husband on 9/11 so I'm not single by choice, which is probably another reason I hate the word."

"I'm so sorry, Kate. Wow, 9/11. One of the towers or...?"

"No, no. He just happened to be in a freak pedestrian accident on that morning."

263

"But still. What a horrible thing. On such an ominous day." He fiddled with his silverware and napkin. "I wasn't meaning anything by calling you single."

"Oh, no, not at all. No offense taken. I'm just too sensitive about it and find this dating thing such a drag. I hadn't dated at all until this past year or so. I feel like I have to keep it all a secret, given my position at work. The minute anyone there finds out, it will be all over the department and I would hate that. So, I sort of feel like I'm having an affair with everyone I go out with, ya know?"

"That's kind of exciting, though, isn't it? Well you know, I'm not saying affairs are good..."

Mike's nervousness was beginning to overtake mine.

"Of course, but I really don't want that kind of excitement in my life. I am a no-drama kind of girl."

"So, good thing I sat facing the door, huh? In case one of your co-workers walks in?" He grinned big and I noticed how perfectly his teeth were spaced. Not perfectly white, but nearly.

"You're laughing, but I actually thought about that on the way over."

"No, you didn't."

"I did. I did." I shook my head and picked up the wine list to search for something that might calm the nerves.

"Yes, let's order a drink." He motioned to the server.

We talked for nearly an hour and a half over a shared plate of Pad Thai and two glasses of pinot. I knew halfway through dinner that I probably would not see Mike again, but I was thankful for the company. For this evening. For the interest. For not having to sign up with a dating service to find my own damn date!

Mike got up to use the restroom after taking care of the check. I took the last sip of my wine and thought about our conversation and how I had no idea if he was divorced or never married. I was embarrassed that I had been so self-centered. When he returned, I brought it up.

"So, I apologize, but we talked so much about me and my life and work, I didn't ask about your past. Are you divorced? Never married? Children?"

"I'm sorry, I should have volunteered that. Definitely nothing to hide. Yes, I divorced three years ago, but we get along pretty well. High school sweethearts that just grew apart, ya know?" He pulled out his wallet and produced a photo.

"And these are the best things that ever happened to me." It was a picture of a teenage girl and boy, maybe 16 and 14, I guessed.

"Aw, they are great looking kids."

"Yeah they're awesome. I couldn't be prouder."

"I think he looks like you," I said, studying Mike's face.

"That's a great compliment, but they're both adopted."

"Oh, gosh." I put my hand over my mouth, embarrassed by my blunder.

"Oh, it's okay. I get that all the time. They say even adopted kids can take on the mannerisms and facial expressions of their adoptive parents. That grin he has comes from me grinning at him all the time." His pride was palpable.

"What are their names?"

He pointed to the girl. "That's Deirdre, she's the sensitive kid who worries about what everyone is feeling."

I felt tears rim my eyes at the sound of her name.

"This is Sean. He's the smarty. Will probably ace the SAT. You know the type?"

I absolutely did. For a moment the room stood still, and I felt like my head was under water. Is this guy for real? Deirdre and Sean? What kind of coincidence is this?

"Kate...is everything all right?"

"I...uh...I...yeah. I'm okay. Maybe it was the curry. I'll be right back."

I rose to find the restroom and once I did, rushed into the stall and lost all of the Pad Thai right then and there. I took a few minutes to compose myself and splash cold water on my face before returning to Mike. Was this a joke? A message of some sort? I straightened my top and fluffed my hair, checking to ensure my makeup was still intact. I made my way back to the table trying to appear unscathed.

"Hey," Mike said, concerned. He stood up again as I approached.

"Sorry, I suddenly felt ill, but I'm okay now."

"Is it something I said?"

"No, not at all. Listen, I have a lot of history and seeing your children reminded me of some things that got the best of me. Definitely not your fault."

"Okay, well..."

"You are so lucky to have them. Don't ever take them for granted."

"Well sometimes I think I do, with all the traveling, ya know, with my work."

"The time goes by so fast. Before you know it, they'll be getting married and having babies of their own. Cherish every moment."

It was clear that Mike was somewhat uncomfortable with my sudden waxing philosophical.

"I intend to. Thanks." He thought for a moment and then reached across the table and took my hand in his. It felt unusually soft and warm, reminding me of the man with the soft round face.

"Whatever happened. In your past. It's okay. You've done great things for a lot of people who will never know it was you who saved them. None of us live perfect lives. We do the best we can with the time we have. You have done well." He paused. "Very well."

With that, Mike got up and walked toward the door, placing the palm of his right hand on my shoulder and patting it as he walked by. That familiar wave of peace came over me, sustaining me for another day...maybe another year.

I whispered, "Thank you."

twenty-six

2010

THERE THEY WERE...RIGHT BEFORE ME, BUT I couldn't touch them. Either of them. I saw Sean cradling a child in his arms. Rocking. Yes, he was rocking. A woman, I presume his wife, stood nearby smiling as if to approve of his rocking technique. Everything was black and white and gray. Deirdre was off to the side, crying. Why? Why was she crying? For a moment, I felt like Dorothy peering through the giant crystal ball in the Wizard of Oz. I needed to get back home. Where were my ruby slippers? There's no place like home, I wanted to scream. But nothing came out.

I awoke with the same audible Dorothy-inspired "Oh!", when the house fell on top of the Wicked Witch of the East. I opened my eyes and I was in my bedroom in Rockville, Maryland. The colors were muted as the first morning light shone through the sheers covering the east window.

I'm not at home. They were right there. Right. There. But I couldn't touch them. I buried my face in the pillow and sobbed as loud as I ever had. I wished I had asked more questions of the man with the soft round face. Would it keep me out of Quietude to end my life? Would that prevent me from reuniting with my kids at some point? I wish I knew, so I could end this craziness. I felt no more in-the-know about these things than I did the first time around. What kind of justice is that? The pain felt unbearable. I got out of bed, went to the bathroom, and fished for a bottle of Benadryl. If I could get back to sleep, maybe I could see them again. I took two and then one more for good measure. I knew I would hate the drowsy feeling later on, but it was Saturday and I just didn't care. I wanted to try again. I needed to see them again, even if I couldn't touch them.

ى

"You okay?" I had asked my dad, who had called me out of my dreamless coma to give me the latest update on my mother and Danny.

"Yeah, I'm fine. Just tired."

"You said that last time we talked. When was the last time you had a physical?"

"A physical. Why do I need a physical? If it ain't broke, I don't need to fix it, right?"

"How do you know if it's broke or not unless you have someone check you out?"

"I said I'm fine."

"I know, but you seem tired all the time now."

"Well, you'd be tired too if you had to put up with the drama around here."

He was right. Danny ended up doing two years in the state prison for theft and writing bad checks. My mother isolated herself in her own prison during that time, leaving my dad alone to drink too much. Danny, a man now in his forties, was back home with my parents and not much had changed. I had little energy to hear about it, but I felt sorry for my dad, so I indulged him one more time. I'm not sure why I didn't have similar feelings for my mom. After all, I am a mom, too. If Sean had been a troubled man, would I have reacted similarly? I guessed not, but who can know? My annoyance with my mom stemmed from her harsh attitude and words toward me, growing up. That became more painfully clear to me in this life than it was in the first. I was much more forgiving of her after Danny died. Somehow it felt like she had the right to be withdrawn and pitiful then. But this time, I couldn't muster the same sympathy. It was almost as if she needed something, some tragedy, in order to act out her innate sorrow. If he had been a happy, well-adjusted kid, she would have found something to grieve. Or was that unfair?

"So, how are things with Danny back in the house?" I asked, indifferently.

"Same as usual. He's changed. He's found God. He's gonna stick to treatment this time. But we all know he's a ticking time bomb and as soon as he gets frustrated that he can't get good employment or some girl rubs him the wrong way, he'll be back at it. I hate to sound so cynical, but..."

My father referring to a "girl" of Danny's was revealing in itself. He still saw my brother as an immature teenager who is not in control of his reactions.

"I understand. Believe me. You have nothing to feel bad about. Is there anything I can do?" I hated to ask, but it was my family. I couldn't ignore the obvious.

"Nah, honey. I'll let you know if something comes up."

"What about money? Can I help that way? I know having an extra adult to feed is not cheap."

"Well, so far, we're hanging in there. Thank goodness we were good savers."

I wanted to say, *you* were a good saver but didn't want my dad to pick up on my momentary annoyance with my mom. I had to admit that aside from my mother's prescription needs, she wasn't a big spender or shopper, so at least I could give her that.

"Yeah, I guess that's one way to look at it. Well, I need to go. I've gotta get some work done around this neglected house, Dad." I lied. "Promise me you'll get that physical, will you? For me?"

"Okay, princess. I'll do that."

I wasn't convinced but made a mental note to check back with him in a week.

"I love you. Tell Mom I said, Hi."

"I think I just heard her get up. You want me to go get her?"

"No, I'll catch up with her later." I wasn't in the mood for that much indulgence. In my first life, my mother had died in 2010, and in recent weeks I wondered, and sometimes wished, for the call about her stroke. At other times, I knew I should be cherishing every minute I could get with her. I didn't feel like cherishing today and as cold as that felt, I knew I had made a strange peace with accepting who she was without much guilt. Emphasis on much.

"Love you, Dad. Talk to you soon."

"Okay, love you, too," he said, hinting at disappointment.

That was that. Within a month, my dad was diagnosed with prostate cancer and we were considering his options.

૭

I have a Harvard education and have been fighting this dreaded disease most of my adult life, but that little six-letter word could still bring me to my knees. I wanted to eliminate the word from our vocabulary completely, but unfortunately the fear it elicits makes it more prominent and evil, and nearly impossible to ever forget, even if we were to eradicate it from society.

As I sat nervously one day, waiting to hear from Dad's doctors in Columbus, I Googled the word *cancer* just to see what was trending on the web. The first reference was its definition and origin. I was reminded that Hippocrates originally called malignant cells *karkinos*, which is Greek for crab. There are various explanations about why he used that term, some of which point to the hardness of malignant tumors, representing the hard shell of a crab. Others have said it has to do with the pain a crab can inflict with its pinching claws. Some say the crab is tenacious and stubborn in how it bites and won't let go. I felt all of those personally in the moment. Then four hundred and fifty years later, Greco-Roman philosopher, Celsus, wrote a medical encyclopedia and renamed the disease *cancer*, the Latin word for crab. I marveled at how long we have been fighting this stealth enemy – thousands of years. And I once thought I could single-handedly defeat it. Yep. I often felt like David trying to slay Goliath with a slingshot. But I only injured him. I don't know what it will take to bring the giant down.

I thought about how much of my life I spent hating cancer and wondered if I might be coming into a period in life when I needed to let go of the hate. But I didn't know how. Every time I saw or heard of another child succumbing to its stubborn bite, I seethed and was motivated once again to go on the angry hunt for a way to paralyze the claws of this relentless foe. The phone rang to release me from the momentary rage.

"It's stage three," said the physician, Dr. Cho, on the other end. "But not metastatic, which is good news."

"Stage three. Okay." Not metastatic. Good. That meant the tumor was invasive, but the cancer had not spread to other areas of his body.

I quickly morphed into practitioner mode, asking clinical questions, getting the details and the numbers, finding out what knowledge they had about the newer treatments and so on. I thought I detected some resistance on the other end and didn't want this to be a battle of the medical egos.

"Listen," I said more calmly and less like a clinician. "This is my dad. So, I'm not trying to ruffle anyone's feathers there. I just want to..." My voice cracked and the lump in my throat prevented me from getting any air out to go on.

"Dr. Mulligan," she replied warmly after giving me a moment. "We *want* you consulting on this. Why wouldn't we?"

"You do?"

"Of course. It would be an honor. If I was giving any other impression, I apologize. Actually, I'm probably more intimidated than threatened." She laughed nervously.

"Oh." I was speechless and didn't know why. "Thank you. I appreciate that more than you know."

"We all have the same goals here, but you know as well as I do that when it's a family member, we have to step back because we really can't be objective."

"You're right. Of course, you're right." I was relieved and scared at the same time. She sounded like she was in her twenties. But maybe that was a good thing – maybe she wouldn't be afraid of thinking outside the box.

We discussed next steps and appropriate treatments for my dad's age and particular type of cancer. So much had changed just in the last few years regarding treatments. We used to think of cancer as one big nasty crab. Now we know there are more than a hundred types of cancer, characterized by abnormal cell growth, that make up this crab family. Many species, many stubborn weapons, many defenses against treatment, and ways to spread the chaos. I was encouraged that my father could beat this based on applying customized treatment, but I worried most about how alcohol had ravaged his body and immune system over the years, not to mention the stress of my mother and brother on his potential healing.

Shortly after hearing the news, I called him and suggested he come to Rockville to live with me during his treatment. I could ensure he got the best care and could monitor his treatment without having to take leave from my position at the NCI. He wouldn't even consider it.

"I can't leave your mother alone with Danny," he said worriedly.

I almost enjoyed the thought of the two of them battling it out on a daily basis, without my dad's constant mediation. But when he suggested they all come, I balked at the idea. I definitely didn't want to be a witness to the toxicity.

"I don't think that would work. Dad, I think you need to get away from them. I'm worried all of that stress is going to affect your healing."

"Katie, it's something I've been dealing with for almost fifty years now. I'm used to it. Ah, hell, I ignore it most of the time and deal with each thing as it comes along. You know how it is."

I did. But there was an exhaustion in his voice that made me really sad. Guilt washed over me. What had I done to my father? Why couldn't my mother see the gift she had been given? Maybe if she had embraced that, Danny wouldn't have needed to rebel.

I remembered the words, "That will be up to her," spoken so wisely by the man with the soft round face when I asked if I might save my mother from her depression. That was a cue and I missed it. I should have known she was too weak. Sarah Mulligan was not the woman I hoped she could be. She was not me. I zoned out of the conversation with my dad for a second to process that revelation. He continued.

"I like my doctors in Columbus. They seem really smart and they talk loud enough that I can hear them." He was almost yelling at me to get his point across. I smiled, since I knew that was as important to him as the information the doctors were delivering. He was smart, too, and wanted to understand.

"Okay, well, just know that I will be conferring with them regularly and I'll try to make it back every month or so to check in on all of you. Deal?"

"Don't you worry. You've got important things to do there, so we'll be fine."

"Okay, Daddy. Stay strong and we'll talk soon, okay?"

"You got it. Go find some way to beat this devil, will ya?"

"We're working on it."

And I went into overdrive to work on it.

twenty-seven

2012

LYING THERE, HELPLESS AND PEACEFUL, HIS breathing rhythmic and steady, I felt sorry for him, an emotion I was not used to feeling when it came to my brother. All of my former angst toward Danny melted away. He couldn't hurt anyone in this state, so there was some comfort and relief in that. Part of me wanted him to wake up, since losing him like this would crush me. The other part hoped he would be put out of his misery. But I was learning, or attempting to learn, that it's not about me. My whole return to the former life was all about me, and it took me years to admit it. Saving Danny to keep my mom from being so mean and to assuage my own guilt was all about wanting to like myself. It was a selfish proposition and I had jumped at the chance to control everyone else to save myself, but in the end, all it did was make me dislike me even more. For the first time ever, sitting next to the hospital bed watching Danny fight for his life, I loved him more than I needed to love myself.

"I'm sorry," I whispered, just like I did when I saw him in that pond about to meet his fate. "I'm sorry I saved you."

I held his rough and frail hand in both of mine, while wayward tears stung my cheeks. I longed to see the ending credits to this horror film of my brother's life. But not before I had the chance to really love him. Right before this last overdose, he had disappeared again for about three months. We all assumed, and rightly so, that he was using. But years of this roller coaster taught us all that there was no way to find him or bring him out of it. It was always on his terms. It would either be in a jail or a hospital that we would reunite.

When I got the call that this time might be the last straw for him, I came right away, angry and frustrated, and unforgiving. But seeing him like this, softened me. I noticed things about him in this state that were not apparent most of the time when I was lecturing him about his screwed-up life. He had lost about twenty pounds since I saw him last. I never took time to notice how he had wrecked his body, with the deep wrinkles around his eyes and forehead, that made him look ten years older than me, and the needle marks in both arms – and apparently in other more vulnerable places – that were tattooed evidence of his constant state of desperation. His sandy blonde hair, now streaked with grey, was thinning like my father's, and the spider veins around his nose and mouth were bright red and spindly. His lips, dry and cracked, looked like they had been sunburned recently. His clay-colored neck was leathery and lined like a farmer's. This was the body of a man who had no real home. Who probably scrapped for food, but scrapped for his daily drug fix even more. While I was living the life of an elitist, my own brother was committing a slow and deliberate suicide. *How many lives do I have to live to fix that?*

In the midst of wallowing in my guilt, my father entered the room.

"Hey sweet pea," he said cheerfully.

"Dad." I got up, wiped my eyes and squeezed him harder than I ever had. "You look great!"

"Thanks to those docs, and you my dear, I feel pretty great."

He was my one victory if I had one in this life. After months of hormone and immunotherapy, he had been declared cancer free, which was a personal and professional accomplishment for me. Personal because I had managed to at least free my father from one burden in his life. Professional because my scientific contribution had led to what saved him and had become a common treatment way before its time. Our discovery years ago in Pittsburgh, that certain drugs can prevent cancer cells from binding to and paralyzing immune cells, led to hundreds of other studies and trials and to where we are today. That had saved my dad. It was something I knew about going into this life that I would capitalize on, and it worked. But seeing my robust father standing next to my dying brother, represented success and failure juxtaposed. I had to live with that -- somehow find a way to be okay with that.

"Where's Mom?"

"Oh, she'll be here a little later."

That was code for she isn't out of bed yet. It was noon.

"We were here late last night, and they told us to go home once they got him stabilized. I got back here around ten, I guess."

"Yeah, I talked to the attending, and he said he's probably out of the woods, but we won't know until he wakes up and they can assess his brain function. Right now, I'm just glad his vitals are cooperating."

My dad looked at me curiously. "You okay? You look worn out."

278

"Yeah, just doing a lot of thinking, you know, about how we got here. How he got here."

"Well that's a rabbit hole that leads to nowhere. You, of all people, should understand that."

"I know. I guess it's because I've been away. I don't deal with it on a regular basis like you and Mom. Seeing him here, and how weak and frail he looks, just got to me, ya know?"

"Well don't let him fool ya. The minute he wakes up, he'll be telling you how it is and anxious to get out of here to get...his needs met." He looked away so I wouldn't see his pain.

"What happens after that? I mean when they are done with him here?" I didn't like the way I had phrased that, but it's how we tended to talk about Danny in these moments.

"The social worker came in this morning before you arrived and is trying to arrange for him to go right to drug rehab while he waits for his court hearing."

"Court hearing?"

"Yeah, he not only overdosed, but they found enough cocaine and opioids on him that make it look like more than simple possession. They can't ignore that, Kate."

"I know. Geez. So how are you keeping him out of jail right now?"

"You remember my friend, the attorney, Joe Butler? He showed up in court for Danny and convinced the judge he was a good candidate for rehab and the new drug court program they began not too long ago in this county. So, he should count his blessings that somebody is going to have faith in him. But he has to stay out of trouble and follow everything they ask or he'll end up facing long prison time, I suppose."

"I'm sorry Dad. I'm really sorry."

"Nothing for you to be sorry about. This is your brother's doing. No one else to blame but him."

That was my dad's good defense. But we were both feeling guilt for very different reasons.

I sighed heavily. This was a prison sentence for my father, and I felt like the one who put him there.

twenty-eight

2013

THIS WAS MY FIFTIETH YEAR AND THE ONE that had ended my first life, so on New Year's Eve, 2012, I said a prayer, in sort of a drunken state, that I would survive this one. My friends, unaware of my secret, all laughed at that sentiment and assured me I had another fifty to go. *God, I hope not.* Truth be told, I was ready to go. In total, I had lived eighty-seven years and although my body didn't show it, the emotional scars from the sum of both lives were thick and unsightly in my mind's eye. There's not enough therapy in the world that can remedy the cascade of consequences that flow from that kind of damage. I wish I knew then what I know now, but I've never been one to cry over spilt milk, so I accepted with as much grace as possible the beautiful mess I had made of my lives.

My work at the NCI had become more rewarding as the discoveries continued to amaze even those of us who were the most seasoned researchers. The Obama administration was as equally enthusiastic or even more so, as the former administration was, to secure funding for research -- although the drug companies continued to play hard ball. I had learned how to put that in perspective unlike my earlier days when my more socialistic point of view could not co-exist with the demands of capitalism. I had learned how to play in the same sandbox with those who had a different point of view, even if I occasionally thought it disingenuous. It made me a team player and a good leader. And appreciated, for that matter, which fed my need to like myself. Work served to ground me in what I loved, but also to prove my intelligence in a world in which the clash of so many cultures could make your head spin. There were perceived racial and feminist struggles, just to name a couple. I say perceived because I learned most of the time the struggle was more with the insecure person who used those as covers than reality bore out. I, a white female with a black male assistant director, did not feel the struggles of many, which isn't to say there weren't any. But they were not as prominent as many would have wanted the world to believe. That complication alone could minimize the real victims and unfairly bolster those who needed a crutch. Added to that were the normal corporate frustrations, plus cut-throat Washington politics, with a side order of greed and power, topped off with different economic and social ideologies for dessert – which made for a menu no sane person could eat from without a serious case of food poisoning! After a few bouts of it myself, I settled into learning how to take my portions lightly and do the best I could to just be a decent human being. That always won in the end, no matter who I was dealing with or how differently we thought. I just tried to be decent and many people followed that lead. When they didn't, I smiled and moved on to the next possibly successful encounter.

My love life was not so easily navigated. I could manage hundreds of people, talk to world leaders, dine with the best negotiators and manipulators, but I still got weak in the knees anytime a prospective date said, "Hey would you like to go get a cup of coffee?" I became a teenage girl every time, which I came to learn was normal. At one point, I sought out the help of a therapist to find out what was wrong with me. She laughed and said "You're human. Just be yourself" and I tried to, but somehow that decent human being that worked so well in my career fell short in the dating world that seemed tainted with men who just wanted a hook-up. So, I settled into enjoying being single, with my cat and recently acquired Labradoodle, Roxy. I had a few male friends who I could count on when I just wanted a movie and dinner date. They may have secretly wanted more, but I was clear, and they were willing, so it was enough male companionship to fill the void. I continued to talk to Ken about everything I was struggling with, and his well-remembered voice got me through most of the rough spots.

Even Jodi gave up pushing me to find a husband and said she admired the fact that I could be single and fulfilled. She and Trent had weathered a few storms, separating at one point but now back together. She said she was in no position to judge or try to live vicariously through me. She had grown, too, and it felt like we were all discovering our own sense of peace amidst the scars.

I wasn't sure, then, why I felt the pull to be done with life just when it seemed the stars were lining up like they were supposed to. Maybe I had been so conditioned over the years to respond to drama or crisis, that I didn't really know how to respond to quiet. Maybe there was something in the chaos and the constant questioning of myself that was vitalizing, keeping me on my toes, waiting for the next challenge. I used to think life would be easier if it was settled. Now I was questioning how that had any value. One could live a hundred lives, but the wisdom you learn in one is not applicable to another. Maybe we are meant to be spontaneous responders and not always have a plan of protection. That's how we learn to be human. To grasp the experiences of others. Maybe that's how we learn to love.

৵

Despite all I had settled in my mind, though, Danny was my first and last mistake, my Achille's heel. I had spent two lifetimes trying to make sense of the senseless and, for all intents and purposes, failed miserably. On September 13, 2013, I sat in my corner office, daydreaming, hoping to get through it without feeling the weight of what the day meant. Each year, June nineteenth and September thirteenth were a double whammy. June was the month Danny died in one life and I saved him in another. September was the month I apparently died and made the monumental decision to have another go of it. Both bittersweet. Both more than I could wrap my brain around. This year was different because it was the exact day and year of my accident. My decision to come back to life and return to make things better happened on this very day and year. It was difficult to process over a normal cup of coffee. I felt eerily detached from the world. For some reason, I couldn't be certain I would go on living after today. I wondered if this day would mark something different since it would be the beginning of a part of life I had never lived before. There was something both exciting and daunting about it. I thought about Deirdre and how on this day I had been looking forward to her wedding and stressing about the cost. I wondered, and hoped, that she had gone through with the wedding as planned, despite her mother getting hit by a bus. I thought about how selfish it was to leave her that way. I hoped I would have a chance some day to tell her I was sorry for that. And Sean? He was just getting his adult life started. He and his dad were on the outs. He needed me and I left him.

These guilt feelings usually drove my motivation to take off both days from work in June and September just to find a path toward acceptance without losing my mind. Even though today was a Friday, and normally would have been a perfect day to take off leading into the weekend, I had a ton of meetings and issues to address that required my presence. Honestly, I think I knew this was going to be a very rough day and subconsciously did not plan to be alone. Yet another part of me was secretly hoping for a migraine or some excuse to not be expected to think too hard as I muddled through the business of the day.

I looked up at the large clock on the wall above the two overstuffed chairs facing my well-appointed mahogany desk. It was 8:03 am, probably about the exact time I had encountered the bus in my frantic run to get to that meeting on time so many years ago. I sighed heavily and leaned back. The soft leather chair around me was supple and supportive, a tangible symbol of what I had accomplished in my career. I thought about Cam Fletcher and wished he could see me now. I'm not sure why, but I had never made an attempt to look up anyone I had worked with at the ad agency in my first life. Curious, I turned to my computer and Googled Schuster and Bates in Pittsburgh. To my surprise, it came up as Schuster, Bates and Fletcher. I nearly laughed out loud. *Huh.* I was never able to understand why some things were different this time around, but on this account, I could assume that in my first life, I may have been the one who had held Fletcher back from making partner. *Well, good for him.* I clicked on the executive staff link and then on his name. The photo popped up and I swallowed hard at the image. I had a visceral reaction to it but wasn't sure what it meant. Fletcher represented another time in my life, when I was a different person. I guess it was true I *was* another person then. On second thought, maybe I was the same person, but less confident, less able to hold my own with men like Fletcher. He looked good. Happy. I felt strangely uneasy.

Just then Shawna pulled me out of my parallel world and beeped me to say I had a personal call. My dad.

"Kate, can you come? Can you come home?" He was out of breath and frantic.

"Dad, what's going on?"

"Just come...Danny...He's out of control."

"Are you hurt?"

"No, it's just that I can't handle this anymore."

That was not something I ever heard my dad utter. He was my hero. He could handle anything. I looked at my calendar full of meetings.

"Can this wait until the tomorrow? I've got..."

He interrupted. "No! I'm afraid...I'm afraid that..."

The call was disconnected. My heart raced. I tried to call back, but no answer. I called 911.

"911, what is your emergency?"

"Hi, my parents and brother live in Clearfield...Ohio. I know this is a lot to ask, but my father just phoned me sounding out of breath and frantic. It sounded like he was afraid my brother was going to hurt him. Can you get in touch with the police department there and have someone do a welfare check? I'm here in Rockville and can't get there right away. Please."

I gave her the address and their names. I let her know that my brother was a drug addict currently free on bail.

286

"Yes, I'll get someone dispatched soon."

"Can I stay on the phone while you do that?"

"Sure, please hold."

It was the longest sixty seconds of my life.

"Ma'am, we have someone in Clearfield on the way."

"Thank you so much."

I hung up and grabbed my purse. On the way out, I told Shawna I needed a flight back home as soon as possible and asked her to book it right away to Pittsburgh and I'd drive from there if she could secure a rental.

"I'll call ya when I have a minute." I ran out of the office just barely hearing her reply.

"Okay, be safe," she said as she picked up the receiver to dial Delta.

It's usually about a forty-minute drive to Reagan National if traffic cooperates. I was lucky that it wasn't too bad and got there in about forty-five. Shawna had booked a 10:00 am flight, scheduled to get into Pittsburgh at 11:15. It would be another hour drive to Clearfield from there.

Once I got to the gate, I called Shawna to tell her I had a family emergency and would call who I needed to call later to explain. I then called my dad's phone again for the tenth time with no luck. I hoped the police had arrived and calmed down the situation.

I was able to get in touch with the Clearfield Police Department who assured me police had been to the home, and that all was fine. I debated at that point if I should go back to the office and just wait to hear from my dad. But my need to have an excuse for the day helped me decide to go on. This was definitely a distraction, but I worried about how it would feel to see Danny, in an agitated state, on this fateful day. The image both saddened and angered me.

The flight was uneventful, but my patience was thin. I wanted to have my own wings to fly home. Thankfully, Shawna had called someone in Pittsburgh to deliver a rental car to the airport so I could jump in right out of the terminal and begin driving home. She had asked me if I would rather her secure a driver for me because she was worried that I was too upset, but I insisted on driving. I wanted to be alone. I wanted to scream and cry and beat on the steering wheel. Maybe listen to some angry music to get it all out. I had made a playlist like that for just these kinds of moments. Surprisingly, I didn't indulge myself. I tried to remain positive. My dad sounded out of breath. Had he been running from Danny? Where was my mother? Well, that was a moot point. The words, "I'm afraid," kept haunting me. What was he afraid of? What was Danny up to now? I had to stay calm. I had to make it okay.

I drove faster than normal, even though there was a steady rain most of the way. I was careful when getting close to Clearfield. It was famous for being a speed trap. The last thing I needed was to be delayed. I looked at the clock and it was 12:23 pm.

I pulled into the driveway and saw both of my parents' cars, which was somewhat of a relief, but it also could signal something else. I wasn't sure. I darted out of the car, wrapping my jacket around me to shield my body from the cold rainy mist in the air. I was in the house in seconds.

"Dad?" I called out, with no response. It was quiet except for what sounded like heavy breathing coming from the living room.

I pulled off my wet jacket and laid it and my purse down on the settee in the foyer. I made my way to the living area, which was the first room on the left past the hall stairs. When I turned into it, I gasped.

"Dad!" I shouted, staring at him sitting in his recliner, frail and frightened. Danny stood next to him, with a gun pointed at my father's head. The look of fear on my dad's face was something I had never witnessed. My mouth went dry and I swallowed hard.

Something happens to us in those moments when a life-saving decision must be made. Like when I saw the bus driver looking in his side mirror, about to steer into my running body. I saw it. I knew instantly what it meant, but I was speechless. Paralyzed with fear. A hostage to the moment that was unfolding without my permission.

I felt an amazing calm flow over me. In a very soft voice, I spoke to my brother.

"Danny. Let's talk. I know you're upset. Let's talk, okay?"

My voice was coming from somewhere else. I was having a panic attack inside, but this other being was speaking to him like he was a child she cared for. I stayed quiet and let her talk for me.

"Danny? Please?"

"Go away!" he shouted. He was sweating profusely. I suspected he was in withdrawal but couldn't be sure.

"Just put the gun down. Whatever you're upset about, we'll figure it out. Dad doesn't deserve this." It was the wrong thing to say.

"Oh, of course. Perfect Katie. Who are you to judge what anyone deserves? You're as guilty as the rest of us."

He was right.

"I know. This is my fault, too." I took a step closer, hoping he wouldn't notice.

Danny was nervous and kept putting the gun down and then raising it again. Each time, my father winced, and I gasped.

"What do you need, Danny? Whatever it is, I'll make sure you get it."

"Oh, that's right. Like you called the police? I know it was you. I know he called you, and what do you do? Just call the cops. That's all you know to do, isn't it?"

So, they had been there, but I didn't know why they hadn't done anything. Danny seemed to read my mind.

"Well, wrong again, Katie. They came and we were calm. Business as usual. Dad kept his mouth shut like I told him to and they left. Simple. I've become a pro at manipulating the cops. You should know that by now. But I guess you don't know everything do you?"

"No, I don't, Danny. I can't imagine what you've been through. I know it's been really hard. When I saw you last time in the hospital, I realized how much I love you. How much I want you to be okay. For you. Not me."

"Doesn't that sound nice?" He touched the gun to my dad's head. Another wince and gasp followed. "She loves me. Just like you do, Dad. So much that you'll let me live in hell before you'll give me something to help me live."

My dad's face had turned white and more frightful. I was genuinely concerned that he would collapse under the pressure.

"Please Danny, give me the gun." I held out my hands.

"You would love that, wouldn't you? You like to be in control. Well, this time, I'm in control. I'm probably going to prison for a long time anyway, so killing him and the rest of you won't mean a hill of beans to me."

"That's not true. You're not a murderer. You're not." I pleaded with him through the tears. My voice was hoarse, and my calmness was turning to primal fear. Fight, flee or freeze. I couldn't flee and leave my dad here. I wanted to fight but didn't know how without someone getting hurt.

"Where's mom for God's sake?" I was back in my natural voice.

My dad managed a strained response. "She's in her room. Probably asleep."

"Probably?" Danny laughed sarcastically. "She's dead to the world. She gets to do that legally. Ain't that ironic? Why isn't she going to jail for being an addict? Huh?" he yelled while pointing the gun at me. This time I winced, and my dad gasped.

"You're right about that, too. It's not fair. Danny, you can't help this. Look at our parents. They both struggle with this stuff. I was the lucky one. I didn't get that gene, but you did. Had I known it would be like this, I would have..."

"You would have what?" he interrupted. "Fixed it? You're not God, Katie. You might have some big important job and all, thinkin' you can save the world, but you're just as broken as I am. This whole family is fucking broken. I can put us all out of our misery right now." He began to roll his head in agony as he waved the gun around, sweat now dripping from his forehead. He looked confused and desperate. At the end of his rope.

My God. He's going to do it.

I had another out of body moment in which my instincts took over and I was no longer in control. Danny raised the gun to my father's head, and I heard it cock. I lunged toward them, hoping to knock the gun out of his hand.

In slow motion, I felt my body in mid-air and my father shout in a low guttural voice, "No, Sarah, no!"

Mom?

A shot rang out and I felt an instant burn, first in my back, and then in my chest. Everything turned from slow back to fast in that second. Suddenly my hearing was clear, and all my senses heightened. I fell to the ground, feeling my face hit the carpet. It smelled of cigarette smoke and dog hair.

"Oh my God," I heard my dad's high-pitched voice say. "What have you done?"

Then silence. And darkness.

twenty-nine

MY NECK HURT. SOMETHING WAS PRESSING against it. Hard. Fingers. *What's going on?*

"There's a pulse," a gruff voice declared.

"Paramedics just arrived," a younger man replied.

"Let's give them some room."

"Is she going to be okay?" asked a familiar but fearful voice.

Daddy?

"Paramedics are here, let's give them some room."

I felt the jolt of feet pounding against the floor. Then there were hands all over me.

"Let's get her turned on her side."

"BP?"

"Blood pressure is 62 over 40 and falling."

"Epinephrine coming," a female replied.

A sharp sting.

"What's her name?" one yelled out.

"Kate...it's Kate," my father shouted in distress. "Oh, dear God," his voice cracked.

"Kate, stay with us. We're going to get you to the hospital. Stay with us, okay Kate?"

Okay. How do I do that?

I tried to make sense of the voices. I could hear several in the other room. Definitely the gruff one talking and my father answering in an annoyed tone. I gasped as something was placed over my face. Loud swooshing sounds. Air being forced into my lungs. Think, Kate. Think. I could still hear their faint words, some clear, some lost.

Gun to my head...wife came in the room...gun went off...next thing I know, Kate's on the floor...oh God.

Then mother's voice with intermittent sobs.

I don't know...don't know how...just tried to stop him...wanted it to stop.

"You shot her!" my dad screamed.

Who was shot?

Warrant for his arrest...where is your son, Mrs. Mulligan?

At the mention of Danny, my heart skipped a beat and I coughed.

"BP still falling. More epi, please."

"Stay with us, Kate."

At the sting, memories flashed like a strobe light, bright but frantic, not lasting long enough to see the images clearly.

"Yeah, Daniel Mulligan," the younger guy said loudly, after some radio noise. "Be on the lookout. Twenty-ten white Ford F150 with plates Charlie, Nancy, Victor, four, two, zero."

Danny. In trouble again. Another flash. *Oh God. Daddy. The gun.*

I felt the pressure of hands on both sides of me.

"One, two, three..."

Up I went up in sudden levitation and then down again on something in motion. It dawned on me then. *This is a gurney.*

Again, I willed myself to see and speak, but nothing came of it.

"Okay, let's get her on board," one of the voices declared.

"Watch the side here...the door is narrow," said another.

"Gotcha."

I heard a lot of heavy breathing. I wanted to scream out. *What's wrong with me? Where am I going?* My mouth was so dry. *I'm tired. So tired.* The coolness of a light mist in the outside air surprised me.

"Can I ride with..." my father begged from inside the house.

"No, you both need to come to the station with us," the gruff one interrupted. "We'll keep you and your wife informed of her status."

Her status. *My status?*

There was barking in the distance, reminding me of Max. No, Bugles. *I don't know.* I longed for Deirdre and Sean. Ken. I wanted to sob, but something crowded the lump in my throat.

Another jolt. The air was different. Compressed. Then competing voices, with a familiar one from before.

"Gun shot to the back. Punctured lung. Got her intubated. Blood pressure unstable, most recent 65 over 47. We're on our way."

Doors slammed shut, one then the other.

"Hang in there, Kate," a female voice whispered as she squeezed my hand.

I sensed flashing lights, then quiet, then speed. Then peace. *Finally some peace and quiet.*

"Are you still with us, Kate?" She said breathless. "We're nearly there. Keep breathing...just keep breathing. God in heaven, help this one," her voice cracked.

I heard him. Soft and assuring. *Katherine.*

epilogue

THERE IS SOMETHING EERIE ABOUT A COLD and misty morning, especially when it ends in your death. I had not planned for this turn of events, but that's no surprise, is it? Again, I was too late. Too late to save my brother. Or to save the world from him.

In the moments before I let go of life as I knew it, I wish I could say that I made myself right with God. Right with the world. Instead, I was just afraid. I guess that's human. There was no road to Damascus epiphany that allowed it all to make sense, nor could I claim that I was wiser, stronger or better for having lived the second life. If I learned anything profound, it is that the wisdom you gain in life is only good for that particular life. Try as I did to apply it in another, it fell devastatingly short.

Oh, and I thought I would be different, which is the second lesson learned. We are made the way we are for a purpose. I just didn't happen to like my original one, so I thought I could re-tool, refurbish, re-something, and I would be more pleased with myself. But I didn't know. This Monday-morning quarterbacking sucks, by the way. If I only knew then what I know now – the very sentiment that made reliving my life so tempting – I would have let well enough alone. If only.

Ultimately, what I didn't know was that some of my well-intentioned good choices would have poor consequences for those I loved. I would have never chosen them if I knew. But in my selfish quest to assuage my guilt, I hurt people. I didn't know how it all worked beyond my small space on earth. I didn't know I was already loved beyond measure. Or that one life was enough because it was more about grace and forgiveness than about doing it right. I didn't know that different choices would mean different mistakes, and that turned out to be a gamble. Which mistakes yielded the most pain? I still can't answer that. Pain is pain, regardless of the end result. But pain is the beginning of healing. And healing gives way to hope. And hope is the only reason to live. Neither life was more or less painful. Just different. Both lives hurtful and hopeful at the same time. Both closed without answers, but with the hope of a perfect ending. At the same time.

As I drifted in and out of consciousness, I saw my second life pass before me, much different from the first. Still no feeding starving children in Kenya. But more smiles. Definitely more smiles.

There I am on my Scwhinn, speeding down our country road, so full of hope for a new life. *Freedom.* Danny smiling and playing in the pond. *Priceless.* Danny having his tenth birthday party. *Relief.* My mom sleeping her life away. *Disappointing.* Cherry's last breath. *Guilt.* My dad smiling during my Harvard graduation. *Proud.* Look how happy I am at my wedding? *Beautiful.* Kentaro. *Perfect.* Cancer treatment discovery. *Miraculous.* Losing the baby. *Devastating.* Not being able to stop world events. *Guilty, again.* Losing Ken. *Out of breath.* Danny with a gun to my father's head. *Regret.*

Then I saw myself on the gurney. *Wait.* There was Deidre and Sean again, just like the first time. Crying. Then my father appeared. *Wait.* Where was Danny? My mother? *Wait. Don't let me go.* Everyone is crying. *Why? When? Which life?* There was a bright light, just like before. I heard the monitor alarm, the sound of my heart flat-lining. Then two deafening, but steady tones at once, almost in harmony. One more faint than the other. *Wait.*

I looked toward the light and he was there. Same as before. That familiar face. Those kind eyes. That voice. Soft, assuring, loving. *It's over.*

His arms extended toward me. I hesitated.

"Don't be afraid."

Strangely, calm replaced the fear.

I raised my arms toward him, and he took me in his. And with a hint of sweet anticipation, he proclaimed, "Now, Katherine, you are ready."

∽

When it comes your time to die, be not like those whose hearts are filled with the fear of death, so that when their time comes, they weep and pray for a little more time to live their lives over again in a different way. Sing your death song and die like a hero going home.

Tecumseh
1768-1813
Native American leader of the Shawnee

acknowledgments

I am grateful to my daughter, Laura, who sat with me in a Savannah bed and breakfast over a decade ago and helped me map out the characters for this book. It took me a long time to bring it to fruition, but her encouragement and ideas along the way have been so valuable as the manuscript took shape. I also want to thank my parents, Ruth and Bud, who are my biggest fans, no matter what crazy project I am working on; and my husband, Eric, who lovingly gives me the time and space I need to work out my therapeutic creativity. Thanks also to my son, Justin and his wife, Nicola, as well as my son-in-law, Jeff, and beautiful granddaughters, Rachel and Ashley, who all keep me grounded and remembering what is important in life.

I appreciate the wonderful ladies who pre-read the manuscript and gave me thoughtful and constructive feedback: Brandi, Ruth, Laura, Barbara, Pat, Tina, and Sarah. Thank you to Sandra O'Donnell at RO Literary, who decided not to take me on as a client, but she said the story was intriguing and my writing was "lovely," which was just enough professional encouragement to move me toward publication.

Finally, I thank the good Lord for giving me the ability to write stories that allow me to escape into a world other than the one I've been placed in, but also Who keeps me humble and assured that no matter how many mistakes I make, His grace is sufficient for another day. For that, I am most thankful as there is no comparison to this wonderful, messy world I call my life.

Book Club Discussion Questions

1. What specific themes did the author emphasize throughout *Back to Life*?

2. What role did Kate's parents play in how she lived life the first time around? How did that change in her second life?

3. How did you feel about Kate's brother Danny?

4. Does Kate's character seem real and believable? Can you relate to her predicaments? To what extent do they remind you of yourself or someone you know?

5. How did Kate change, grow or evolve throughout the course of the story? What events trigger such changes?

6. In what ways do the events in *Back to Life* reveal evidence of the author's world view?

7. Did any parts of the book make you uncomfortable? If so, why did you feel that way? Did this lead to a new understanding or awareness of some aspect of your life you might not have thought about before?